About the Author

FLANN O'BRIEN was one of the two pseudonyms of Brian O'Nolan. The other was Myles na gCopaleen, which he used as a celebrated Irish newspaper columnist. Born in County Tyrone before the First World War, the author settled in Dublin, and in 1939, his masterpiece, *At Swim-Two-Birds* (also available in a Plume edition), established him as a major English-language novelist. His other notable works include *The Third Policeman, The Hard Life* and *The Dalkey Archive*, as well as a classic work in Gaelic, *An Béal Bocht*. Of him John Updike has written: "He was five years younger than Samuel Beckett, sounded his genius earlier, husbanded it less thriftily, and died young, at the age of fifty-four. As with Scott Fitzgerald, there is a brilliant ease in his prose, a poignant grace glimmering off every page. . . . Like Beckett, he has the gift of the perfect sentence, the art, which they both learned from Joyce, of tuning plain language to a lyric pitch." Renowned critic V. S. Pritchett has commented: "His gifts are startling and heartless. He has the astounding Irish genius for describing the human animal . . ." To which novelist Anthony Burgess has added: "If we don't cherish the work of Flann O'Brien we are stupid fools who don't deserve to have great men. Flann O'Brien is a very great man."

THE
THIRD
POLICEMAN

THE
THIRD
POLICEMAN

by Flann O'Brien

A PLUME BOOK

PLUME
Published by the Penguin Group
Penguin Books USA Inc., 375 Hudson Street, New York, New York 10014, U.S.A.
Penguin Books Ltd, 27 Wrights Lane, London W8 5TZ, England
Penguin Books Australia Ltd, Ringwood, Victoria, Australia
Penguin Books Canada Ltd, 10 Alcorn Avenue, Toronto, Ontario, Canada M4V 3B2
Penguin Books (N.Z.) Ltd, 182–190 Wairau Road, Auckland 10, New Zealand

Penguin Books Ltd, Registered Offices: Harmondsworth, Middlesex, England

First Plume Printing, October, 1976

13 15 17 19 20 18 16 14 12

All the characters and events portrayed in this book are fictitious.

This is an authorized reprint of a hardcover edition
published by Walker and Company.

BOOKS ARE AVAILABLE AT QUANTITY DISCOUNTS WHEN USED
TO PROMOTE PRODUCTS OR SERVICES. FOR INFORMATION PLEASE
WRITE TO PREMIUM MARKETING DIVISION, PENGUIN BOOKS USA INC.,
375 HUDSON STREET, NEW YORK, NEW YORK 10014.

Human existence being an hallucination containing in itself the secondary hallucinations of day and night (the latter an insanitary condition of the atmosphere due to accretions of black air) it ill becomes any man of sense to be concerned at the illusory approach of the supreme hallucination known as death.

DE SELBY

Since the affairs of men rest still uncertain,
Let's reason with the worst that may befall.

SHAKESPEARE

THE
THIRD
POLICEMAN

I

Not everybody knows how I killed old Phillip Mathers, smashing his jaw in with my spade; but first it is better to speak of my friendship with John Divney because it was he who first knocked old Mathers down by giving him a great blow in the neck with a special bicycle-pump which he manufactured himself out of a hollow iron bar. Divney was a strong civil man but he was lazy and idle-minded. He was personally responsible for the whole idea in the first place. It was he who told me to bring my spade. He was the one who gave the orders on the occasion and also the explanations when they were called for.

I was born a long time ago. My father was a strong farmer and my mother owned a public house. We all lived in the public house but it was not a strong house at all and was closed most of the day because my father was out at work on the farm and my mother was always in the kitchen and for some reason the customers never came until it was nearly bed-time; and well after it at Christmas-time and on other unusual days like that. I never saw my mother outside the kitchen in my life and never saw a customer during the day and even at night I never saw more than two or three together. But then I was in bed part of the time and it is possible that things happened differently with my mother and with the customers late at night. My father I do not remember well but he was a strong man and did not talk much except on Saturdays when he would mention Parnell with the customers and say that Ireland was a queer country. My mother I can recall perfectly. Her face was always red and sore-looking from bending at the fire; she spent her life making tea to pass the time and singing snatches of old songs to pass the meantime. I knew her well but my father and I were strangers and did not converse much; often indeed when I would be studying in the kitchen at night I could hear him through the thin door to the shop talking there from his seat under the oil-lamp for hours on end to Mick the sheepdog. Always it was only the drone of his voice I heard, never the separate bits of words. He was a man who understood all dogs thoroughly and treated them like human beings. My mother owned a cat but it was a foreign outdoor animal and was rarely seen and my mother never took any notice of it. We were all happy enough in a queer separate way.

Then a certain year came about the Christmas-time and when the year was gone my father and mother were gone also. Mick the sheepdog was very tired and sad after my father went and would not do his work with the sheep at all; he too went the next year. I was young and foolish at the time and did not know properly why these people had all left me, where they had gone and why they did not give explanations beforehand. My mother was the first to go and I can remember a fat man with a red face and a black suit telling my father that there was no doubt where she was, that he could be as sure of that as he could of anything else in this vale of tears. But he did not mention where and as I thought the whole thing was very private and that she might be back on Wednesday, I did not ask him where. Later, when my father went, I thought he had gone to fetch her with an outside car but when neither of them came back on the next Wednesday, I felt sorry and disappointed. The man in the black suit was back again. He stayed in the house for two nights and was continually washing his hands in the bedroom and reading books. There were two other men, one a small pale man and one a tall black man in leggings. They had pockets full of pennies and they gave me one every time I asked them questions. I can remember the tall man in the leggings saying to the other man:

'The poor misfortunate little bastard.'

I did not understand this at the time and thought that they were talking about the other man in the black clothes who was always working at the wash-stand in the bedroom. But I understood it all clearly afterwards.

After a few days I was brought away myself on an outside car and sent to a strange school. It was a boarding school filled with people I did not know, some young and some older. I soon got to know that it was a good school and a very

8

expensive one but I did not pay over any money to the people who were in charge of it because I had not any. All this and a lot more I understood clearly later.

My life at this school does not matter except for one thing. It was here that I first came to know something of de Selby. One day I picked up idly an old tattered book in the science master's study and put it in my pocket to read in bed the next morning as I had just earned the privilege of lying late. I was about sixteen then and the date was the seventh of March. I still think that day is the most important in my life and can remember it more readily than I do my birthday. The book was a first edition of *Golden Hours* with the two last pages missing. By the time I was nineteen and had reached the end of my education I knew that the book was valuable and that in keeping it I was stealing it. Nevertheless I packed it in my bag without a qualm and would probably do the same if I had my time again. Perhaps it is important in the story I am going to tell to remember that it was for de Selby I committed my first serious sin. It was for him that I committed my greatest sin.

I had long-since got to know how I was situated in the world. All my people were dead and there was a man called Divney working the farm and living on it until I should return. He did not own any of it and was given weekly cheques of pay by an office full of solicitors in a town far away. I had never met these solicitors and never met Divney but they were really all working for me and my father had paid in cash for these arrangements before he died. When I was younger I thought he was a generous man to do that for a boy he did not know well.

I did not go home direct from school. I spent some months in other places broadening my mind and finding out what a complete edition of de Selby's works would cost me and whether some of the less important of his commentators' books could be got on loan. In one of the places where I was broadening my mind I met one night with a bad accident. I broke my left leg (or, if you like, it was broken for me) in six places and when I was well enough again to go my way I had one leg made of wood, the left one. I knew that I had only a little money, that I was going home to a rocky farm and that my life would not be easy. But I was certain by this time that farming, even if I had to do it, would not be my life work. I knew that if my name was to be remembered, it would be remembered with de Selby's.

I can recall in every detail the evening I walked back into my own house with a travelling-bag in each hand. I was twenty years of age; it was an evening in a happy yellow summer and the door of the public house was open. Behind the counter was John Divney, leaning forward on the low-down porter dash-board with his fork, his arms neatly folded and his face looking down on a newspaper which was spread upon the counter. He had brown hair and was made hand-somely enough in a small butty way; his shoulders were broadened out with work and his arms were thick like little tree-trunks. He had a quiet civil face with eyes like cow's eyes, brooding, brown, and patient. When he knew that somebody had come in he did not stop his reading but his left hand strayed out and found a rag and began to give the counter slow damp swipes. Then, still reading, he moved his hands one above the other as if he was drawing out a con-certina to full length and said:

'A schooner?'

A schooner was what the customers called a pint of Cole-raine blackjack. It was the cheapest porter in the world. I said that I wanted my dinner and mentioned my name and station. Then we closed the shop and went into the kitchen and we were there nearly all night, eating and talking and drinking whiskey.

The next day was Thursday. John Divney said that his work was now done and that he would be ready to go home to where his people were on Saturday. It was not true to say that his work was done because the farm was in a poor way and most of the year's work had not even been started. But on Saturday he said there were a few things to finish and that he could not work on Sunday but that he would be in a posi-tion to hand over the place in perfect order on Tuesday even-ing. On Monday he had a sick pig to mind and that delayed him. At the end of the week he was busier than ever and the passing of another two months did not seem to lighten or reduce his urgent tasks. I did not mind much because if he was idle-minded and a sparing worker, he was satisfactory so far as company was concerned and he never asked for pay. I did little work about the place myself, spending all my time arranging my papers and re-reading still more closely the pages of de Selby.

A full year had not passed when I noticed that Divney was using the word ' we ' in his conversation and worse than that, the word ' our '. He said that the place was not everything that it might be and talked of getting a hired man. I did not agree with this and told him so, saying that there was no necessity for more than two men on a small farm and adding, most unhappily for myself, that we were poor. After that it was useless trying to tell him that it was I who owned everything. I began to tell myself that even if I did own everything, he owned me.

Four years passed away happily enough for each of us. We had a good house and plenty of good country food but little money. Nearly all my own time was spent in study. Out of my savings I had now bought the complete works of the two principal commentators, Hatchjaw and Bassett, and a photostat of the de Selby Codex. I had also embarked upon the task of learning French and German thoroughly in order to read the works of other commentators in those languages. Divney had been working after a fashion on the farm by day and talking loudly in the public house by night and serving drinks there. Once I asked him what about the public house and he said he was losing money on it every day. I did not understand this because the customers, judging by their voices through the thin door, were plentiful enough and Divney was continually buying himself suits of clothes and fancy tiepins. But I did not say much. I was satisfied to be left in peace because I knew that my own work was more important than myself.

One day in early winter Divney said to me:

' I cannot lose very much more of my own money on that bar. The customers are complaining about the porter. It is very bad porter because I have to drink a little now and again myself to keep them company and I do not feel well in my health over the head of it. I will have to go away for two days and do some travelling and see if there is a better brand of porter to be had.'

He disappeared the next morning on his bicycle and when he came back very dusty and travel-worn at the end of three days, he told me that everything was all right and that four barrels of better porter could be expected on Friday. It came punctually on that day and was well bought by the customers in the public house that night. It was manufactured in some town in the south and was known as ' The Wrastler '. If you drank three or four pints of it, it was nearly bound to win. The customers praised it highly and when they had it inside them they sang and shouted and sometimes lay down on the floor or on the roadway outside in a great stupor. Some of them complained afterwards that they had been robbed while in this state and talked angrily in the shop the next night about stolen money and gold watches which had disappeared off their strong chains. John Divney did not say much on this subject to them and did not mention it to me at all. He printed the words—BEWARE OF PICKPOCKETS— in large letters on a card and hung it on the back of shelves beside another notice that dealt with cheques. Nevertheless a week rarely passed without some customer complaining after an evening with ' The Wrastler '. It was not a satisfactory thing.

As time went on Divney became more and more despondent about what he called ' the bar '. He said that he would be satisfied if it paid its way but he doubted seriously if it ever would. The Government were partly responsible for the situation owing to the high taxes. He did not think that he could continue to bear the burden of the loss without some assistance. I said that my father had some old-fashioned way of management which made possible a profit but that the shop should be closed if now continuing to lose money. Divney only said that it was a very serious thing to surrender a licence.

It was about this time, when I was nearing thirty, that Divney and I began to get the name of being great friends. For years before that I had rarely gone out at all. This was because I was so busy with my work that I hardly ever had the time; also my wooden leg was not very good for walking with. Then something very unusual happened to change all this and after it had happened, Divney and I never parted company for more than one minute either night or day. All day I was out with him on the farm and at night I sat on my father's old seat under the lamp in a corner of the public house doing what work I could with my papers in the middle of the blare and the crush and the hot noises which went always with 'The Wrastler'. If Divney went for a walk on Sunday to a neighbour's house I went with him and came home with him again, never before or after him. If he went away to a town on his bicycle to order porter or seed potatoes or even 'to see a certain party', I went on my own bicycle beside him. I brought my bed into his room and took the trouble to sleep only after he was sleeping and to be wide-awake a good hour before he stirred. Once I nearly failed in my watchfulness. I remember waking up with a start in the small hours of a black night and finding him quietly dressing himself in the dark. I asked him where he was going and he said he could not sleep and that he thought a walk would do him good. I said I was in the same condition myself and the two of us went for a walk together into the coldest and wettest night I ever experienced. When we returned drenched I said it was foolish for us to sleep in different beds in such bitter weather and got into his bed beside him. He did not say much, then or at any other time. I slept with him always after that. We were friendly and smiled at each other but the situation was a queer one and neither of us liked it. The neighbours were not long noticing how inseparable we were. We had been in that condition of being always together for nearly three years and they said that we were the best two Christians in all Ireland. They said that human friendship was a beautiful thing and that Divney and I were the noblest example of it in the history of the world. If other people fell out or fought or disagreed, they were asked why they could not be like me and Divney. It would have been a great shock for everybody if Divney had appeared in any place at any time without myself beside him. And it is not strange that two people never came to dislike each other as bitterly as did I and Divney. And two people were never so polite to each other, so friendly in the face.

I must go back several years to explain what happened

to bring about this peculiar situation. The 'certain party' whom Divney went to visit once a month was a girl called Pegeen Meers. For my part I had completed my definitive 'De Selby Index' wherein the views of all known commentators on every aspect of the savant and his work had been collated. Each of us therefore had a large thing on the mind. One day Divney said to me:

'That is a powerful book you have written I don't doubt.'

'It is useful,' I admitted, 'and badly wanted.' In fact it contained much that was entirely new and proof that many opinions widely held about de Selby and his theories were misconceptions based on misreadings of his works.

'It might make your name in the world and your golden fortune in copyrights?'

'It might.'

'Then why do you not put it out?'

I explained that money is required to 'put out' a book of this kind unless the writer already has a reputation. He gave me a look of sympathy that was not usual with him and sighed.

'Money is hard to come by these days,' he said, 'with the drink trade on its last legs and the land starved away to nothing for the want of artificial manures that can't be got for love or money owing to the trickery of the Jewmen and the Freemasons.'

I knew that it was not true about the manures. He had already pretended to me that they could not be got because he did not want the trouble of them. After a pause he said:

'We will have to see what we can do about getting money for your book and indeed I am in need of some myself because you can't expect a girl to wait until she is too old to wait any longer.'

I did not know whether he meant to bring a wife, if he got one, into the house. If he did and I could not stop him, then I would have to leave. On the other hand if marriage meant that he himself would leave I think I would be very glad of it.

It was some days before he talked on this subject of money again. Then he said:

'What about old Mathers?'

'What about him?'

I had never seen the old man but knew all about him. He had spent a long life of fifty years in the cattle trade and now lived in retirement in a big house three miles away. He still did large business through agents and the people said that he carried no less than three thousand pounds with him every time he hobbled to the village to lodge his money. Little as I knew of social proprieties at the time, I would not dream of asking him for assistance.

'He is worth a packet of potato-meal,' Divney said.

'I do not think we should look for charity,' I answered.

'I do not think so either,' he said. He was a proud man in his own way, I thought, and no more was said just then. But after that he took to the habit of putting occasionally into conversations on other subjects some irrelevant remark about our need for money and the amount of it which Mathers carried in his black cash-box; sometimes he would revile the old man, accusing him of being in 'the artificial manure ring' or of being dishonest in his business dealings. Once he said something about 'social justice' but it was plain to me that he did not properly understand the term.

I do not know exactly how or when it became clear to me that Divney, far from seeking charity, intended to rob Mathers; and I cannot recollect how long it took me to realise that he meant to kill him as well in order to avoid the possibility of being identified as the robber afterwards. I only know that within six months I had come to accept this grim plan as a commonplace of our conversation. Three further months passed before I could bring myself to agree to the proposal and three months more before I openly admitted to Divney that my misgivings were at an end. I cannot recount the tricks and wiles he used to win me to his side. It is sufficient to say that he read portions of my 'De Selby Index' (or pretended to) and discussed with me afterwards the serious responsibility of any person who declined by mere reason of personal whim to give the 'Index' to the world.

Old Mathers lived alone. Divney knew on what evening and at what deserted stretch of road near his house we would meet him with his box of money. The evening when it came was in the depth of winter; the light was already waning as we sat at our dinner discussing the business we had in hand.

Divney said that we should bring our spades tied on the crossbars of our bicycles because this would make us look like men out after rabbits; he would bring his own iron pump in case we should get a slow puncture.

There is little to tell about the murder. The lowering skies seemed to conspire with us, coming down in a shroud of dreary mist to within a few yards of the wet road where we were waiting. Everything was very still with no sound in our ears except the dripping of the trees. Our bicycles were hidden. I was leaning miserably on my spade and Divney, his iron pump under his arm, was smoking his pipe contentedly. The old man was upon us almost before we realised there was anybody near. I could not see him well in the dim light but I could glimpse a spent bloodless face peering from the top of the great black coat which covered him from ear to ankle. Divney went forward at once and pointing back along the road said:

' Would that be your parcel on the road?'

The old man turned his head to look and received a blow in the back of the neck from Divney's pump which knocked him clean off his feet and probably smashed his neck-bone. As he collapsed full-length in the mud he did not cry out. Instead I heard him say something softly in a conversational tone—something like ' I do not care for celery ' or ' I left my glasses in the scullery '. Then he lay very still. I had been watching the scene rather stupidly, still leaning on my spade. Divney was rummaging savagely at the fallen figure and then stood up. He had a black cash-box in his hand. He waved it in the air and roared at me:

' Here, wake up! Finish him with the spade! '

I went forward mechanically, swung the spade over my shoulder and smashed the blade of it with all my strength against the protruding chin. I felt and almost heard the fabric of his skull crumple up crisply like an empty eggshell. I do not know how often I struck him after that but I did not stop until I was tired.

I threw the spade down and looked around for Divney. He was nowhere to be seen. I called his name softly but he did not answer. I walked a little bit up the road and called again. I jumped on the rising of a ditch and peered around into the gathering dusk. I called his name once more as loudly as I dared but there was no answer in the stillness. He was gone. He had made off with the box of money, leaving me alone with the dead man and with a spade which was now probably tinging the watery mud around it with a weak pink stain.

My heart stumbled painfully in its beating. A chill of fright ran right through me. If anybody should come, nothing in the world would save me from the gallows. If Divney was with me still to share my guilt, even that would not protect me. Numb with fear I stood for a long time looking at the crumpled heap in the black coat.

Before the old man had come Divney and I had dug a deep hole in the field beside the road, taking care to preserve the sods of grass. Now in a panic I dragged the heavy sodden figure from where it lay and got it with a tremendous effort across the ditch into the field and slumped it down into the hole. Then I rushed back for my spade and started to throw and push the earth back into the hole in a mad blind fury.

The hole was nearly full when I heard steps. Looking round in great dismay I saw the unmistakable shape of Divney making his way carefully across the ditch into the field. When he came up I pointed dumbly to the hole with my spade. Without a word he went to where our bicycles were, came back with his own spade and worked steadily with me until the task was finished. We did everything possible to hide any trace of what had happened. Then we cleaned our boots with grass, tied the spades and walked home. A few people who came against us on the road bade us good evening in the dark. I am sure they took us for two tired labourers making for home after a hard day's work. They were not far wrong.

On our way I said to Divney:

' Where were you that time?'

' Attending to important business,' he answered. I thought he was referring to a certain thing and said:

' Surely you could have kept it till after.'

' It is not what you are thinking of,' he answered.

' Have you got the box?'

He turned his face to me this time, screwed it up and put a finger on his lip.

'Not so loud,' he whispered. 'It is in a safe place.'

'But where?'

The only reply he gave me was to put the finger on his lip more firmly and make a long hissing noise. He gave me to understand that mentioning the box, even in a whisper, was the most foolish and reckless thing it was possible for me to do.

When we reached home he went away and washed himself and put on one of the several blue Sunday suits he had. When he came back to where I was sitting, a miserable figure at the kitchen fire, he came across to me with a very serious face, pointed to the window and cried:

'Would that be your parcel on the road?'

Then he let out a bellow of laughter which seemed to loosen up his whole body, turn his eyes to water in his head and shake the whole house. When he had finished he wiped the tears from his face, walked into the shop and made a noise which can only be made by taking the cork quickly out of a whiskey bottle.

In the weeks which followed I asked him where the box was a hundred times in a thousand different ways. He never answered in the same way but the answer was always the same. It was in a very safe place. The least said about it the better until things quietened down. Mum was the word. It would be found all in good time. For the purpose of safe-keeping the place it was in was superior to the Bank of England. There was a good time coming. It would be a pity to spoil everything by hastiness or impatience.

And that is why John Divney and I became inseparable friends and why I never allowed him to leave my sight for three years. Having robbed me in my own public house (having even robbed my customers) and having ruined my farm, I knew that he was sufficiently dishonest to steal my share of Mathers' money and make off with the box if given the opportunity. I knew that there was no possible necessity for waiting until ' things quietened down ' because very little notice was taken of the old man's disappearance. People said he was a queer mean man and that going away without telling anybody or leaving his address was the sort of thing he would do.

I think I have said before that the peculiar terms of physical intimacy upon which myself and Divney found ourselves had become more and more intolerable. In latter months I had hoped to force him to capitulate by making my company unbearably close and unrelenting but at the same time I took to carrying a small pistol in case of accidents. One Sunday night when both of us were sitting in the kitchen—both, incidentally, on the same side of the fire—he took his pipe from his mouth and turned to me:

'Do you know,' he said, 'I think things have quietened down.'

I only gave a grunt.

'Do you get my meaning?' he asked.

'Things were never any other way,' I answered shortly. He looked at me in a superior way.

'I know a lot about these things,' he said, 'and you would be surprised at the pitfalls a man will make if he is in too big a hurry. You cannot be too careful but all the same I think things have quietened down enough to make it safe.'

'I am glad you think so.'

'There are good times coming. I will get the box tomorrow and then we will divide the money, right here on this table.'

'*We* will get the box,' I answered, saying the first word with great care. He gave me a long hurt look and asked me sadly did I not trust him. I replied that both of us should finish what both had started.

'All right,' he said in a very vexed way. 'I am sorry you don't trust me after all the work I have done to try to put this place right but to show you the sort I am I will let you get the box yourself, I will tell you where it is tomorrow.'

I took care to sleep with him as usual that night. The next morning he was in a better temper and told me with great simplicity that the box was hidden in Mathers' own empty house, under the floorboards of the first room on the right from the hall.

'Are you sure?' I asked.

'I swear it,' he said solemnly, raising his hand to heaven.

I thought the position over for a moment, examining the possibility that it was a ruse to part company with me at last and then make off himself to the real hiding-place. But his face for the first time seemed to wear a look of honesty.

'I am sorry if I injured your feelings last night,' I said, 'but to show that there is no ill-feeling I would be glad if you would come with me at least part of the way. I honestly think that both of us should finish what the two of us started.'

'All right,' he said. 'It is all the same but I would like you to get the box with your own hands because it is only simple justice after not telling you where it was.'

As my own bicycle was punctured we walked the distance. When we were about a hundred yards from Mathers' house, Divney stopped by a low wall and said that he was going to sit on it and smoke his pipe and wait for me.

'Let you go alone and get the box and bring it back here. There are good times coming and we will be rich men tonight. It is sitting under a loose board in the floor of the first room on the right, in the corner forenenst the door.'

Perched as he was on the wall I knew that he need never leave my sight. In the brief time I would be away I could see him any time I turned my head.

'I will be back in ten minutes,' I said.

'Good man,' he answered. 'But remember this. If you meet anybody, you don't know what you're looking for, you don't know in whose house you are, you don't know anything.'

'I don't even know my own name,' I answered.

This was a very remarkable thing for me to say because the next time I was asked my name I could not answer. I did not know.

II

D E S E L B Y has some interesting things to say on the subject of houses.[1] A row of houses he regards as a row of
necessary evils. The softening and degeneration of the
human race he attributes to its progressive predilection for
interiors and waning interest in the art of going out and stay-
ing there. This in turn he sees as the result of the rise of
such pursuits as reading, chess-playing, drinking, marriage
and the like, few of which can be satisfactorily conducted
in the open. Elsewhere[2] he defines a house as 'a large
coffin ', ' a warren ', and ' a box '. Evidently his main objection was to the confinement of a roof and four walls. He
ascribed somewhat far-fetched therapeutic values—chiefly
pulmonary—to certain structures of his own design which
he called ' habitats ', crude drawings of which may still be
seen in the pages of the *Country Album*. These structures
were of two kinds, roofless ' houses ' and ' houses ' without
walls. The former had wide open doors and windows with
an extremely ungainly superstructure of tarpaulins loosely
rolled on spars against bad weather—the whole looking like
a foundered sailing-ship erected on a platform of masonry
and the last place where one would think of keeping even
cattle. The other type of ' habitat ' had the conventional
slated roof but no walls save one, which was to be erected
in the quarter of the prevailing wind; around the other sides
were the inevitable tarpaulins loosely wound on rollers suspended from the gutters of the roof, the whole structure
being surrounded by a diminutive moat or pit bearing some
resemblance to military latrines. In the light of present-day
theories of housing and hygiene, there can be no doubt that
de Selby was much mistaken in these ideas but in his own
remote day more than one sick person lost his life in an ill-
advised quest for health in these fantastic dwellings.[3]

---

[1] *Golden Hours,* ii, 261.   [2] *Country Album,* p. 1,034.
[3] Le Fournier, the reliable French commentator (in *De Selby—
l'Énigme de l'Occident*) has put forward a curious theory regarding

My recollections of de Selby were prompted by my visit to the home of old Mr Mathers. As I approached it along the road the house appeared to be a fine roomy brick building of uncertain age, two storeys high with a plain porch and eight or nine windows to the front of each floor.

I opened the iron gate and walked as softly as I could up the weed-tufted gravel drive. My mind was strangely empty. I did not feel that I was about to end successfully a plan I had worked unrelentingly at night and day for three years. I felt no glow of pleasure and was unexcited at the prospect of becoming rich. I was occupied only with the mechanical task of finding a black box.

The hall-door was closed and although it was set far back in a very deep porch the wind and rain had whipped a coating of gritty dust against the panels and deep into the crack where the door opened, showing that it had been shut for years. Standing on a derelict flower-bed, I tried to push up the sash of the first window on the left. It yielded to my strength, raspingly and stubbornly. I clambered through the opening and found myself, not at once in a room, but crawling along the deepest window-ledge I have ever seen. When I reached the floor and jumped noisily down upon it, the open window seemed very far away and much too small to have admitted me.

The room where I found myself was thick with dust, musty and deserted of all furniture. Spiders had erected great stretchings of their web about the fireplace. I made my way quickly to the hall, threw open the door of the room where the box was and paused on the threshold. It was a dark morning and the weather had stained the windows with blears of grey wash which kept the brightest part of the weak light from coming in. The far corner of the room was

---

these 'habitats'. He suggests that de Selby, when writing the *Album*, paused to consider some point of difficulty and in the meantime engaged in the absent-minded practice known generally as 'doodling', then putting his manuscript away. The next time he took it up he was confronted with a mass of diagrams and drawings which he took to be the plans of a type of dwelling he always had in mind and immediately wrote many pages explaining the sketches. 'In no other way,' adds the severe Le Fournier, 'can one explain so regrettable a lapse.'

a blur of shadow. I had a sudden urge to have done with my task and be out of this house forever. I walked across the bare boards, knelt down in the corner and passed my hands about the floor in search of the loose board. To my surprise I found it easily. It was about two feet in length and rocked hollowly under my hand. I lifted it up, laid it aside and struck a match. I saw a black metal cash-box nestling dimly in the hole. I put my hand down and crooked a finger into the loose reclining handle but the match suddenly flickered and went out and the handle of the box, which I had lifted up about an inch slid heavily off my finger. Without stopping to light another match I thrust my hand bodily into the opening and just when it should be closing about the box, something happened.

I cannot hope to describe what it was but it had frightened me very much long before I had understood it even slightly. It was some change which came upon me or upon the room, indescribably subtle, yet momentous, ineffable. It was as if the daylight had changed with unnatural suddenness, as if the temperature of the evening had altered greatly in an instant or as if the air had become twice as rare or twice as dense as it had been in the winking of an eye; perhaps all of these and other things happened together for all my senses were bewildered all at once and could give me no explanation. The fingers of my right hand, thrust into the opening in the floor, had closed mechanically, found nothing at all and came up again empty. The box was gone!

I heard a cough behind me, soft and natural yet more disturbing than any sound that could ever come upon the human ear. That I did not die of fright was due, I think, to two things, the fact that my senses were already disarranged and able to interpret to me only gradually what they had perceived and also the fact that the utterance of the cough seemed to bring with it some more awful alteration in everything, just as if it had held the universe standstill for an instant, suspending the planets in their courses, halting the sun and holding in mid-air any falling thing the earth was pulling towards it. I collapsed weakly from my kneeling backwards into a limp sitting-down upon the floor. Sweat broke upon my brow and my eyes remained open for a long time without a wink, glazed and almost sightless.

In the darkest corner of the room near the window a man was sitting in a chair, eyeing me with a mild but unwavering interest. His hand had crept out across the small table by his side to turn up very slowly an oil-lamp which was standing on it. The oil-lamp had a glass bowl with the wick dimly visible inside it, curling in convolutions like an intestine. There were tea things on the table. The man was old Mathers. He was watching me in silence. He did not move or speak and might have been still dead save for the slight movement of his hand at the lamp, the very gentle screwing of his thumb and forefinger against the wick-wheel. The hand was yellow, the wrinkled skin draped loosely upon the bones. Over the knuckle of his forefinger I could clearly see the loop of a skinny vein.

It is hard to write of such a scene or to convey with known words the feelings which came knocking at my numbed mind. How long we sat there, for instance, looking at one another I do not know. Years or minutes could be swallowed up with equal ease in that indescribable and unaccountable interval. The light of morning vanished from my sight, the dusty floor was like nothingness beneath me and my whole body dissolved away, leaving me existing only in the stupid spellbound gaze that went steadily from where I was to the other corner.

I remember that I noticed several things in a cold mechanical way as if I was sitting there with no worry save to note everything I saw. His face was terrifying but his eyes in the middle of it had a quality of chill and horror which made his other features look to me almost friendly. The skin was like faded parchment with an arrangement of puckers and wrinkles which created between them an expression of fathomless inscrutability. But the eyes were horrible. Looking at them I got the feeling that they were not genuine eyes at all but mechanical dummies animated by electricity or the like, with a tiny pinhole in the centre of the ' pupil ' through which the real eye gazed out secretively and with great coldness. Such a conception, possibly with no foundation at all in fact, disturbed me agonisingly and gave rise in my mind to interminable speculations as to the colour and quality of the real eye and as to whether, indeed, it was real at all or merely another dummy with its pinhole on the same plane as the first one so that the real eye, possibly behind thousands of these absurd disguises, gazed out through a barrel of serried peep-holes. Occasionally the heavy cheese-like lids would drop down slowly with great languor and then rise again. Wrapped loosely around the body was an old wine-coloured dressing-gown.

In my distress I thought to myself that perhaps it was his twin brother but at once I heard someone say:

Scarcely. If you look carefully at the left-hand side of his neck you will notice that there is sticking-plaster or a bandage there. His throat and chin are also bandaged.

Forlornly, I looked and saw that this was true. He was the man I had murdered beyond all question. He was sitting on a chair four yards away watching me. He sat stiffly without a move as if afraid to hurt the gaping wounds which covered his body. Across my own shoulders a stiffness had spread from my exertions with the spade.

But who had uttered these words? They had not frightened me. They were clearly audible to me yet I knew they did not ring out across the air like the chilling cough of the old man in the chair. They came from deep inside me, from my soul. Never before had I believed or suspected that I had a soul but just then I knew I had. I knew also that my soul was friendly, was my senior in years and was solely concerned for my own welfare. For convenience I called him Joe. I felt a little reassured to know that I was not altogether alone. Joe was helping me.

I will not try to tell of the space of time which followed. In the terrible situation I found myself, my reason could give me no assistance. I knew that old Mathers had been felled by an iron bicycle-pump, hacked to death with a heavy spade and then securely buried in a field. I knew also that the same man was now sitting in the same room with me, watching me in silence. His body was bandaged but his eyes were alive and so was his right hand and so was all of him. Perhaps the murder by the roadside was a bad dream.

There is nothing dreamy about your stiff shoulders. No,

I replied, but a nightmare can be as strenuous physically as the real thing.

I decided in some crooked way that the best thing to do was to believe what my eyes were looking at rather than to place my trust in a memory. I decided to show unconcern, to talk to the old man and to test his own reality by asking about the black box which was responsible, if anything could be, for each of us being the way we were. I made up my mind to be bold because I knew that I was in great danger. I knew that I would go mad unless I got up from the floor and moved and talked and behaved in as ordinary a way as possible. I looked away from old Mathers, got carefully to my feet and sat down on a chair that was not far away from him. Then I looked back at him, my heart pausing for a time and working on again with slow heavy hammer-blows which seemed to make my whole frame shudder. He had remained perfectly still but the live right hand had gripped the pot of tea, raised it very awkwardly and slapped a filling into the empty cup. His eyes had followed me to my new position and were now regarding me again with the same unwavering languorous interest.

Suddenly I began to talk. Words spilled out of me as if they were produced by machinery. My voice, tremulous at first, grew hard and loud and filled the whole room. I do not remember what I said at the beginning. I am sure that most of it was meaningless but I was too pleased and reassured at the natural healthy noise of my tongue to be concerned about the words.

Old Mathers did not move or say anything at first but I was certain that he was listening to me. After a while he began to shake his head and then I was sure I had heard him say No. I became excited at his responses and began to speak carefully. He negatived my inquiry about his health, refused to say where the black box had gone and even denied that it was a dark morning. His voice had a peculiar jarring weight like the hoarse toll of an ancient rusty bell in an ivy-smothered tower. He had said nothing beyond the one word No. His lips hardly moved; I felt sure he had no teeth behind them.

'Are you dead at present?' I asked.

' I am not.'

' Do you know where the box is?'

' No.'

He made another violent movement with his right arm, slapping hot water into his teapot and pouring forth a little more of the feeble brew into his cup. He then relapsed into his attitude of motionless watching. I pondered for a time.

' Do you like weak tea?' I asked.

' I do not,' he said.

' Do you like tea at all?' I asked, ' strong or weak or half-way tea?'

' No,' he said.

' Then why do you drink it?'

He shook his yellow face from side to side sadly and did not say anything. When he stopped shaking he opened up his mouth and poured the cupful of tea in as one would pour a bucket of milk into a churn at churning-time.

Do you notice anything?

No, I replied, nothing beyond the eeriness of this house and the man who owns it. He is by no means the best con-versationalist I have met.

I found I spoke lightly enough. While speaking inwardly or outwardly or thinking of what to say I felt brave and normal enough. But every time a silence came the horror of my situation descended upon me like a heavy blanket flung upon my head, enveloping and smothering me and making me afraid of death.

But do you notice nothing about the way he answers your questions?

No.

Do you not see that every reply is in the negative? No matter what you ask him he says No.

That is true enough, I said, but I do not see where that leads me.

Use your imagination.

When I brought my whole attention back to old Mathers I thought he was asleep. He sat over his teacup in a more stooped attitude as if he were a rock or part of the wooden chair he sat on, a man completely dead and turned to stone. Over his eyes the limp lids had drooped down, almost closing them. His right hand resting on the table lay lifeless and abandoned. I composed my thoughts and addressed to him a sharp noisy interrogation.

' Will you answer a straight question?' I asked. He stirred somewhat, his lids opening slightly.

' I will not,' he replied.

I saw that this answer was in keeping with Joe's shrewd suggestion. I sat thinking for a moment until I had thought the same thought inside out.

' Will you refuse to answer a straight question?' I asked.

' I will not,' he replied.

This answer pleased me. It meant that my mind had got to grips with his, that I was now almost arguing with him and that we were behaving like two ordinary human beings. I did not understand all the terrible things which had happened to me but I now began to think that I must be mistaken about them.

' Very well,' I said quietly, ' Why do you always answer No?'

He stirred perceptibly in his chair and filled the teacup up again before he spoke. He seemed to have some difficulty in finding words.

' " No " ' is, generally speaking, a better answer than " Yes ",' he said at last. He seemed to speak eagerly, his words coming out as if they had been imprisoned in his mouth for a thousand years. He seemed relieved that I had found a way to make him speak. I thought he even smiled slightly at me but this was doubtless the trickery of the bad morning light or a mischief worked by the shadows of the lamp. He swallowed a long draught of tea and sat waiting, looking at me with his queer eyes. They were now bright and active and moved about restlessly in their yellow wrinkled sockets.

' Do you refuse to tell me why you say that?' I asked.

' No,' he said. ' When I was a young man I led an unsatisfactory life and devoted most of my time to excesses of one kind or another, my principal weakness being Number One. I was also party to the formation of an artificial manure-ring.'

My mind went back at once to John Divney, to the farm

and the public house and on from that to the horrible after-noon we had spent on the wet lonely road. As if to inter-rupt my unhappy thoughts I heard Joe's voice again, this time severe:

No need to ask him what Number One is, we do not want lurid descriptions of vice or anything at all in that line. Use your imagination. Ask him what all this has to do with Yes and No.

'What has that got to do with Yes and No?'

'After a time,' said old Mathers disregarding me, 'I mercifully perceived the error of my ways and the unhappy destination I would reach unless I mended them. I retired from the world in order to try to comprehend it and to find out why it becomes more unsavoury as the years accumulate on a man's body. What do you think I discovered at the end of my meditations?'

I felt pleased again. He was now questioning me.

'What?'

'That No is a better word than Yes,' he replied.

This seemed to leave us where we were, I thought.

On the contrary, very far from it. I am beginning to agree with him. There is a lot to be said for No as a General Prin-ciple. Ask him what he means.

'What do you mean?' I inquired.

'When I was meditating,' said old Mathers, 'I took all my sins out and put them on the table, so to speak. I need not tell you it was a big table.'

He seemed to give a very dry smile at his own joke. I chuckled to encourage him.

'I gave them all a strict examination, weighed them and viewed them from all angles of the compass. I asked myself how I came to commit them, where I was and whom I was with when I came to do them.'

This is very wholesome stuff, every word a sermon in it-self. Listen very carefully. Ask him to continue.

'Continue,' I said.

I confess I felt a click inside me very near my stomach as if Joe had put a finger to his lip and pricked up a pair of limp spaniel ears to make sure that no syllable of the wisdom escaped him. Old Mathers continued talking quietly.

'I discovered,' he said, 'that everything you do is in response to a request or a suggestion made to you by some other party either inside you or outside. Some of these suggestions are good and praiseworthy and some of them are undoubtedly delightful. But the majority of them are definitely bad and are pretty considerable sins as sins go. Do you understand me?'

'Perfectly.'

'I would say that the bad ones outnumber the good ones by three to one.'

Six to one if you ask me.

'I therefore decided to say No henceforth to every suggestion, request or inquiry whether inward or outward. It was the only simple formula which was sure and safe. It was difficult to practise at first and often called for heroism but I persevered and hardly ever broke down completely. It is now many years since I said Yes. I have refused more requests and negatived more statements than any man living or dead. I have rejected, reneged, disagreed, refused and denied to an extent that is unbelievable.'

An excellent and original régime. This is all extremely interesting and salutary, every syllable a sermon in itself. Very very wholesome.

'Extremely interesting,' I said to old Mathers.

'The system leads to peace and contentment,' he said. 'People do not trouble to ask you questions if they know the answer is a foregone conclusion. Thoughts which have no chance of succeeding do not take the trouble to come into your head at all.'

'You must find it irksome in some ways,' I suggested. 'If, for instance, I were to offer you a glass of whiskey . . .'

'Such few friends as I have,' he answered, 'are usually good enough to arrange such invitations in a way that will enable me to adhere to my system and also accept the whiskey. More than once I have been asked whether I would refuse such things.'

'And the answer is still NO?'

'Certainly.'

Joe said nothing at this stage but I had the feeling that this confession was not to his liking; he seemed to be uneasy inside me. The old man seemed to get somewhat restive also. He bent over his teacup with abstraction as if he were engaged in accomplishing a sacrament. Then he drank with his hollow throat, making empty noises.

A saintly man.

I turned to him again, fearing that his fit of talkativeness had passed.

'Where is the black box which was under the floor a moment ago?' I asked. I pointed to the opening in the corner. He shook his head and did not say anything.

'Do you refuse to tell me?'

'No.'

'Do you object to my taking it?'

'No.'

'Then where is it?'

'What is your name?' he asked sharply.

I was surprised at this question. It had no bearing on my own conversation but I did not notice its irrelevance because I was shocked to realise that, simple as it was, I could not answer it. I did not know my name, did not remember who I was. I was not certain where I had come from or what my business was in that room. I found I was sure of nothing save my search for the black box. But I knew that the other man's name was Mathers and that he had been killed with a pump and a spade. I had no name.

'I have no name,' I replied.

'Then how could I tell you where the box was if you could not sign a receipt? That would be most irregular. I might as well give it to the west wind or to the smoke from a pipe. How could you execute an important Bank document?'

'I can always get a name,' I replied. 'Doyle or Spaldman is a good name and so is O'Sweeny and Hardiman and O'Gara. I can take my choice. I am not tied down for life to one word like most people.'

'I do not care much for Doyle,' he said absently.

The name is Bari. Signor Bari, the eminent tenor. Five hundred thousand people crowded the great piazza when the great artist appeared on the balcony of St. Peter's Rome.

Fortunately these remarks were not audible in the ordinary sense of the word. Old Mathers was eyeing me.

' What is your colour?' he asked.

' My colour?'

' Surely you know you have a colour?'

' People often remark on my red face.'

' I do not mean that at all.'

Follow this closely, this is bound to be extremely interesting. Very edifying also.

I saw it was necessary to question old Mathers carefully.

' Do you refuse to explain this question about the colours?'

' No,' he said. He slapped more tea in his cup.

' No doubt you are aware that the winds have colours,' he said. I thought he settled himself more restfully in his chair and changed his face till it looked a little bit benign.

' I never noticed it.'

' A record of this belief will be found in the literature of all ancient peoples.[4] There are four winds and eight sub-winds, each with its own colour. The wind from the east is a deep purple, from the south a fine shining silver. The north wind is a hard black and the west is amber. People in the old days had the power of perceiving these colours and could spend a day sitting quietly on a hillside watching the beauty of the winds, their fall and rise and changing hues, the magic of neighbouring winds when they are interweaved like ribbons at a wedding. It was a better occupation than gazing at newspapers. The sub-winds had colours of indescribable delicacy, a reddish-yellow half-way between silver and purple, a greyish-green which was related equally to black and brown. What could be more exquisite than a

---

[4] It is not clear whether de Selby had heard of this but he suggests (*Garcia*, p. 12) that night, far from being caused by the commonly accepted theory of planetary movements, was due to accumulations of ' black air ' produced by certain volcanic activities of which he does not treat in detail. See also p. 79 and 945, *Country Album*. Le Fournier's comment (in *Homme ou Dieu*) is interesting. ' On ne saura jamais jusqu'à quel point de Selby fut cause de la Grande Guerre, mais, sans aucun doute, ses théories excentriques—spécialement celle que nuit n'est pas un phénomène de nature, mais dans l'atmosphère un état malsain amené par un industrialisme cupide et sans pitié—aurent l'effet de produire un trouble profond dans les masses.'

countryside swept lightly by cool rain reddened by the
south-west breeze!'

'Can *you* see these colours?' I asked.

'No.'

'You were asking me what my colour was. How do
people get their colours?'

'A person's colour,' he answered slowly, 'is the colour of
the wind prevailing at his birth.'

'What is your own colour?'

'Light yellow.'

'And what is the point of knowing your colour or having
a colour at all?'

'For one thing you can tell the length of your life from
it. Yellow means a long life and the lighter the better.'

*This is very edifying, every sentence a sermon in itself.
Ask him to explain.*

'Please explain.'

'It is a question of making little gowns,' he said informatively.

'Little gowns?'

'Yes. When I was born there was a certain policeman
present who had the gift of wind-watching. The gift is
getting very rare these days. Just after I was born he went
outside and examined the colour of the wind that was blowing across the hill. He had a secret bag with him full of
certain materials and bottles and he had tailor's instruments
also. He was outside for about ten minutes. When he came
in again he had a little gown in his hand and he made my
mother put it on me.'

'Where did he get this gown?' I asked in surprise.

'He made it himself secretly in the backyard, very likely
in the cowhouse. It was very thin and slight like the very
finest of spider's muslin. You would not see it at all if you
held it against the sky but at certain angles of the light you
might at times accidentally notice the edge of it. It was the
purest and most perfect manifestation of the outside skin
of light yellow. This yellow was the colour of my birth-
wind.'

'I see,' I said.

A very beautiful conception.

' Every time my birthday came,' old Mathers said, ' I was presented with another little gown of the same identical quality except that it was put on over the other one and not in place of it. You may appreciate the extreme delicacy and fineness of the material when I tell you that even at five years old with five of these gowns together on me, I still appeared to be naked. It was, however, an unusual yellowish sort of nakedness. Of course there was no objection to wearing other clothes over the gown. I usually wore an overcoat. But every year I got a new gown.'

' Where did you get them?' I asked.

' From the police. They were brought to my own home until I was big enough to call to the barracks for them.'

' And how does all this enable you to predict your span of life?'

' I will tell you. No matter what your colour is, it will be represented faithfully in your birth-gown. With each year and each gown, the colour will get deeper and more pronounced. In my own case I had attained a bright full-blown yellow at fifteen although the colour was so light at birth as to be imperceptible. I am now nearing seventy and the colour is a light brown. As my gowns come to me through the years ahead, the colour will deepen to dark brown, then a dull mahogany and from that ultimately to that very dark sort of brownness one associates usually with stout.'

' Yes?'

' In a word the colour gradually deepens gown by gown and year by year until it appears to be black. Finally a day will come when the addition of one further gown will actually achieve real and full blackness. On that day I will die.'

Joe and I were surprised at this. We pondered it in silence, Joe, I thought, seeking to reconcile what he had heard with certain principles he held respecting morality and religion.

' That means,' I said at last, ' that if you get a number of these gowns and put them all on together, reckoning each as a year of life, you can ascertain the year of your death?'

' Theoretically, yes,' he replied, ' but there are two difficulties. First of all the police refuse to let you have the gowns together on the ground that the general ascertainment of death-days would be contrary to the public interest. They

34

talk of breaches of the peace and so forth. Secondly, there is a difficulty about stretching.'

'Stretching?'

'Yes. Since you will be wearing as a grown man the tiny gown that fitted you when you were born, it is clear that the gown has stretched until it is perhaps one hundred times as big as it was originally. Naturally this will affect the colour; making it many times rarer than it was. Similarly there will be a proportionate stretch and a corresponding diminution in colour in all the gowns up to manhood—perhaps twenty or so in all.'

I wonder whether it can be taken that this accretion of gowns will have become opaque at the incidence of puberty.

I reminded him that there was always an overcoat.

'I take it, then,' I said to old Mathers, 'that when you say you can tell the length of life, so to speak, from the colour of your shirt, you mean that you can tell roughly whether you will be long-lived or short-lived?'

'Yes,' he replied. 'But if you use your intelligence you can make a very accurate forecast. Naturally some colours are better than others. Some of them, like purple or maroon, are very bad and always mean an early grave. Pink, however, is excellent, and there is a lot to be said for certain shades of green and blue. The prevalence of such colours at birth, however, usually connote a wind that brings bad weather— thunder and lightning, perhaps—and there might be difficulties such, for instance, as getting a woman to come in time. As you know, most good things in life are associated with certain disadvantages.'

Really very beautiful, everything considered.

'Who are these policemen?' I asked.

'There is Sergeant Pluck and another man called Mac-Cruiskeen and there is a third man called Fox that disappeared twenty-five years ago and was never heard of after. The first two are down in the barracks and so far as I know they have been there for hundreds of years. They must be operating on a very rare colour, something that ordinary eyes could not see at all. There is no white wind that I know of. They all have the gift of seeing the winds.

A bright thought came to me when I heard of these

policemen. If they knew so much they would have no difficulty in telling me where I would find the black box. I began to think I would never be happy until I had that box again in my grip. I looked at old Mathers. He had relapsed again to his former passivity. The light had faded from his eyes and the right hand resting on the table looked quite dead.

' Is the barracks far?' I asked loudly.

' No.'

I made up my mind to go there with no delay. Then I noticed a very remarkable thing. The lamplight, which in the beginning had been shining forlornly in the old man's corner only, had now grown rich and yellow and flooded the entire room. The outside light of morning had faded away almost to nothingness. I glanced out of the window and gave a start. Coming into the room I had noticed that the window was to the east and that the sun was rising in that quarter and firing the heavy clouds with light. Now it was setting with last glimmers of feeble red in exactly the same place. It had risen a bit, stopped, and then gone back. Night had come. The policemen would be in bed. I was sure I had fallen among strange people. I made up my mind to go to the barracks the first thing on the morrow. Then I turned again to old Mathers.

' Would you object,' I said to him, ' if I went upstairs and occupied one of your beds for the night? It is too late to go home and I think it is going to rain in any case.'

' No,' he said.

I left him bent at his teaset and went up the stairs. I had got to like him and thought it was a pity he had been murdered. I felt relieved and simplified and certain that I would soon have the black box. But I would not ask the policemen openly about it at first. I would be crafty. In the morning I would go to the barracks and report the theft of my American gold watch. Perhaps it was this lie which was responsible for the bad things that happened to me afterwards. I had no American gold watch.

III

I CREPT OUT of old Mathers' house nine hours afterwards, making my way on to the firm high-road under the
first skies of morning. The dawn was contagious, spreading
rapidly about the heavens. Birds were stirring and the great
kingly trees were being pleasingly interfered with by the first
breezes. My heart was happy and full of zest for high adventure. I did not know my name or where I had come from
but the black box was practically in my grasp. The policemen would direct me to where it was. Ten thousand pounds'
worth of negotiable securities would be a conservative esti-
mate of what was in it. As I walked down the road I was
pleased enough with everything.

The road was narrow, white, old, hard and scarred with
shadow. It ran away westwards in the mist of the early
morning, running cunningly through the little hills and
going to some trouble to visit tiny towns which were not,
strictly speaking, on its way. It was possibly one of the
oldest roads in the world. I found it hard to think of a
time when there was no road there because the trees and
the tall hills and the fine views of bogland had been
arranged by wise hands for the pleasing picture they made
when looked at from the road. Without a road to have
them looked at from they would have a somewhat aimless
if not a futile aspect.

De Selby has some interesting things to say on the subject of roads.[1] Roads he regards as the most ancient of
human monuments, surpassing by many tens of centuries
the oldest thing of stone that man has reared to mark his
passing. The tread of time, he says, levelling all else, has
beaten only to a more enduring hardness the pathways that
have been made throughout the world. He mentions in passing a trick the Celts had in ancient times—that of ' throwing
a calculation ' upon a road. In those days wise men could

[1] *Golden Hours*, vi. 156.

37

tell to a nicety the dimension of a host which had passed by in the night by looking at their tracks with a certain eye and judging them by their perfection and imperfection, the way each footfall was interfered with by each that came after. In this way they could tell the number of men who had passed, whether they were with horse or heavy with shields and iron weapons, and how many chariots; thus they could say the number of men who should be sent after them to kill them. Elsewhere[2] de Selby makes the point that a good road will have character and a certain air of destiny, an indefinable intimation that it is going somewhere, be it east or west, and not coming back from there. If you go with such a road, he thinks, it will give you pleasant travelling, fine sights at every corner and a gentle ease of peregrination that will persuade you that you are walking forever on falling ground. But if you go east on a road that is on its way west, you will marvel at the unfailing bleakness of every prospect and the great number of sore-footed inclines that confront you to make you tired. If a friendly road should lead you into a complicated city with nets of crooked streets and five hundred other roads leaving it for unknown destinations, your own road will always be discernible for its own self and will lead you safely out of the tangled town.

I walked quietly for a good distance on this road, thinking my own thoughts with the front part of my brain and at the same time taking pleasure with the back part in the great and widespread finery of the morning. The air was keen, clear, abundant and intoxicating. Its powerful presence could be discerned everywhere, shaking up the green things jauntily, conferring greater dignity and definition on the stones and boulders, forever arranging and re-arranging the clouds and breathing life into the world. The sun had climbed steeply out of his hiding and was now standing benignly in the lower sky pouring down floods of enchanting light and preliminary tinglings of heat.

I came upon a stone stile beside a gate leading into a field and sat down to rest upon the top of it. I was not sitting there long until I became surprised; surprising ideas

[2] *A Memoir of Garcia*, p. 27.

were coming into my head from nowhere. First of all I remembered who I was—not my name but where I had come from and who my friends were. I recalled John Divney, my life with him and how we came to wait under the dripping trees on the winter's evening. This led me to reflect in wonder that there was nothing wintry about the morning in which I was now sitting. Furthermore, there was nothing familiar about the good-looking countryside which stretched away from me at every view. I was now but two days from home—not more than three hours' walking—and yet I seemed to have reached regions which I had never seen before and of which I had never even heard. I could not understand this because although my life had been spent mostly among my books and papers, I had thought that there was no road in the district I had not travelled, no road whose destination was not well-known to me. There was another thing. My surroundings had a strangeness of a peculiar kind, entirely separate from the mere strangeness of a country where one has never been before. Everything seemed almost too pleasant, too perfect, too finely made. Each thing the eye could see was unmistakable and unambiguous, incapable of merging with any other thing or of being confused with it. The colour of the bogs was beautiful and the greenness of the green fields supernal. Trees were arranged here and there with far-from-usual consideration for the fastidious eye. The senses took keen pleasure from merely breathing the air and discharged their functions with delight. I was clearly in a strange country but all the doubts and perplexities which strewed my mind could not stop me from feeling happy and heart-light and full of an appetite for going about my business and finding the hiding-place of the black box. The valuable contents of it, I felt, would secure me for life in my own house and afterwards I could revisit this mysterious townland upon my bicycle and probe at my leisure the reasons for all its strangenesses. I got down from the stile and continued my walk along the road. It was pleasant easeful walking. I felt sure I was not going against the road. It was, so to speak, accompanying me.

Before going to sleep the previous night I had spent a long time in puzzled thought and also in carrying on inward conversations with my newly-found soul. Strangely enough, I was not thinking about the baffling fact that I was enjoying the hospitality of the man I had murdered (or whom I was sure I had murdered) with my spade. I was reflecting about my name and how tantalising it was to have forgotten it. All people have names of one kind or another. Some are arbitrary labels related to the appearance of the person, some represent purely genealogical associations but most of them afford some clue as to the parents of the person named and confer a certain advantage in the execution of legal documents.[3] Even a dog has a name which dissociates him from other dogs and indeed my own soul, whom nobody has ever seen on the road or standing at the counter of a public house, had apparently no difficulty in assuming a name which distinguished him from other people's souls.

A thing not easy to account for is the unconcern with which I turned over my various perplexities in my mind. Blank anonymity coming suddenly in the middle of life should be at best alarming, a sharp symptom that the mind is in decay. But the unexplainable exhilaration which I drew from my surroundings seemed to invest this situation merely with the genial interest of a good joke. Even now as I walked along contentedly I sensed a solemn question on this subject from within, one similar to many that had been asked

[3] De Selby (*Golden Hours*, p. 93, *et seq.*) has put forward an interesting theory on names. Going back to primitive times, he regards the earliest names as crude onomatopaeic associations with the appearance of the person or object named—thus harsh or rough manifestations being represented by far from pleasant gutturalities and vice versa. This idea he pursued to rather fanciful lengths, drawing up elaborate paradigms of vowels and consonants purporting to correspond to certain indices of human race, colour and temperament and claiming ultimately to be in a position to state the physiological 'group' of any person merely from a brief study of the letters of his name after the word had been 'rationalised' to allow for variations of language. Certain 'groups' he showed to be universally 'repugnant' to other 'groups'. An unhappy commentary on the theory was furnished by the activities of his own nephew, whether through ignorance or contempt for the humanistic researches of his uncle. The nephew set about a Swedish servant, from whom he was completely excluded by the paradigms, in the pantry of a Portsmouth hotel to such purpose that de Selby had to open his purse to the tune of five or six hundred pounds to avert an unsavoury law case.

the night before. It was a mocking inquiry. I light-heartedly
gave a list of names which, for all I knew, I *might* hear:

Hugh Murray.

Constantin Petrie.

Peter Small.

Signor Beniamino Bari.

The Honourable Alex O'Brannigan, Bart.

Kurt Freund.

Mr John P. de Salis, M.A.

Dr Solway Garr.

Bonaparte Gosworth.

Legs O'Hagan.

Signor Beniamino Bari, Joe said, *the eminent tenor. Three
baton-charges outside La Scala at great tenor's première.
Extraordinary scenes were witnessed outside La Scala Opera
House when a crowd of some ten thousand devotées, in-
censed by the management's statement that no more stand-
ing-room was available, attempted to rush the barriers.
Thousands were injured, 79 fatally, in the wild mêlée. Con-
stable Peter Coutts sustained injuries to the groin from which
he is unlikely to recover. These scenes were comparable only
to the delirium of the fashionable audience inside after
Signor Bari had concluded his recital. The great tenor was
in admirable voice. Starting with a phase in the lower register
with a husky richness which seemed to suggest a cold, he
delivered the immortal strains of Che Gelida Manina,
favourite aria of the beloved Caruso. As he warmed to his
God-like task, note after golden note spilled forth to the
remotest corner of the vast theatre, thrilling all and sundry
to the inner core. When he reached the high C where heaven
and earth seem married in one great climax of exaltation, the
audience arose in their seats and cheered as one man, show-
ering hats, programmes and chocolate-boxes on the great
artist.*

Thank you very much, I murmured, smiling in wild
amusement.

*A bit overdone, perhaps, but it is only a hint of the pre-
tensions and vanity that you inwardly permit yourself.*

Indeed?

Or what about Dr Solway Garr? The duchess has fainted.

Is there a doctor in the audience? The spare figure, thin nervous fingers and iron-grey hair, making its way quietly through the pale excited onlookers. A few brief commands, quietly spoken but imperious. Inside five minutes the situation is well in hand. Wan but smiling, the duchess murmurs her thanks. Expert diagnosis has averted still another tragedy. A small denture has been extracted from the thorax. All hearts go out to the quiet-spoken servant of humanity. His Grace, summoned too late to see aught but the happy ending, is opening his cheque-book and has already marked a thousand guineas on the counterfoil as a small token of his esteem. His cheque is taken but torn to atoms by the smiling medico. A lady in blue at the back of the hall begins to sing O Peace Be Thine and the anthem, growing in volume and sincerity, peals out into the quiet night, leaving few eyes that are dry and hearts that are not replete with yearning ere the last notes fade. Dr Garr only smiles, shaking his head in deprecation.

I think that is quite enough, I said.

I walked on unperturbed. The sun was maturing rapidly in the east and a great heat had started to spread about the ground like a magic influence, making everything, including my own self, very beautiful and happy in a dreamy drowsy way. The little beds of tender grass here and there by the roadside and the dry sheltery ditches began to look seductive and inviting. The road was being slowly baked to a greater hardness, making my walking more and more laborious. After not long I decided that I must now be near the police barracks and that another rest would fit me better for the task I had on hand. I stopped walking and spread my body out evenly in the shelter of the ditch. The day was brand new and the ditch was feathery. I lay back unstintingly, stunned with the sun. I felt a million little influences in my nostril, hay-smells, grass-smells, odours from distant flowers, the reassuring unmistakability of the abiding earth beneath my head. It was a new and a bright day, the day of the world. Birds piped without limitation and incomparable stripe-coloured bees passed above me on their missions and hardly ever came back the same way home. My eyes were shuttered and my head was buzzing with the spinning of the universe.

I was not long lying there until my wits deserted me and I fell far into my sleep. I slept there for a long time, as motionless and as devoid of feeling as the shadow of myself which slept behind me.

When I awoke again it was later in the day and a small man was sitting beside me watching me. He was tricky and smoked a tricky pipe and his hand was quavery. His eyes were tricky also, probably from watching policemen. They were very unusual eyes. There was no palpable divergence in their alignment but they seemed to be incapable of giving a direct glance at anything that was straight, whether or not their curious incompatibility was suitable for looking at crooked things. I knew he was watching me only by the way his head was turned; I could not meet his eyes or challenge them. He was small and poorly dressed and on his head was a cloth cap of pale salmon colour. He kept his head in my direction without speaking and I found his presence disquieting. I wondered how long he had been watching me before I awoke.

Watch your step here. A very slippery-looking customer.

I put my hand into my pocket to see if my wallet was there. It was, smooth and warm like the hand of a good friend. When found that I had not been robbed, I decided to talk to him genially and civilly, see who he was and ask him to direct me to the barracks. I made up my mind not to despise the assistance of anybody who could help me, in however small a way, to find the black box. I gave him the time of day and, so far as I could, a look as intricate as any he could give himself.

' More luck to you,' I said.

' More power to yourself,' he answered dourly.

Ask him his name and occupation and inquire what is his destination.

' I do not desire to be inquisitive, sir,' I said, ' but would it be true to mention that you are a bird-catcher?'

' Not a bird-catcher,' he answered.

' A tinker?'

' Not that.'

' A man on a journey?'

' No, not that.'

43

'A fiddler?'

'Not that one.'

I smiled at him in good-humoured perplexity and said:

'Tricky-looking man, you are hard to place and it is not easy to guess your station. You seem very contented in one way but then again you do not seem to be satisfied. What is your objection to life?'

He blew little bags of smoke at me and looked at me closely from behind the bushes of hair which were growing about his eyes.

'Is it life?' he answered. 'I would rather be without it,' he said, 'for there is a queer small utility in it. You cannot eat it or drink it or smoke it in your pipe, it does not keep the rain out and it is a poor armful in the dark if you strip it and take it to bed with you after a night of porter when you are shivering with the red passion. It is a great mistake and a thing better done without, like bed-jars and foreign bacon.'

'That is a nice way to be talking on this grand lively day,' I chided, 'when the sun is roaring in the sky and sending great tidings into our weary bones.'

'Or like feather-beds,' he continued, 'or bread manufactured with powerful steam machinery. Is it life you say? Life?'

Explain the difficulty of life yet stressing its essential sweetness and desirability.

What sweetness?

Flowers in the spring, the glory and fulfilment of human life, bird-song at evening—you know very well what I mean. I am not so sure about the sweetness all the same.

'It is hard to get the right shape of it,' I said to the tricky man, 'or to define life at all but if you identify life with enjoyment I am told that there is a better brand of it in the cities than in the country parts and there is said to be a very superior brand of it to be had in certain parts of France. Did you ever notice that cats have a lot of it in them when they are quite juveniles?'

He was looking in my direction crossly.

'Is it life? Many a man has spent a hundred years trying to get the dimensions of it and when he understands it at last

44

and entertains the certain pattern of it in his head, by the hokey he takes to his bed and dies! He dies like a poisoned sheepdog. There is nothing so dangerous, you can't smoke it, nobody will give you tuppence-halfpenny for the half of it and it kills you in the wind-up. It is a queer contraption, very dangerous, a certain death-trap. Life?'

He sat there looking very vexed with himself and stayed for a while without talking behind a little grey wall he had built for himself by means of his pipe. After an interval I made another attempt to find out what his business was.

'Or a man out after rabbits?' I asked.

'Not that. Not that.'

'A travelling man with a job of journey-work?'

'No.'

'Driving a steam thrashing-mill?'

'Not for certain.'

'Tin-plates?'

'No.'

'A town clerk?'

'No.'

'A water-works inspector?'

'No.'

'With pills for sick horses?'

'Not with pills.'

'Then by Dad,' I remarked perplexedly, 'your calling is very unusual and I cannot think of what it is at all, unless you are a farmer like myself, or a publican's assistant or possibly something in the drapery line. Are you an actor or a mummer?'

'Not them either.'

He sat up suddenly and looked at me in a manner that was almost direct, his pipe sticking out aggressively from his tight jaws. He had the world full of smoke. I was uneasy but not altogether afraid of him. If I had my spade with me I knew I would soon make short work of him. I thought the wisest thing to do was to humour him and to agree with everything he said.

'I am a robber,' he said in a dark voice, 'a robber with a knife and an arm that's as strong as an article of powerful steam machinery.'

'A robber?' I exclaimed. My forebodings had been borne out.

Steady here. Take no chances.

'As strong as the bright moving instruments in a laundry. A black murderer also. Every time I rob a man I knock him dead because I have no respect for life, not a little. If I kill enough men there will be more life to go round and maybe then I will be able to live till I am a thousand and not have the old rattle in my neck when I am quite seventy. Have you a money-bag with you?'

Plead poverty and destitution. Ask for the loan of money.

That will not be difficult, I answered.

'I have no money at all, or coins or sovereigns or bankers' drafts,' I replied, 'no pawn-masters' tickets, nothing that is negotiable or of any value. I am as poor a man as yourself and I was thinking of asking you for two shillings to help me on my way.'

I was now more nervous than I was before as I sat looking at him. He had put his pipe away and had produced a long farmer's knife. He was looking at the blade of it and flashing lights with it.

'Even if you have no money,' he cackled, 'I will take your little life.'

'Now look here till I tell you,' I rejoined in a stern voice, 'robbery and murder are against the law and furthermore my life would add little to your own because I have a disorder in my chest and I am sure to be dead in six months. As well as that, there was a question of a dark funeral in my teacup on Tuesday. Wait till you hear a cough.'

I forced out a great hacking cough. It travelled like a breeze across the grass near at hand. I was now thinking that it might be wise to jump up quickly and run away. It would at least be a simple remedy.

'There is another thing about me,' I added, 'part of me is made of wood and has no life in it at all.'

The tricky man gave out sharp cries of surprise, jumped up and gave me looks that were too tricky for description. I smiled at him and pulled up my left trouser-leg to show him my timber shin. He examined it closely and ran his hard finger along the edge of it. Then he sat down very quickly, put his knife away and took out his pipe again. It had been burning away all the time in his pocket because he started to smoke it without any delay and after a minute he had so much blue smoke made, and grey smoke, that I thought his clothes had gone on fire. Between the smoke I could see that he was giving friendly looks in my direction. After a few moments he spoke cordially and softly to me.

' I would not hurt you, little man,' he said.

' I think I got the disorder in Mullingar,' I explained. I knew that I had gained his confidence and that the danger of violence was now passed. He then did something which took me by surprise. He pulled up his own ragged trouser and showed me his own left leg. It was smooth, shapely and fairly fat but it was made of wood also.

' That is a funny coincidence,' I said. I now perceived the reason for his sudden change of attitude.

' You are a sweet man,' he responded, ' and I would not lay a finger on your personality. I am the captain of all the one-leggèd men in the country. I knew them all up to now except one—your own self—and that one is now also my friend into the same bargain. If any man looks at you sideways, I will rip his belly.'

' That is very friendly talk,' I said.

' Wide open,' he said, making a wide movement with his hands. ' If you are ever troubled, send for me and I will save you from the woman.'

' Women I have no interest in at all,' I said smiling.

' A fiddle is a better thing for diversion.'

' It does not matter. If your perplexity is an army or a dog, I will come with all the one-leggèd men and rip the bellies. My real name is Martin Finnucane.'

' It is a reasonable name,' I assented.

' Martin Finnucane,' he repeated, listening to his own voice as if he were listening to the sweetest music in the world. He lay back and filled himself up to the ears with dark smoke and when he was nearly bursting he let it out again and hid himself in it.

' Tell me this,' he said at last. ' Have you a desideratum?'

This queer question was unexpected but I answered it quickly enough. I said I had.

'What desideratum?'

'To find what I am looking for.'

'That is a handsome desideratum,' said Martin Finnucane. 'What way will you bring it about or mature its mutandum and bring it ultimately to passable factivity?'

'By visiting the police barracks,' I said, 'and asking the policemen to direct me to where it is. Maybe you might instruct me on how to get to the barrack from where we are now?'

'Maybe indeed,' said Mr Finnucane. 'Have you an ultimatum?'

'I have a secret ultimatum,' I replied.

'I am sure it is a fine ultimatum,' he said, 'but I will not ask you to recite it for me if you think it is a secret one.'

He had smoked away all his tobacco and was now smoking the pipe itself, judging by the surly smell of it. He put his hand into a pocket at his crotch and took out a round thing.

'Here is a sovereign for your good luck,' he said, 'the golden token of your golden destiny.'

I gave him, so to speak, my golden thank-you but I noticed that the coin he gave me was a bright penny. I put it carefully into my pocket as if it were highly prized and very valuable. I was pleased at the way I had handled this eccentric queerly-spoken brother of the wooden leg. Near the far side of the road was a small river. I stood up and looked at it and watched the white water. It tumbled in the stony bedstead and jumped in the air and hurried excitedly round a corner.

'The barracks are on this same road,' said Martin Finnucane, 'and I left it behind me a mile away this today morning. You will discover it at the place where the river runs away from the road. If you look now you will see the fat trout in their brown coats coming back from the barracks at this hour because they go there every morning for the fine breakfast that is to be had from the slops and the throwings of the two policemen. But they have their dinners down the other way where a man called MacFeeterson has a bakery shop in a village of houses with their rears to the water. Three bread vans he has and a light dog-cart for the high

48

mountain and he attends at Kilkishkeam on Mondays and Wednesdays.'

'Martin Finnucane,' I said, 'a hundred and two difficult thoughts I have to think between this and my destination and the sooner the better.'

He sent me up friendly glances from the smokey ditch.

'Good-looking man,' he said, 'good luck to your luck and do not entertain danger without sending me cognisance.'

I said 'Good-bye, Good-bye' and left him after a handshake. I looked back from down the road and saw nothing but the lip of the ditch with smoke coming from it as if tinkers were in the bottom of it cooking their what-they-had. Before I was gone I looked back again and saw the shape of his old head regarding me and closely studying my disappearance. He was amusing and interesting and had helped me by directing me to the barracks and telling me how far it was. And as I went upon my way I was slightly glad that I had met him.

A droll customer.

IV

O F   A L L   the many striking statements made by de Selby,
I do not think that any of them can rival his assertion that
'a journey is an hallucination'. The phrase may be found in
the *Country Album*[1] cheek by jowl with the well-known
treatise on 'tent-suits', those egregious canvas garments
which he designed as a substitute alike for the hated houses
and ordinary clothing. His theory, insofar as I can understand it, seems to discount the testimony of human experience and is at variance with everything I have learnt myself
on many a country walk. Human existence de Selby has
defined as 'a succession of static experiences each infinitely
brief', a conception which he is thought to have arrived at
from examining some old cinematograph films which belonged probably to his nephew.[2] From this premise he discounts the reality or truth of any progression or serialism in
life, denies that time can pass as such in the accepted sense
and attributes to hallucinations the commonly experienced
sensation of progression as, for instance, in journeying from
one place to another or even 'living'. If one is resting at A,
he explains, and desires to rest in a distant place B, one
can only do so by resting for infinitely brief intervals in innumerable intermediate places. Thus there is no difference
essentially between what happens when one is resting at A
before the start of the 'journey' and what happens when
one is 'en route', i.e., resting in one or other of the intermediate places. He treats of these 'intermediate places' in
a lengthy footnote. They are not, he warns us, to be taken
as arbitrarily-determined points on the A-B axis so many
inches or feet apart. They are rather to be regarded as points

[1] Page 822.
[2] These are evidently the same films which he mentions in *Golden
Hours* (p. 155) as having 'a strong repetitive element' and as being
'tedious'. Apparently he had examined them patiently picture by picture and imagined that they would be screened in the same way, fail-
ing at that time to grasp the principle of the cinematograph.

infinitely near each other yet sufficiently far apart to admit of the insertion between them of a series of other 'inter-intermediate' places, between each of which must be imagined a chain of other resting-places—not, of course, strictly adjacent but arranged so as to admit of the application of this principle indefinitely. The illusion of progression he attributes to the inability of the human brain—'as at present developed'—to appreciate the reality of these separate 'rests', preferring to group many millions of them together and calling the result motion, an entirely indefensible and impossible procedure since even two separate positions cannot obtain simultaneously of the same body. Thus motion is also an illusion. He mentions that almost any photograph is conclusive proof of his teachings.

Whatever about the soundness of de Selby's theories, there is ample evidence that they were honestly held and that several attempts were made to put them into practice. During his stay in England, he happened at one time to be living in Bath and found it necessary to go from there to Folkestone on pressing business.[3] His method of doing so was far from conventional. Instead of going to the railway station and inquiring about trains, he shut himself up in a room in his lodgings with a supply of picture postcards of the areas which would be traversed on such a journey, together with an elaborate arrangement of clocks and barometric instruments and a device for regulating the gaslight in conformity with the changing light of the outside day. What happened in the room or how precisely the clocks and other machines were manipulated will never be known. It seems that he emerged after a lapse of seven hours convinced that he was in Folkestone and possibly that he had evolved a formula for travellers which would be extremely distasteful to railway and shipping companies. There is no record of the extent of his disillusionment when he found himself still in the familiar surroundings of Bath but one authority[4] relates that he claimed without turning a hair to have been to Folkestone and back again. Reference is made to a man (un-

[3] See Hatchjaw's *De Selby's Life and Times.*
[4] Bassett: *Lux Mundi: A Memoir of de Selby.*

51

named) declaring to have actually seen the savant coming out of a Folkestone bank on the material date.

Like most of de Selby's theories, the ultimate outcome is inconclusive. It is a curious enigma that so great a mind would question the most obvious realities and object even to things scientifically demonstrated (such as the sequence of day and night) while believing absolutely in his own fantastic explanations of the same phenomena.

Of my own journey to the police-barracks I need only say that it was no hallucination. The heat of the sun played incontrovertibly on every inch of me, the hardness of the road was uncompromising and the country changed slowly but surely as I made my way through it. To the left was brown bogland scarred with dark cuttings and strewn with rugged clumps of bushes, white streaks of boulder and here and there a distant house half-hiding in an assembly of little trees. Far beyond was another region sheltering in the haze, purple and mysterious. The right-hand side was a greener country with the small turbulent river accompanying the road at a respectful distance and on the other side of it hills of rocky pasture stretching away into the distance up and down. Tiny sheep could be discerned near the sky far away and crooked lanes ran hither and thither. There was no sign whatever of human life. It was still early morning, perhaps. If I had not lost my American gold watch it would be possible for me to tell the time.

You have no American gold watch.

Something strange then happened to me suddenly. The road before me was turning gently to the left and as I approached the bend my heart began to behave irregularly and an unaccountable excitement took complete possession of me. There was nothing to see and no change of any kind had come upon the scene to explain what was taking place within me. I continued walking with wild eyes.

As I came round the bend of the road an extraordinary spectacle was presented to me. About a hundred yards away on the left-hand side was a house which astonished me. It looked as if it were painted like an advertisement on a board on the roadside and indeed very poorly painted. It looked completely false and unconvincing. It did not seem to have any depth or breadth and looked as if it would not deceive a child. That was not in itself sufficient to surprise me because I had seen pictures and notices by the roadside before. What bewildered me was the sure knowledge deeply-rooted in my mind, that this was the house I was searching for and that there were people inside it. I had no doubt at all that it was the barracks of the policemen. I had never seen with my eyes ever in my life before anything so unnatural and appalling and my gaze faltered about the thing uncomprehendingly as if at least one of the customary dimensions was missing, leaving no meaning in the remainder. The appearance of the house was the greatest surprise I had encountered since I had seen the old man in the chair and I felt afraid of it.

I kept on walking, but walked more slowly. As I approached, the house seemed to change its appearance. At first, it did nothing to reconcile itself with the shape of an ordinary house but it became uncertain in outline like a thing glimpsed under ruffled water. Then it became clear again and I saw that it began to have some back to it, some small space for rooms behind the frontage. I gathered this from the fact that I seemed to see the front and the back of the ' building' simultaneously from my position approaching what should have been the side. As there was no side that I could see I thought the house must be triangular with its apex pointing towards me but when I was only fifteen yards away I saw a small window apparently facing me and I knew from that that there must be *some* side to it. Then I found myself almost in the shadow of the structure, dry-throated and timorous from wonder and anxiety. It seemed ordinary enough at close quarters except that it was very white and still. It was momentous and frightening; the whole morning and the whole world seemed to have no purpose at all save to frame it and give it some magnitude and position so that I could find it with my simple senses and pretend to myself that I understood it. A constabulary crest above the door told me that it was a police station. I had never seen a police station like it.

I cannot say why I did not stop to think or why my nervousness did not make me halt and sit down weakly by the roadside. Instead I walked straight up to the door and looked in. I saw, standing with his back to me, an enormous policeman. His back appearance was unusual. He was standing behind a little counter in a neat whitewashed day-room; his mouth was open and he was looking into a mirror which hung upon the wall. Again, I find it difficult to convey the precise reason why my eyes found his shape unprecedented and unfamiliar. He was very big and fat and the hair which strayed abundantly about the back of his bulging neck was a pale straw-colour; all that was striking but not unheard of. My glance ran over his great back, the thick arms and legs encased in the rough blue uniform. Ordinary enough as each part of him looked by itself, they all seemed to create together, by some undetectable discrepancy in association or proportion, a very disquieting impression of unnaturalness, amounting almost to what was horrible and monstrous. His hands were red, swollen and enormous and he appeared to have one of them half-way into his mouth as he gazed into the mirror.

'It's my teeth,' I heard him say, abstractedly and half-aloud. His voice was heavy and slightly muffled, reminding me of a thick winter quilt. I must have made some sound at the door or possibly he had seen my reflection in the glass for he turned slowly round, shifting his stance with leisurely and heavy majesty, his fingers still working at his teeth; and as he turned I heard him murmuring to himself:

'Nearly every sickness is from the teeth.'

His face gave me one more surprise. It was enormously fat, red and widespread, sitting squarely on the neck of his tunic with a clumsy weightiness that reminded me of a sack of flour. The lower half of it was hidden by a violent red moustache which shot out from his skin far into the air like the antennae of some unusual animal. His cheeks were red and chubby and his eyes were nearly invisible, hidden from above by the obstruction of his tufted brows and from below by the fat foldings of his skin. He came over ponderously to the inside of the counter and I advanced meekly from the door until we were face to face.

Is it about a bicycle?' he asked.

His expression when I encountered it was unexpectedly

reassuring. His face was gross and far from beautiful but he had modified and assembled his various unpleasant features in some skilful way so that they expressed to me good nature, politeness and infinite patience. In the front of his peaked official cap was an important-looking badge and over it in golden letters was the word SERGEANT. It was Sergeant Pluck himself.

'No,' I answered, stretching forth my hand to lean with it against the counter. The Sergeant looked at me incredulously.

'Are you sure?' he asked.

'Certain.'

'Not about a motor-cycle?'

'No.'

'One with overhead valves and a dynamo for light? Or with racing handle-bars?'

'No.'

'In that circumstantial eventuality there can be no question of a motor-bicycle,' he said. He looked surprised and puzzled and leaned sideways on the counter on the prop of his left elbow, putting the knuckles of his right hand between his yellow teeth and raising three enormous wrinkles of perplexity on his forehead. I decided now that he was a simple man and that I would have no difficulty in dealing with him exactly as I desired and finding out from him what had happened to the black box. I did not understand clearly the reason for his questions about bicycles but I made up my mind to answer everything carefully, to bide my time and to be cunning in all my dealings with him. He moved away abstractedly, came back and handed me a bundle of differently-coloured papers which looked like application forms for bull-licences and dog-licences and the like.

'It would be no harm if you filled up these forms,' he said. 'Tell me,' he continued, 'would it be true that you are an itinerant dentist and that you came on a tricycle?'

'It would not,' I replied.

'On a patent tandem?'

'No.'

'Dentists are an unpredictable coterie of people,' he said. 'Do you tell me it was a velocipede or a penny-farthing?'

'I do not,' I said evenly. He gave me a long searching look as if to see whether I was serious in what I was saying, again wrinkling up his brow.

'Then maybe you are no dentist at all,' he said, 'but only a man after a dog licence or papers for a bull?'

'I did not say I was a dentist,' I said sharply, 'and I did not say anything about a bull.'

The Sergeant looked at me incredulously.

'That is a great curiosity,' he said, 'a very difficult piece of puzzledom, a snorter.'

He sat down by the turf fire and began jawing his knuckles and giving me sharp glances from under his bushy brows. If I had horns upon my head or a tail behind me he could not have looked at me with more interest. I was unwilling to give any lead to the direction of the talk and there was complete silence for five minutes. Then his expression eased a bit and he spoke to me again.

'What is your pronoun?' he inquired.

'I have no pronoun,' I answered, hoping I knew his meaning.

'What is your cog?'

'My cog?'

'Your surnoun?'

'I have not got that either.'

My reply again surprised him and also seemed to please him. He raised his thick eyebrows and changed his face into what could be described as a smile. He came back to the counter, put out his enormous hand, took mine in it and shook it warmly.

'No name or no idea of your originality at all?'

'None.'

'Well, by the holy Hokey!'

Signor Bari, the eminent one-leggèd tenor!

'By the holy Irish-American Powers,' he said again, 'by the Dad! Well carry me back to old Kentucky!'

He then retreated from the counter to his chair by the fire and sat silently bent in thought as if examining one by one the by-gone years stored up in his memory.

'I was once acquainted with a tall man,' he said to me at last, 'that had no name either and you are certain to be his son and the heir to his nullity and all his nothings. What way is your pop today and where is he?'

It was not, I thought, entirely unreasonable that the son of a man who had no name should have no name also but it was clear that the Sergeant was confusing me with somebody else. This was no harm and I decided to encourage him. I considered it desirable that he should know nothing about me but it was even better if he knew several things which were quite wrong. It would help me in using him for my own purposes and ultimately in finding the black box.

'He is gone to America,' I replied.

'Is that where,' said the sergeant. 'Do you tell me that? He was a true family husband. The last time I interviewed him it was about a missing pump and he had a wife and ten sonnies and at that time he had the wife again in a very advanced state of sexuality.'

'That was me,' I said, smiling.

'That was you,' he agreed. 'What way are the ten strong sons?'

'All gone to America.'

'That is a great conundrum of a country,' said the Sergeant, 'a very wide territory, a place occupied by black men and strangers. I am told they are very fond of shooting-matches in that quarter.'

'It is a queer land,' I said.

At this stage there were footsteps at the door and in marched a heavy policeman carrying a small constabulary lamp. He had a dark Jewish face and hooky nose and masses of black curly hair. He was blue-jowled and black-jowled and looked as if he shaved twice a day. He had white enamelled teeth which came, I had no doubt, from Manchester, two rows of them arranged in the interior of his mouth and when he smiled it was a fine sight to see, like delph on a neat country dresser. He was heavy-fleshed and gross in body like the Sergeant but his face looked far more intelligent. It was unexpectedly lean and the eyes in it were penetrating and observant. If his face alone were in question he would look more like a poet than a policeman but the rest of his body looked anything but poetical.

'Policeman MacCruiskeen,' said Sergeant Pluck.

Policeman MacCruiskeen put the lamp on the table, shook hands with me and gave me the time of day with great gravity. His voice was high, almost feminine, and he spoke with a delicate careful intonation. Then he put the little lamp on the counter and surveyed the two of us.

'Is it about a bicycle?' he asked.

'Not that,' said the Sergeant. 'This is a private visitor who says he did not arrive in the townland upon a bicycle. He has no personal name at all. His dadda is in far Amurikey.'

'Which of the two Amurikeys?' asked MacCruiskeen.

'The Unified Stations,' said the Sergeant.

'Likely he is rich by now if he is in that quarter,' said MacCruiskeen, 'because there's dollars there, dollars and bucks and nuggets in the ground and any amount of rackets and golf games and musical instruments. It is a free country too by all accounts.'

'Free for all,' said the Sergeant. 'Tell me this,' he said to the policeman, 'Did you take any readings today?'

'I did,' said MacCruiskeen.

'Take out your black book and tell me what it was, like a good man,' said the Sergeant. 'Give me the gist of it till I see what I see,' he added.

MacCruiskeen fished a small black notebook from his breast pocket.

'Ten point six,' he said.

'Ten point six,' said the Sergeant. 'And what reading did you notice on the beam?'

'Seven point four.'

'How much on the lever?'

'One point five.'

There was a pause here. The Sergeant put on an expression of great intricacy as if he were doing far-from-simple sums and calculations in his head. After a time his face cleared and he spoke again to his companion.

'Was there a fall?'

'A heavy fall at half-past three.'

'Very understandable and commendably satisfactory,' said the Sergeant. 'Your supper is on the hob inside and be sure to stir the milk before you take any of it, the way the rest of us after you will have our share of the fats of it, the health and the heart of it.'

Policeman MacCruiskeen smiled at the mention of food and went into the back room loosening his belt as he went; after a moment we heard the sounds of coarse slobbering as if he was eating porridge without the assistance of spoon or hand. The Sergeant invited me to sit at the fire in his company and gave me a wrinkled cigarette from his pocket.

'It is lucky for your pop that he is situated in Amurikey,' he remarked, 'if it is a thing that he is having trouble with the old teeth. It is very few sicknesses that are not from the teeth.'

'Yes,' I said. I was determined to say as little as possible and let these unusual policemen first show their hand. Then I would know how to deal with them.

'Because a man can have more disease and germination in his gob than you'll find in a rat's coat and Amurikey is a country where the population do have grand teeth like shaving-lather or like bits of delph when you break a plate.'

'Quite true,' I said.

'Or like eggs under a black crow.'

'Like eggs,' I said.

'Did you ever happen to visit the cinematograph in your travels?'

'Never,' I answered humbly, 'but I believe it is a dark quarter and little can be seen at all except the photographs on the wall.'

'Well it is there you see the fine teeth they do have in Amurikey,' said the Sergeant.

He gave the fire a hard look and took to handling absently his yellow stumps of teeth. I had been wondering about his mysterious conversation with MacCruiskeen.

'Tell me this much,' I ventured. 'What sort of readings were those in the policeman's black book?'

The Sergeant gave me a keen look which felt almost hot from being on the fire previously.

'The first beginnings of wisdom,' he said, 'is to ask questions but never to answer any. *You* get wisdom from asking and *I* from not answering. Would you believe that there is a great increase in crime in this locality? Last year we had sixty-nine cases of no lights and four stolen. This year we have eighty-two cases of no lights, thirteen cases of riding on the footpath and four stolen. There was one case of wanton damage to a three-speed gear, there is sure to be a claim at the next Court and the area of charge will be the parish. Before the year is out there is certain to be a pump stolen, a very depraved and despicable manifestation of criminality and a blot on the county.'

'Indeed,' I said.

'Five years ago we had a case of loose handlebars. Now there is a rarity for you. It took the three of us a week to frame the charge.'

'Loose handlebars,' I muttered. I could not clearly see the reason for such talk about bicycles.

'And then there is the question of bad brakes. The country is honeycombed with bad brakes, half of the accidents are due to it, it runs in families.'

I thought it would be better to try to change the conversation from bicycles.

'You told me what the first rule of wisdom is,' I said. 'What is the second rule?'

'That can be answered,' he said. 'There are five in all. Always ask any questions that are to be asked and never answer any. Turn everything you hear to your own advantage. Always carry a repair outfit. Take left turns as much as possible. Never apply your front brake first.'

'These are interesting rules,' I said dryly.

'If you follow them,' said the Sergeant, 'you will save your soul and you will never get a fall on a slippy road.'

'I would be obliged to you,' I said, 'if you would explain to me which of these rules covers the difficulty I have come here today to put before you.'

'This is not today, this is yesterday,' he said, 'but which of the difficulties is it? What is the *crux rei*?'

Yesterday? I decided without any hesitation that it was a waste of time trying to understand the half of what he said. I persevered with my inquiry.

'I came here to inform you officially about the theft of my American gold watch.'

He looked at me through an atmosphere of great surprise

60

and incredulity and raised his eyebrows almost to his hair.

'That is an astonishing statement,' he said at last.

'Why?'

'Why should anybody steal a watch when they can steal a bicycle?'

Hark to his cold inexorable logic.

'Search me,' I said.

'Who ever heard of a man riding a watch down the road or bringing a sack of turf up to his house on the crossbar of a watch?'

'I did not say the thief wanted my watch to ride it,' I expostulated. 'Very likely he had a bicycle of his own and that is how he got away quietly in the middle of the night.'

'Never in my puff did I hear of any man stealing anything but a bicycle when he was in his sane senses,' said the Sergeant, '—except pumps and clips and lamps and the like of that. Surely you are not going to tell me at my time of life that the world is changing?'

'I am only saying that my watch was stolen,' I said crossly.

'Very well,' the Sergeant said with finality, 'we will have to institute a search.'

He smiled brightly at me. It was quite clear that he did not believe any part of my story, and that he thought I was in delicate mental health. He was humouring me as if I were a child.

'Thank you,' I muttered.

'But the trouble will only be beginning when we find it,' he said severely.

'How is that?'

'When we find it we will have to start searching for the owner.'

'But I am the owner.'

Here the Sergeant laughed indulgently and shook his head.

'I know what you mean,' he said. 'But the law is an extremely intricate phenomenon. If you have no name you cannot own a watch and the watch that has been stolen does not exist and when it is found it will have to be restored to its rightful owner. If you have no name you possess nothing and you do not exist and even your trousers are not on you although they look as if they were from where I am sitting. On the other separate hand you can do what you like and the law cannot touch you.'

'It had fifteen jewels,' I said despairingly.

'And on the first hand again you might be charged with theft or common larceny if you were mistaken for somebody else when wearing the watch.'

'I feel extremely puzzled,' I said, speaking nothing less than the truth. The Sergeant gave his laugh of good humour.

'If we ever find the watch,' he smiled, 'I have a feeling that there will be a bell and a pump on it.'

I considered my position with some misgiving. It seemed to be impossible to make the Sergeant take cognisance of anything in the world except bicycles. I thought I would make a last effort.

'You appear to be under the impression,' I said coldly and courteously, 'that I have lost a golden bicycle of American manufacture with fifteen jewels. I have lost a watch and there is no bell on it. Bells are only on alarm clocks and I have never in my life seen a watch with a pump attached to it.'

The Sergeant smiled at me again.

'There was a man in this room a fortnight ago,' he said, 'telling me that he was at the loss of his mother, a lady of eighty-two. When I asked him for a description—just to fill up the blanks in the official form we get for half-nothing from the Stationery Office—he said she had rust on her rims and that her back brakes were subject to the jerks.'

This speech made my position quite clear to me. When I was about to say something else, a man put his face in and looked at us and then came in completely and shut the door carefully and came over to the counter. He was a bluff red man in a burly coat with twine binding his trousers at the knees. I discovered afterwards that his name was Michael Gilhaney. Instead of standing at the counter as he would in a public house, he went to the wall, put his arms akimbo and leaned against it, balancing his weight on the point of one elbow.

' Well, Michael,' said the Sergeant pleasantly.

' That is a cold one,' said Mr Gilhaney.

Sounds of shouting came to the three of us from the inner room where Policeman MacCruiskeen was engaged in the task of his early dinner.

' Hand me in a fag,' he called.

The Sergeant gave me another wrinkled cigarette from his pocket and jerked his thumb in the direction of the back room. As I went in with the cigarette I heard the Sergeant opening an enormous ledger and putting questions to the red-faced visitor.

' What was the make,' he was saying, ' and the number of the frame and was there a lamp and a pump on it into the same bargain?'

V

THE LONG and unprecedented conversation I had with
Policeman MacCruiskeen after I went in to him on my
mission with the cigarette brought to my mind afterwards
several of the more delicate speculations of de Selby, notably
his investigation of the nature of time and eternity by a
system of mirrors.[1] His theory as I understand it is as follows

If a man stands before a mirror and sees in it his reflection, what he sees is not a true reproduction of himself but a
picture of himself when he was a younger man. De Selby's
explanation of this phenomenon is quite simple. Light, as
he points out truly enough, has an ascertained and finite rate
of travel. Hence before the reflection of any object in a
mirror can be said to be accomplished, it is necessary that
rays of light should first strike the object and subsequently
impinge on the glass, to be thrown back again to the object
—to the eyes of a man, for instance. There is therefore an
appreciable and calculable interval of time between the
throwing by a man of a glance at his own face in a mirror
and the registration of the reflected image in his eye.

So far, one may say, so good. Whether this idea is right
or wrong, the amount of time involved is so negligible that
few reasonable people would argue the point. But de Selby

---

[1] Hatchjaw remarks (unconfirmed, however, by Bassett) that throughout the whole ten years that went to the writing of *The Country Album*
de Selby was obsessed with mirrors and had recourse to them so frequently that he claimed to have two left hands and to be living in a
world arbitrarily bounded by a wooden frame. As time went on he
refused to countenance a direct view of anything and had a small
mirror permanently suspended at a certain angle in front of his eyes
by a wired mechanism of his own manufacture. After he had resorted
to this fantastic arrangement, he interviewed visitors with his back
to them and with his head inclined towards the ceiling; he was even
credited with long walks backwards in crowded thoroughfares. Hatchjaw claims that his statement is supported by the MS. of some three
hundred pages of the *Album,* written backwards, 'a circumstance that
made necessary the extension of the mirror principle to the bench of
the wretched printer.' (*De Selby's Life and Times,* p. 221.) This
manuscript cannot now be found.

ever loath to leave well enough alone, insists on reflecting the first reflection in a further mirror and professing to detect minute changes in this second image. Ultimately he constructed the familiar arrangement of parallel mirrors, each reflecting diminishing images of an interposed object indefinitely. The interposed object in this case was de Selby's own face and this he claims to have studied backwards through an infinity of reflections by means of ' a powerful glass '. What he states to have seen through his glass is astonishing. He claims to have noticed a growing youthfulness in the reflections of his face according as they receded, the most distant of them—too tiny to be visible to the naked eye—being the face of a beardless boy of twelve, and, to use his own words, ' a countenance of singular beauty and nobility '. He did not succeed in pursuing the matter back to the cradle ' owing to the curvature of the earth and the limitations of the telescope.'

So much for de Selby. I found MacCruiskeen with a red face at the kitchen table panting quietly from all the food he had hidden in his belly. In exchange for the cigarette he gave me searching looks. ' Well, now,' he said.

He lit the cigarette and sucked at it and smiled covertly at me.

' Well, now,' he said again. He had his little lamp beside him on the table and he played his fingers on it.

' That is a fine day,' I said. ' What are you doing with a lamp in the white morning?'

' I can give you a question as good as that,' he responded. ' Can you notify me of the meaning of a bulbul?'

' A bulbul?'

' What would you say a bulbul is?'

This conundrum did not interest me but I pretended to rack my brains and screwed my face in perplexity until I felt it half the size it should be.

' Not one of those ladies who take money?' I said.

' No.'

' Not the brass knobs on a German steam organ?'

' Not the knobs.'

' Nothing to do with the independence of America or such-like?'

' No.'

' A mechanical engine for winding clocks?'

' No.'

' A tumour, or the lather in a cow's mouth, or those elastic articles that ladies wear?'

' Not them by a long chalk.'

' Not an eastern musical instrument played by Arabs?' He clapped his hands.

' Not that but very near it,' he smiled, ' something next door to it. You are a cordial intelligible man. A bulbul is a Persian nightingale. What do you think of that now?'

' It is seldom I am far out,' I said dryly.

He looked at me in admiration and the two of us sat in silence for a while as if each was very pleased with himself and with the other and had good reason to be.

' You are a B.A. with little doubt?' he questioned.

I gave no direct answer but tried to look big and learned and far from simple in my little chair.

' I think you are a sempiternal man,' he said slowly.

He sat for a while giving the floor a strict examination and then put his dark jaw over to me and began questioning me about my arrival in the parish.

' I do not want to be insidious,' he said, ' but would you inform me about your arrival in the parish? Surely you had a three-speed gear for the hills?'

' I had no three-speed gear,' I responded rather sharply, ' and no two-speed gear and it is also true that I had no bicycle and little or no pump and if I had a lamp itself it would not be necessary if I had no bicycle and there would be no bracket to hang it on.'

' That may be,' said MacCruiskeen, ' but likely you were laughed at on the tricycle?'

' I had neither bicycle nor tricycle and I am not a dentist,' I said with severe categorical thoroughness, ' and I do not believe in the penny-farthing or the scooter, the velocipede or the tandem-tourer.'

MacCruiskeen got white and shaky and gripped my arm and looked at me intensely.

' In my natural puff,' he said at last, in a strained voice, ' I have never encountered a more fantastic epilogue or a queerer story. Surely you are a queer far-fetched man. To my dying night I will not forget this today morning. Do not tell me that you are taking a hand at me?'

'No,' I said.

'Well Great Crikes!'

He got up and brushed his hair with a flat hand back along his skull and looked out of the window for a long interval, his eyes popping and dancing and his face like an empty bag with no blood in it.

Then he walked around to put back the circulation and took a little spear from a place he had on the shelf.

'Put your hand out,' he said.

I put it out idly enough and he held the spear at it. He kept putting it near me and nearer and when he had the bright point of it about half a foot away, I felt a prick and gave a short cry. There was a little bead of my red blood in the middle of my palm.

'Thank you very much,' I said. I felt too surprised to be annoyed with him.

'That will make you think,' he remarked in triumph, 'unless I am an old Dutchman by profession and nationality.'

He put his little spear back on the shelf and looked at me crookedly from a sidewise angle with a certain quantity of what may be called *roi-s'amuse*.

'Maybe you can explain that?' he said.

'That is the limit,' I said wonderingly.

'It will take some analysis,' he said, 'intellectually.'

'Why did your spear sting when the point was half a foot away from where it made me bleed?'

'That spear,' he answered quietly, 'is one of the first things I ever manufactured in my spare time. I think only a little of it now but the year I made it I was proud enough and would not get up in the morning for any sergeant. There is no other spear like it in the length and breadth of Ireland and there is only one thing like it in Amurikey but I have not heard what it is. But I cannot get over the no-bicycle. Great Crikes!'

'But the spear,' I insisted, 'give me the gist of it like a good man and I will tell no one.'

'I will tell you because you are a confidential man,' he said, 'and a man that said something about bicycles that I never heard before. What you think is the point is not the point at all but only the beginning of the sharpness.'

'Very wonderful,' I said, 'but I do not understand you.'

'The point is seven inches long and it is so sharp and thin that you cannot see it with the old eye. The first half of the sharpness is thick and strong but you cannot see it either because the real sharpness runs into it and if you saw the one you could see the other or maybe you would notice the joint.'

'I suppose it is far thinner than a match?' I asked.

'There *is* a difference,' he said. 'Now the proper sharp part is so thin that nobody could see it no matter what light is on it or what eye is looking. About an inch from the end it is so sharp that sometimes—late at night or on a soft bad day especially—you cannot think of it or try to make it the subject of a little idea because you will hurt your box with the excruciation of it.'

I gave a frown and tried to make myself look like a wise person who was trying to comprehend something that called for all his wisdom.

'You cannot have fire without bricks,' I said, nodding.

'Wisely said,' MacCruiskeen answered.

'It was sharp sure enough,' I conceded, 'it drew a little bulb of the red blood but I did not feel the pricking hardly at all. It must be very sharp to work like that.'

MacCruiskeen gave a laugh and sat down again at the table and started putting on his belt.

'You have not got the whole gist of it at all,' he smiled. 'Because what gave you the prick and brought the blood was not the point at all; it was the place I am talking about that is a good inch from the reputed point of the article under our discussion.'

'And what is this inch that is left?' I asked. 'What in heaven's name would you call that?'

'That is the real point,' said MacCruiskeen, 'but it is so thin that it could go into your hand and out in the other extremity externally and you would not feel a bit of it and you would see nothing and hear nothing. It is so thin that maybe

it does not exist at all and you could spend half an hour trying to think about it and you could put no thought around it
in the end. The beginning part of the inch is thicker than
the last part and is nearly there for a fact but I don't think it
is if it is my private opinion that you are anxious to enlist.'

I fastened my fingers around my jaw and started to think
with great concentration, calling into play parts of my brain
that I rarely used. Nevertheless I made no progress at all as
regards the question of the points. MacCruiskeen had been
at the dresser a second time and was back at the table with a
little black article like a leprechaun's piano with diminutive
keys of white and black and brass pipes and circular revolv-
ing cogs like parts of a steam engine or the business end of a
thrashing-mill. His white hands were moving all over it and
feeling it as if they were trying to discover some tiny lump
on it, and his face was looking up in the air in a spiritual attitude and he was paying no attention to my personal existence
at all. There was an overpowering tremendous silence as if
the roof of the room had come down half-way to the floor,
he at his queer occupation with the instrument and myself
still trying to comprehend the sharpness of the points and
to get the accurate understanding of them.

After ten minutes he got up and put the thing away. He
wrote for a time in his notebook and then lit his pipe.

'Well now,' he remarked expansively.

'Those points,' I said.

'Did I happen to ask you what a bulbul is?'

'You did,' I responded, 'but the question of those points
is what takes me to the fair.'

'It is not today or yesterday I started pointing spears,' he
said, 'but maybe you would like to see something else that
is a medium fair example of supreme art?'

'I would indeed,' I answered.

'But I cannot get over what you confided in me privately
sub-rosa about the no-bicycle, that is a story that would
make your golden fortune if you wrote down in a book
where people could pursue it literally.'

He walked back to the dresser, opened the lower part of
it, and took out a little chest till he put it on the table for
my inspection. Never in my life did I inspect anything more

ornamental and well-made. It was a brown chest like those owned by seafaring men or lascars from Singapore, but it was diminutive in a very perfect way as if you were looking at a full-size one through the wrong end of a spy-glass. It was about a foot in height, perfect in its proportions and without fault in workmanship. There were indents and carving and fanciful excoriations and designs on every side of it and there was a bend on the lid that gave the article great distinction. At every corner there was a shiny brass corner-piece and on the lid there were brass corner-pieces beautifully wrought and curved impeccably against the wood. The whole thing had the dignity and the satisfying quality of true art.

' There now,' said MacCruiskeen.

' It is nearly too nice,' I said at last, ' to talk about it.'

' I spent two years manufacturing it when I was a lad,' said MacCruiskeen, ' and it still takes me to the fair.'

' It is unmentionable,' I said.

' Very nearly,' said MacCruiskeen.

The two of us then started looking at it and we looked at it for five minutes so hard that it seemed to dance on the table and look even smaller than it might be.

' I do not often look at boxes or chests,' I said, simply, ' but this is the most beautiful box I have ever seen and I will always remember it. There might be something inside it?'

' There might be,' said MacCruiskeen.

He went to the table and put his hands around the article in a fawning way as if he were caressing a sheepdog and he opened the lid with a little key but shut it down again before I could inspect the inside of it.

' I will tell you a story and give you a synopsis of the ramification of the little plot,' he said. ' When I had the chest made and finished, I tried to think what I would keep in it and what I would use it for at all. First I thought of them letters from Bridie, the ones on the blue paper with the strong smell but I did not think it would be anything but a sacrilege in the end because there was hot bits in them letters. Do you comprehend the trend of my observations?'

' I do,' I answered.

' Then there was my studs and the enamel badge and my presentation iron-pencil with a screw on the end of it to push the point out, an intricate article full of machinery and a Present from Southport. All these things are what are called Examples of the Machine Age.'

' They would be contrary to the spirit of the chest,' I said.

' They would be indeed. Then there was my razor and the spare plate in case I was presented with an accidental bash on the gob in the execution of me duty . . .'

' But not them.'

' Not them. Then there was my certificates and me cash and the picture of Peter the Hermit and the brass thing with straps that I found on the road one night near Matthew O'Carahan's. But not them either.'

' It is a hard conundrum,' I said.

' In the end I found there was only one thing to do to put myself right with my private conscience.'

' It is a great thing that you found the right answer at all,' I countered.

' I decided to myself,' said MacCruiskeen, ' that the only sole correct thing to contain in the chest was another chest of the same make but littler in cubic dimension.'

' That was very competent masterwork,' I said, endeavouring to speak his own language.

He went to the little chest and opened it up again and put his hands down sideways like flat plates or like the fins on a fish and took out of it a smaller chest but one resembling its mother-chest in every particular of appearance and dimension. It almost interfered with my breathing, it was so delightfully unmistakable. I went over and felt it and covered it with my hand to see how big its smallness was. Its brasswork had a shine like the sun on the sea and the colour of the wood was a rich deep richness like a colour deepened and toned only by the years. I got slightly weak from looking at it and sat down on a chair and for the purpose of pretending that I was not disturbed I whistled *The Old Man Twangs His Braces*.

MacCruiskeen gave me a smooth inhuman smile.

' You may have come on no bicycle,' he said, ' but that does not say that you know everything.'

'Those chests,' I said, 'are so like one another that I do not believe they are there at all because that is a simpler thing to believe than the contrary. Nevertheless the two of them are the most wonderful two things I have ever seen.'

'I was two years manufacturing it,' MacCruiskeen said.

'What is in the little one?' I asked.

'What would you think now?'

'I am completely half afraid to think,' I said, speaking truly enough.

'Wait now till I show you,' said MacCruiskeen, 'and give you an exhibition and a personal inspection individually.'

He got two thin butter-spades from the shelf and put them down into the little chest and pulled out something that seemed to me remarkably like another chest. I went over to it and gave it a close examination with my hand, feeling the same identical wrinkles, the some proportions and the same completely perfect brasswork on a smaller scale. It was so faultless and delightful that it reminded me forcibly, strange and foolish as it may seem, of something I did not understand and had never even heard of.

'Say nothing,' I said quickly to MacCruiskeen, 'but go ahead with what you are doing and I will watch here and I will take care to be sitting down.'

He gave me a nod in exchange for my remark and got two straight-handled teaspoons and put the handles into his last chest. What came out may well be guessed at. He opened this one and took another one out with the assistance of two knives. He worked knives, small knives and smaller knives, till he had twelve little chests on the table, the last of them an article half the size of a matchbox. It was so tiny that you would not quite see the brasswork at all only for the glitter of it in the light. I did not see whether it had the same identical carvings upon it because I was content to take a swift look at it and then turn away. But I knew in my soul that it was exactly the same as the others. I said no word at all because my mind was brimming with wonder at the skill of the policeman.

'That last one,' said MacCruiskeen, putting away the knives, 'took me three years to make and it took me another year to believe that I had made it. Have you got the convenience of a pin?'

I gave him my pin in silence. He opened the smallest of them all with a key like a piece of hair and worked with the pin till he had another little chest on the table, thirteen in all arranged in a row upon the table. Queerly enough they looked to me as if they were all the same size but invested with some crazy perspective. This idea surprised me so much that I got my voice back and said:

'These are the most surprising thirteen things I have ever seen together.'

'Wait now, man,' MacCruiskeen said.

All my senses were now strained so tensely watching the policeman's movements that I could almost hear my brain rattling in my head when I gave a shake as if it was drying up into a wrinkled pea. He was manipulating and prodding with his pin till he had twenty-eight little chests on the table and the last of them so small that it looked like a bug or a tiny piece of dirt except that there was a glitter from it. When I looked at it again I saw another thing beside it like something you would take out of a red eye on a windy dry day and I knew then that the strict computation was then twenty-nine.

'Here is your pin,' said MacCruiskeen.

He put it into my stupid hand and went back to the table thoughtfully. He took a something from his pocket that was too small for me to see and started working with the tiny black thing on the table beside the bigger thing which was itself too small to be described.

At this point I became afraid. What he was doing was no longer wonderful but terrible. I shut my eyes and prayed that he would stop while still doing things that were at least possible for a man to do. When I looked again I was happy that there was nothing to see and that he had put no more of the chests prominently on the table but he was working to the left with the invisible thing in his hand on a bit of the table itself. When he felt my look he came over to me and gave me an enormous magnifying-glass which looked like a basin fixed to a handle. I felt the muscles around my heart tightening painfully as I took the instrument.

'Come over here to the table,' he said, 'and look there till you see what you see infra-ocularly.'

When I saw the table it was bare only for the twenty-nine chest articles but through the agency of the glass I was in a position to report that he had two more out beside the last ones, the smallest of all being nearly half a size smaller than ordinary invisibility. I gave him back the glass instrument and took to the chair without a word. In order to reassure myself and make a loud human noise I whistled the *Corncrake Plays the Bagpipes*.

'There now,' said MacCruiskeen.

He took two wrinkled cigarettes from his fob and lit the two at the same time and handed me one of them.

'Number Twenty-Two,' he said, 'I manufactured fifteen years ago and I have made another different one every year since with any amount of nightwork and overtime and piecework and time-and-a-half incidentally.'

'I understand you clearly,' I said.

'Six years ago they began to get invisible, glass or no glass. Nobody has ever seen the last five I made because no glass is strong enough to make them big enough to be regarded truly as the smallest things ever made. Nobody can see me making them because my little tools are invisible into the same bargain. The one I am making now is nearly as small as nothing. Number One would hold a million of them at the same time and there would be room left for a pair of woman's horse-breeches if they were rolled up. The dear knows where it will stop and terminate.'

'Such work must be very hard on the eyes,' I said, determined to pretend that everybody was an ordinary person like myself.

'Some of these days,' he answered, 'I will have to buy spectacles with gold ear-claws. My eyes are crippled with the small print in the newspapers and in the offeecial forms.'

'Before I go back to the day-room,' I said, 'would it be right to ask you what you were performing with that little small piano-instrument, the article with the knobs, and the brass pins?'

'That is my personal musical instrument,' said MacCruiskeen, 'and I was playing my own tunes on it in order to extract private satisfaction from the sweetness of them.'

'I was listening,' I answered, 'but I did not succeed in hearing you.'

'That does not surprise me intuitively,' said MacCruiskeen, 'because it is an indigenous patent of my own. The vibrations of the true notes are so high in their fine frequencies that they cannot be appreciated by the human ear-cup. Only myself has the secret of the thing and the intimate way of it, the confidential knack of circumventing it. Now what do you think of that?'

I climbed up to my legs to go back to the day-room, passing a hand weakly about my brow.

'I think it is extremely acatalectic,' I answered.

VI

WHEN I penetrated back to the day-room I encountered two gentlemen called Sergeant Pluck and Mr Gilhaney and they were holding a meeting about the question of bicycles.

'I do not believe in the three-speed gear at all,' the Sergeant was saying, 'it is a new-fangled instrument, it crucifies the legs, the half of the accidents are due to it.'

'It is a power for the hills,' said Gilhaney, 'as good as a second pair of pins or a diminutive petrol motor.'

'It is a hard thing to tune,' said the Sergeant, 'you can screw the iron lace that hangs out of it till you get no catch at all on the pedals. It never stops the way you want it, it would remind you of bad jaw-plates.'

'That is all lies,' said Gilhaney.

'Or like the pegs of a fairy-day fiddle,' said the Sergeant, 'or a skinny wife in the craw of a cold bed in springtime.'

'Not that,' said Gilhaney.

'Or porter in a sick stomach,' said the Sergeant.

'So help me not,' said Gilhaney.

The Sergeant saw me with the corner of his eye and turned to talk to me, taking away all his attention from Gilhaney.

'MacCruiskeen was giving you his talk I wouldn't doubt,' he said.

'He was being extremely explanatory,' I answered dryly.

'He is a comical man,' said the Sergeant, 'a walking emporium, you'd think he was on wires and worked with steam.'

'He is,' I said.

'He is a melody man,' the Sergeant added, 'and very temporary, a menace to the mind.'

'About the bicycle,' said Gilhaney.

'The bicycle will be found,' said the Sergeant, 'when I retrieve and restore it to its own owner in due law and possessively. Would you desire to be of assistance in the search?' he asked me.

' I would not mind,' I answered.

The Sergeant looked at his teeth in the glass for a brief intermission and then put his leggings on his legs and took a hold of his stick as an indication that he was for the road. Gilhaney was at the door operating it to let us out. The three of us walked out into the middle of the day.

' In case we do not come up with the bicycle before it is high dinner-time,' said the Sergeant, ' I have left an official memorandum for the personal information of Policeman Fox so that he will be acutely conversant with the *res ipsa*,' he said.

' Do you hold with rat-trap pedals?' asked Gilhaney.

' Who is Fox?' I asked.

' Policeman Fox is the third of us,' said the Sergeant, ' but we never see him or hear tell of him at all because he is always on his beat and never off it and he signs the book in the middle of the night when even a badger is asleep. He is as mad as a hare, he never interrogates the public and he is always taking notes. If rat-trap pedals were universal it would be the end of bicycles, the people would die like flies.'

' What put him that way?' I inquired.

' I never comprehended correctly,' replied the Sergeant, ' or got the real informative information but Policeman Fox was alone in a private room with MacCruiskeen for a whole hour on a certain 23rd of June and he has never spoken to anybody since that day and he is as crazy as tuppence-half-penny and as cranky as thruppence. Did I ever tell you how I asked Inspector O'Corky about rat-traps? Why are they not made prohibitive, I said, or made specialities like arsenic when you would have to buy them at a chemist's shop and sign a little book and look like a responsible personality?'

' They are a power for the hills,' said Gilhaney.

The Sergeant spat spits on the dry road.

' You would want a special Act of Parliament,' said the Inspector, ' a special Act of Parliament.'

' What way are we going?' I asked, ' or what direction are we heading for or are we on the way back from some-where else?'

It was a queer country we were in. There was a number of blue mountains around us at what you might call a respectful distance with a glint of white water coming down the shoulders of one or two of them and they kept hemming us in and meddling oppressively with our minds. Half-way to these mountains the view got clearer and was full of humps and hollows and long parks of fine bogland with civil people here and there in the middle of it working with long instruments, you could hear their voices calling across the wind and the crack of the dull carts on the roadways. White buildings could be seen in several places and cows shambling lazily from here to there in search of pasture. A company of crows came out of a tree when I was watching and flew sadly down to a field where there was a quantity of sheep attired in fine overcoats.

'We are going where we are going,' said the Sergeant, 'and this is the right direction to a place that is next door to it. There is one particular thing more dangerous than the rat-trap pedal.'

He left the road and drew us in after him through a hedge.

'It is dishonourable to talk like that about the rat-traps,' said Gilhaney, 'because my family has had their boots in them for generations of their own posterity backwards and forwards and they all died in their beds except my first cousin that was meddling with the suckers of a steam thrashing-mill.'

'There is only one thing more dangerous,' said the Sergeant, 'and that is a loose plate. A loose plate is a scorcher, nobody lives very long after swallowing one and it leads indirectly to asphyxiation.'

'There is no danger of swallowing a rat-trap?' said Gilhaney.

'You would want to have good strong clips if you have a plate,' said the Sergeant, 'and plenty of red sealing-wax to stick it to the roof of your jaws. Take a look at the roots of that bush, it looks suspicious and there is no necessity for a warrant.'

It was a small modest whin-bush, a lady member of the tribe as you might say, with dry particles of hay and sheep's feathers caught in the branches high and low. Gilhaney was on his knees putting his hands through the grass and rooting like one of the lower animals. After a minute he extracted a black instrument. It was long and thin and looked like a large fountain-pen.

' My pump, so help me! ' he shouted.

' I thought as much,' said the Sergeant, ' the finding of the pump is a fortunate clue that may assist us in our mission of private detection and smart policework. Put it in your pocket and hide it because it is possible that we are watched and followed and dogged by a member of the gang.'

' How did you know that it was in that particular corner of the world?' I asked in my extreme simplicity.

' What is your attitude to the high saddle?' inquired Gilhaney.

' Questions are like the knocks of beggarmen, and should not be minded,' replied the Sergeant, ' but I do not mind telling you that the high saddle is all right if you happen to have a brass fork.'

' A high saddle is a power for the hills,' said Gilhaney.

We were in an entirely other field by this time and in the company of white-coloured brown-coloured cows. They watched us quietly as we made a path between them and changed their attitudes slowly as if to show us all of the maps on their fat sides. They gave us to understand that they knew us personally and thought a lot of our families and I lifted my hat to the last of them as I passed her as a sign of my appreciation.

' The high saddle,' said the Sergeant, ' was invented by a party called Peters that spent his life in foreign parts riding on camels and other lofty animals—giraffes, elephants and birds that can run like hares and lay eggs the size of the bowl you see in a steam laundry where they keep the chemical water for taking the tar out of men's pants. When he came home from the wars he thought hard of sitting on a low saddle and one night accidentally when he was in bed he invented the high saddle as the outcome of his perpetual cerebration and mental researches. His Christian name I do not remember. The high saddle was the father of the low handlebars. It crucifies the fork and gives you a blood rush in the head, it is very sore on the internal organs.'

' Which of the organs?' I inquired.

' Both of them,' said the Sergeant.

' I think this would be the tree,' said Gilhaney.

' It would not surprise me,' said the Sergeant, ' put your hands in under its underneath and start feeling promiscuously the way you can ascertain factually if there is anything there in addition to its own nothing.'

Gilhaney lay down on his stomach on the grass at the butt of a blackthorn and was inquiring into its private parts with his strong hands and grunting from the stretch of his exertions. After a time he found a bicycle lamp and a bell and stood up and put them secretly in his fob.

' That is very satisfactory and complacently articulated,' said the Sergeant, ' it shows the necessity for perseverance, it is sure to be a clue, we are certain to find the bicycle.'

' I do not like asking questions,' I said politely, ' but the wisdom that directed us to this tree is not taught in the National Schools.'

' It is not the first time my bicycle was stolen,' said Gilhaney.

' In *my* day,' said the Sergeant, ' half the scholars in the National Schools were walking around with enough disease in their gobs to decimate the continent of Russia and wither a field of crops by only looking at them. That is all stopped now, they have compulsory inspections, the middling ones are stuffed with iron and the bad ones are pulled out with a thing like the claw for cutting wires.'

' The half of it is due to cycling with the mouth open,' said Gilhaney.

' Nowadays,' said the Sergeant, ' it is nothing strange to see a class of boys at First Book with wholesome teeth and with junior plates manufactured by the County Council for half-nothing.'

' Grinding the teeth half-way up a hill,' said Gilhaney, ' there is nothing worse, it files away the best part of them and leads to a hob-nailed liver indirectly.'

' In Russia,' said the Sergeant, ' they make teeth out of old piano-keys for elderly cows but it is a rough land without too much civilisation, it would cost you a fortune in tyres.'

We were now going through a country full of fine enduring trees where it was always five o'clock in the afternoon. It was a soft corner of the world, free from inquisitions and disputations and very soothing and sleepening on the mind. There was no animal there that was bigger than a man's thumb and no noise superior to that which the Sergeant was making with his nose, an unusual brand of music like wind in the chimney. To every side of us there was a green growth of soft ferny carpeting with thin green twines coming in and out of it and coarse bushes putting their heads out here and there and interrupting the urbanity of the presentation not unpleasingly. The distance we walked in this country I do not know but we arrived in the end at some place where we stopped without proceeding farther. The Sergeant put his finger at a certain part of the growth.

'It might be there and it might not,' he said, 'we can only try because perseverance is its own reward and necessity is the unmarried mother of invention.'

Gilhaney was not long at work till he took his bicycle out of that particular part of the growth. He pulled the briers from between the spokes and felt his tyres with red knowing fingers and furbished his machine fastidiously. The three of us walked back again without a particle of conversation to where the road was and Gilhaney put his toe on the pedal to show he was for home.

'Before I ride away,' he said to the Sergeant, 'what is your true opinion of the timber rim?'

'It is a very commendable invention,' the Sergeant said. 'It gives you more of a bounce, it is extremely easy on your white pneumatics.'

'The wooden rim,' said Gilhaney slowly, 'is a death-trap in itself, it swells on a wet day and I know a man that owes his bad wet death to nothing else.'

Before we had time to listen carefully to what he was after saying he was half-way down the road with his forked coat sailing behind him on the sustenance of the wind he was raising by reason of his headlong acceleration.

'A droll man,' I ventured.

'A constituent man,' said the Sergeant, 'largely instrumental but volubly fervous.'

Walking finely from the hips the two of us made our way home through the afternoon, impregnating it with the smoke of our cigarettes. I reflected that we would be sure to have lost our way in the fields and parks of bogland only that the road very conveniently made its way in advance of us back to the barrack. The Sergeant was sucking quietly at his stumps and carried a black shadow on his brow as if it were a hat.

As he walked he turned in my direction after a time.

' The County Council has a lot to answer for,' he said.

I did not understand his meaning, but I said that I agreed with him.

' There is one puzzle,' I remarked, ' that is hurting the back of my head and causing me a lot of curiosity. It is about the bicycle. I have never heard of detective-work as good as that being done before. Not only did you find the lost bicycle but you found all the clues as well. I find it is a great strain for me to believe what I see, and I am becoming afraid occasionally to look at some things in case they would have to be believed. What is the secret of your constabulary virtuosity?'

He laughed at my earnest inquiries and shook his head with great indulgence at my simplicity.

' It was an easy thing,' he said.

' How easy?'

' Even without the clues I could have succeeded in ultimately finding the bicycle.'

' It seems a very difficult sort of easiness,' I answered. ' Did you know where the bicycle was?'

' I did.'

' How?'

' Because I put it there.'

' You stole the bicycle yourself?'

' Certainly.'

' And the pump and the other clues?'

' I put them where they were finally discovered also.'

' And why?'

He did not answer in words for a moment but kept on walking strongly beside me looking as far ahead as possible.

' The County Council is the culprit,' he said at last.

I said nothing, knowing that he would blame the County Council at greater length if I waited till he had the blame thought out properly. It was not long till he turned in my direction to talk to me again. His face was grave.

'Did you ever discover or hear tell of the Atomic Theory?' he inquired.

'No,' I answered.

He leaned his mouth confidentially over to my ear.

'Would it surprise you to be told,' he said darkly, 'that the Atomic Theory is at work in this parish?'

'It would indeed.'

'It is doing untold destruction,' he continued, 'the half of the people are suffering from it, it is worse than the small-pox.'

I thought it better to say *something*.

'Would it be advisable,' I said, 'that it should be taken in hand by the Dispensary Doctor or by the National Teachers or do you think it is a matter for the head of the family?'

'The lock stock and barrel of it all,' said the Sergeant, 'is the County Council.'

He walked on looking worried and preoccupied as if what he was examining in his head was unpleasant in a very intricate way.

'The Atomic Theory,' I sallied, 'is a thing that is not clear to me at all.'

'Michael Gilhaney,' said the Sergeant, 'is an example of a man that is nearly banjaxed from the principle of the Atomic Theory. Would it astonish you to hear that he is nearly half a bicycle?'

'It would surprise me unconditionally,' I said.

'Michael Gilhaney,' said the Sergeant, 'is nearly sixty years of age by plain computation and if he is itself, he has spent no less than thirty-five years riding his bicycle over the rocky roadsteads and up and down the hills and into the deep ditches when the road goes astray in the strain of the winter. He is always going to a particular destination or other on his bicycle at every hour of the day or coming back from there at every other hour. If it wasn't that his bicycle was stolen every Monday he would be sure to be more than half-way now.'

'Half-way to where?'

'Half-way to being a bicycle himself,' said the Sergeant.

'Your talk,' I said, 'is surely the handiwork of wisdom because not one word of it do I understand.'

'Did you never study atomics when you were a lad?' asked the Sergeant, giving me a look of great inquiry and surprise.

'No,' I answered.

'That is a very serious defalcation,' he said, 'but all the same I will tell you the size of it. Everything is composed of small particles of itself and they are flying around in concentric circles and arcs and segments and innumerable other geometrical figures too numerous to mention collectively, never standing still or resting but spinning away and darting hither and thither and back again, all the time on the go. These diminutive gentlemen are called atoms. Do you follow me intelligently?'

'Yes.'

'They are lively as twenty leprechauns doing a jig on top of a tombstone.'

A very pretty figure, Joe murmured.

'Now take a sheep,' the Sergeant said. 'What is a sheep only millions of little bits of sheepness whirling around and doing intricate convolutions inside the sheep? What else is it but that?'

'That would be bound to make the beast dizzy,' I observed, 'especially if the whirling was going on inside the head as well.'

The Sergeant gave me a look which I am sure he himself would describe as one of *non-possum* and *noli-me-tangere.*

'That remark is what may well be called buncombe,' he said sharply, 'because the nerve-strings and the sheep's head itself are whirling into the same bargain and you can cancel out one whirl against the other and there you are—like simplifying a division sum when you have fives above and below the bar.'

'To say the truth I did not think of that,' I said.

'Atomics is a very intricate theorem and can be worked out with algebra but you would want to take it by degrees because you might spend the whole night proving a bit of it with rulers and cosines and similar other instruments and then at the wind-up not believe what you had proved at all. If that happened you would have to go back over it till you got a place where you could believe your own facts and figures as delineated from Hall and Knight's Algebra and then go on again from that particular place till you had the whole thing properly believed and not have bits of it half-believed or a doubt in your head hurting you like when you lose the stud of your shirt in bed.'

' Very true,' I said.

' Consecutively and consequentially,' he continued, ' you can safely infer that you are made of atoms yourself and so is your fob pocket and the tail of your shirt and the instrument you use for taking the leavings out of the crook of your hollow tooth. Do you happen to know what takes place when you strike a bar of iron with a good coal hammer or with a blunt instrument?'

' What?'

' When the wallop falls, the atoms are bashed away down to the bottom of the bar and compressed and crowded there like eggs under a good clucker. After a while in the course of time they swim around and get back at last to where they were. But if you keep hitting the bar long enough and hard enough they do not get a chance to do this and what happens then?'

' That is a hard question.'

' Ask a blacksmith for the true answer and he will tell you that the bar will dissipate itself away by degrees if you persevere with the hard wallops. Some of the atoms of the bar will go into the hammer and the other half into the table or the stone or the particular article that is underneath the bottom of the bar.'

' That is well-known,' I agreed.

' The gross and net result of it is that people who spent most of their natural lives riding iron bicycles over the rocky roadsteads of this parish get their personalities mixed up with the personalities of their bicycle as a result of the interchanging of the atoms of each of them and you would be surprised at the number of people in these parts who nearly are half people and half bicycles.'

I let go a gasp of astonishment that made a sound in the air like a bad puncture.

'And you would be flabbergasted at the number of bicycles that are half-human almost half-man, half-partaking of humanity.'

Apparently there is no limit, Joe remarked. *Anything can be said in this place and it will be true and will have to be believed.*

I would not mind being working this minute on a steamer in the middle of the sea, I said, coiling ropes and doing the hard manual work. I would like to be far away from here.

I looked carefully around me. Brown bogs and black bogs were arranged neatly on each side of the road with rectangular boxes carved out of them here and there, each with a filling of yellow-brown brown-yellow water. Far away near the sky tiny people were stooped at their turf-work, cutting out precisely-shaped sods with their patent spades and building them into a tall memorial twice the height of a horse and cart. Sounds came from them to the Sergeant and myself, delivered to our ears without charge by the west wind, sounds of laughing and whistling and bits of verses from the old bog-songs. Nearer, a house stood attended by three trees and surrounded by the happiness of a coterie of fowls, all of them picking and rooting and disputating loudly in the unrelenting manufacture of their eggs. The house was quiet in itself and silent but a canopy of lazy smoke had been erected over the chimney to indicate that people were within engaged on tasks. Ahead of us went the road, running swiftly across the flat land and pausing slightly to climb slowly up a hill that was waiting for it in a place where there was tall grass, grey boulders and rank stunted trees. The whole overhead was occupied by the sky, serene, impenetrable, ineffable and incomparable, with a fine island of clouds anchored in the calm two yards to the right of Mr Jarvis's outhouse.

The scene was real and incontrovertible and at variance with the talk of the Sergeant, but I knew that the Sergeant was talking the truth and if it was a question of taking my choice, it was possible that I would have to forego the reality of all the simple things my eyes were looking at.

I took a sideways view of him. He was striding on with

signs of anger against the County Council on his coloured face.

'Are you certain about the humanity of the bicycle?' I inquired of him. 'Is the Atomic Theory as dangerous as you say?'

'It is between twice and three times as dangerous as it might be,' he replied gloomily. 'Early in the morning I often think it is four times, and what is more, if you lived here for a few days and gave full play to your observation and inspection, you would know how certain the sureness of certainty is.'

'Gilhaney did not look like a bicycle,' I said. 'He had no back wheel on him and I did not think he had a front wheel either, although I did not give much attention to his front.'

The Sergeant looked at me with some commiseration.

'You cannot expect him to grow handlebars out of his neck but I have seen him do more indescribable things than that. Did you ever notice the queer behaviour of bicycles in these parts?'

'I am not long in this district.'

Thanks be, said Joe.

'Then watch the bicycles if you think it is pleasant to be surprised continuously,' he said. 'When a man lets things go so far that he is half or more than half a bicycle, you will not see so much because he spends a lot of his time leaning with one elbow on walls or standing propped by one foot at kerbstones. Of course there are other things connected with ladies and ladies' bicycles that I will mention to you separately some time. But the man-charged bicycle is a phenomenon of great charm and intensity and a very dangerous article.'

At this point a man with long coat-tails spread behind him approached quickly on a bicycle, coasting benignly down the road past us from the hill ahead. I watched him with the eye of six eagles, trying to find out which was carrying the other and whether it was really a man with a bicycle on his shoulders. I did not seem to see anything, however, that was memorable or remarkable.

The Sergeant was looking into his black notebook.

'That was O'Feersa,' he said at last. 'His figure is only

87

twenty-three per cent.'

' He is twenty-three per cent bicycle?'

' Yes.'

' Does that mean that his bicycle is also twenty-three per cent O'Feersa?'

' It does.'

' How much is Gilhaney?'

' Forty-eight.'

' Then O'Feersa is much lower.'

' That is due to the lucky fact that there are three similar brothers in the house and that they are too poor to have a separate bicycle apiece. Some people never know how fortunate they are when they are poorer than each other. Six years ago one of the three O'Feersas won a prize of ten pounds in *John Bull*. When I got the wind of this tiding, I knew I would have to take steps unless there was to be two new bicycles in the family, because you will understand that I can steal only a limited number of bicycles in the one week. I did not want to have three O'Feersas on my hands. Luckily I knew the postman very well. The postman! Great holy suffering indiarubber bowls of brown stirabout!' The recollection of the postman seemed to give the Sergeant a pretext for unlimited amusement and cause for intricate gesturing wtih his red hands.

' The postman?' I said.

' Seventy-one per cent,' he said quietly.

' Great Scot!'

' A round of thirty-eight miles on the bicycle every single day for forty years, hail, rain or snowballs. There is very little hope of ever getting his number down below fifty again.'

' You bribed him?'

' Certainly. With two of the little straps you put around the hubs of bicycles to keep them spick.'

' And what way do these people's bicycles behave?'

' These people's bicycles?'

' I mean these bicycles' people or whatever is the proper name for them—the ones that have two wheels under them and a handlebars.'

' The behaviour of a bicycle that has a high content of

humanity,' he said, 'is very cunning and entirely remarkable. You never see them moving by themselves but you meet them in the least accountable places unexpectedly. Did you never see a bicycle leaning against the dresser of a warm kitchen when it is pouring outside?'

' I did.'

' Not very far away from the fire?'

' Yes.'

' Near enough to the family to hear the conversation?'

' Yes.'

' Not a thousand miles from where they keep the eatables?'

' I did not notice that. You do not mean to say that these bicycles *eat food*?'

' They were never seen doing it, nobody ever caught them with a mouthful of steak. All I know is that the food disappears.'

' What! '

' It is not the first time I have noticed crumbs at the front wheels of some of these gentlemen.'

' All this is a great blow to me,' I said.

' Nobody takes any notice,' replied the Sergeant. ' Mick thinks that Pat brought it in and Pat thinks that Mick was instrumental. Very few of the people guess what is going on in this parish. There are other things I would rather not say too much about. A new lady teacher was here one time with a new bicycle. She was not very long here till Gilhaney went away into the lonely country on her female bicycle. Can you appreciate the immorality of that?'

' I can.'

' But worse happened. Whatever way Gilhaney's bicycle managed it, it left itself leaning at a place where the young teacher would rush out to go away somewhere on her bicycle in a hurry. Her bicycle was gone but here was Gilhaney's leaning there conveniently and trying to look very small and comfortable and attractive. Need I inform you what the result was or what happened?'

Indeed he need not, Joe said urgently. *I have never heard of anything so shameless and abandoned. Of course the teacher was blameless, she did not take pleasure and did not know.*

'You need not,' I said.

'Well, there you are. Gilhaney has a day out with the lady's bicycle and vice versa contrarily and it is quite clear that the lady in the case had a high number—thirty-five or forty, I would say, in spite of the newness of the bicycle. Many a grey hair it has put into my head, trying to regulate the people of this parish. If you let it go too far it would be the end of everything. You would have bicycles wanting votes and they would get seats on the County Council and make the roads far worse than they are for their own ulterior motivation. But against that and on the other hand, a good bicycle is a great companion, there is a great charm about it.'

'How would you know a man has a lot of bicycle in his veins?'

'If his number is over Fifty you can tell it unmistakable from his walk. He will walk smartly always and never sit down and he will lean against the wall with his elbow out and stay like that all night in his kitchen instead of going to bed. If he walks too slowly or stops in the middle of the road he will fall down in a heap and will have to be lifted and set in motion again by some extraneous party. This is the unfortunate state that the postman has cycled himself into, and I do not think he will ever cycle himself out of it.'

'I do not think I will ever ride a bicycle,' I said.

'A little of it is a good thing and makes you hardy and puts iron on to you. But walking too far too often too quickly is not safe at all. The continual cracking of your feet on the road makes a certain quantity of road come up into you. When a man dies they say he returns to clay but too much walking fills you up with clay far sooner (or buries bits of you along the road) and brings your death half-way to meet you. It is not easy to know what is the best way to move yourself from one place to another.

After he had finished speaking I found myself walking nimbly and lightly on my toes in order to prolong my life. My head was packed tight with fears and miscellaneous apprehensions.

'I never heard of these things before,' I said, 'and never knew these happenings could happen. Is it a new development or was it always an ancient fundamental?'

The Sergeant's face clouded and he spat thoughtfully three yards ahead of him on the road.

'I will tell you a secret,' he said very confidentially in a low voice. 'My great-grandfather was eighty-three when he died. For a year before his death he was a horse!'

'A horse?'

'A horse in everything but extraneous externalities. He would spend the day grazing in a field or eating hay in a stall. Usually he was lazy and quiet but now and again he would go for a smart gallop, clearing the hedges in great style. Did you ever see a man on two legs galloping?'

'I did not.'

'Well, I am given to understand that it is a great sight. He always said he won the Grand National when he was a lot younger and used to annoy his family with stories about the intricate jumps and the great height of them.'

'I suppose your great-grandfather got himself into this condition by too much horse riding?'

'That was the size of it. His old horse Dan was in the contrary way and gave so much trouble, coming into the house at night and interfering with young girls during the day and committing indictable offences, that they had to shoot him. The police were unsympathetic, not comprehending things rightly in these days. They said they would have to arrest the horse and charge him and have him up at the next Petty Sessions unless he was done away with. So my family shot him but if you ask me it was my great-grandfather they shot and it is the horse that is buried up in Cloncoonla Churchyard.'

The Sergeant then became thoughtful at the recollection of his ancestors and had a reminiscent face for the next half-mile till we came to the barracks. Joe and I agreed privately that these revelations were the supreme surprise stored for us and awaiting our arrival in the barracks.

When we reached it the Sergeant led the way in with a sigh. 'The lock, stock and barrel of it all,' he said, 'is the County Council.'

VII

THE SEVERE shock which I encountered soon after re-entry to the barrack with the Sergeant set me thinking afterwards of the immense consolations which philosophy and religion can offer in adversity. They seem to lighten dark places and give strength to bear the unaccustomed load. Not unnaturally my thoughts were never very far from de Selby. All his works—but particularly *Golden Hours*— have what one may term a therapeutic quality. They have a heart-lifted effect more usually associated with spirituous liquors, reviving and quietly restoring the spiritual tissue. This benign property of his prose is not, one hopes, to be attributed to the reason noticed by the eccentric du Garbandier, who said ' the beauty of reading a page of de Selby is that it leads one inescapably to the happy conviction that one is not, of all nincompoops, the greatest.'[1] This is, I think, an overstatement of one of de Selby's most ingratiating qualities. The humanising urbanity of his work has always seemed to me to be enhanced rather than vitiated by the chance obtrusion here and there of his minor failings, all the more pathetic because he regarded some of them as pinnacles of his intellectual prowess rather than indications of his frailty as a human being.

Holding that the usual processes of living were illusory, it is natural that he did not pay much attention to life's adversities and he does not in fact offer much suggestion as to how they should be met. Bassett's anecdote[2] on this point may be worth recounting. During de Selby's Bartown days he had acquired some local reputation as a savant ' due possibly to the fact that he was known never to read newspapers.' A young man in the town was seriously troubled by some question regarding a lady and feeling that this

[1] ' Le Suprème charme qu'on trouve à lire une page de de Selby est qu'elle vous conduit inexorablement a l'heureuse certitude que des sots vous n'êtes pas le plus grand.'
[2] In *Lux Mundi*.

matter was weighing on his mind and threatening to interfere with his reason, he sought de Selby for advice. Instead of exorcising this solitary blot from the young man's mind, as indeed could easily have been done, de Selby drew the young man's attention to some fifty imponderable propositions each of which raised difficulties which spanned many eternities and dwarfed the conundrum of the young lady to nothingness. Thus the young man who had come fearing the possibility of a bad thing left the house completely convinced of the worst and cheerfully contemplating suicide. That he arrived home for his supper at the usual time was a happy intervention on the part of the moon for he had gone home by the harbour only to find that the tide was two miles out. Six months later he earned for himself six calendar months' incarceration with hard labour on foot of eighteen counts comprising larceny and offences bearing on interference with railroads. So much for the savant as a dispenser of advice.

As already said, however, de Selby provides some genuine mental sustenance if read objectively for what there is to read. In the *Layman's Atlas*[3] he deals explicitly with bereavement, old age, love, sin, death and the other saliencies of existence. It is true that he allows them only some six lines but this is due to his devastating assertion that they are all 'unnecessary'.[4] Astonishing as it may seem, he makes this statement as a direct corollary to his discovery that the earth, far from being a sphere, is 'sausage-shaped.'

[3] Now very rare and a collector's piece. The sardonic du Garbandier makes great play of the fact that the man who first printed the *Atlas* (Watkins) was struck by lightning on the day he completed the task. It is interesting to note that the otherwise reliable Hatchjaw has put forward the suggestion that the entire *Atlas* is spurious and the work of 'another hand', raising issues of no less piquancy than those of the Bacon-Shakespeare controversy. He has many ingenious if not quite convincing arguments, not the least of them being that de Selby was known to have received considerable royalties from this book which he did not write, 'a procedure that would be of a piece with the master's ethics.' The theory is, however, not one which will commend itself to the serious student.

[4] Du Garbandier has inquired with his customary sarcasm why a malignant condition of the gall-bladder, a disease which frequently reduced de Selby to a cripple, was omitted from the list of 'unnecessaries'.

Not a few of the critical commentators confess to a doubt as to whether de Selby was permitting himself a modicum of unwonted levity in connection with this theory but he seems to argue the matter seriously enough and with no want of conviction.

He adopts the customary line of pointing out fallacies involved in existing conceptions and then quietly setting up his own design in place of the one he claims to have demolished.

Standing at a point on the postulated spherical earth, he says, one appears to have four main directions in which to move, viz., north, south, east and west. But it does not take much thought to see that there really appear to be only two since north and south are meaningless terms in relation to a spheroid and can connote motion in only *one* direction; so also with west and east. One can reach any point on the north-south band by travelling in either ' direction ', the only apparent difference in the two ' routes ' being extraneous considerations of time and distance, both already shown to be illusory. North-south is therefore one direction and east-west apparently another. Instead of four directions there are only two. It can be safely inferred,[5] de Selby says, that there is a further similar fallacy inherent here and that there is in fact only one possible direction properly so-called, because if one leaves any point on the globe, moving and continuing to move in any ' direction ', one ultimately reaches the point of departure again.

The application of this conclusion to his theory that ' the earth is a sausage ' is illuminating. He attributes the idea that the earth is spherical to the fact that human beings are continually moving in only one known direction (though convinced that they are free to move in any direction) and that this one direction is really around the circular circumference of an earth which is in fact sausage-shaped. It can scarcely be contested that if multi-directionality be admitted to be a fallacy, the sphericity of the earth is another fallacy that would inevitably follow from it. De Selby likens the position of a human on the earth to that of a man on a

---

[5] Possibly the one weak spot in the argument.

tight-wire who must continue walking along the wire or perish, being, however, free in all other respects. Movement in this restricted orbit results in the permanent hallucination known conventionally as 'life' with its innumerable concomitant limitations, afflictions and anomalies. If a way can be found, says de Selby, of discovering the 'second direction', i.e., along the 'barrel' of the sausage, a world of entirely new sensation and experience will be open to humanity. New and unimaginable dimensions will supersede the present order and the manifold 'unnecessaries' of 'one-directional' existence will disappear.

It is true that de Selby is rather vague as to how precisely this new direction is to be found. It is not, he warns us, to be ascertained by any microscopic subdivision of the known points of the compass and little can be expected from sudden darts hither and thither in the hope that a happy chance will intervene. He doubts whether human legs would be 'suitable' for traversing the 'longitudinal celestium' and seems to suggest that death is nearly always present when the new direction is discovered. As Bassett points out justly enough, this lends considerable colour to the whole theory but suggests at the same time that de Selby is merely stating in an obscure and recondite way something that is well-known and accepted.

As usual, there is evidence that he carried out some private experimenting. He seems to have thought at one time that gravitation was the 'jailer' of humanity, keeping it on the one-directional line of oblivion, and that ultimate freedom lay in some upward direction. He examined aviation as a remedy without success and subsequently spent some weeks designing certain 'barometric pumps' which were 'worked with mercury and wires' to clear vast areas of the earth of the influence of gravitation. Happily for the people of the place as well for their movable chattels he does not seem to have had much result. Eventually he was distracted from these occupations by the extraordinary affair of the water-box.*

*See Hatchjaw: *The De Selby Water-Boxes Day by Day*. The calculations are given in full and the daily variations are expressed in admirably clear graphs.

As I have already hinted, I would have given much for a glimpse of a signpost showing the way along the 'barrel' of the sausage after I had been some two minutes back in the white day-room with Sergeant Pluck.

We were not more than completely inside the door when we became fully aware that there was a visitor present. He had coloured stripes of high office on his chest but he was dressed in policeman's blue and on his head he carried a policeman's hat with a special badge of superior office glittering very brilliantly in it. He was very fat and circular, with legs and arms of the minimum, and his large bush of moustache was bristling with bad temper and self-indulgence. The Sergeant gave him looks of surprise and then a military salute.

'Inspector O'Corky!' he said.

'What is the meaning of the vacuity of the station in routine hours?' barked the Inspector.

The sound his voice made was rough like coarse cardboard rubbed on sandpaper and it was clear that he was not pleased with himself or with other people.

'I was out myself,' the Sergeant replied respectfully, 'on emergency duty and policework of the highest gravity.'

'Did you know that a man called Mathers was found in the crotch of a ditch up the road two hours ago with his belly opened up with a knife or sharp instrument?'

To say that this was a surprise which interfered seriously with my heart-valves would be the same as saying that a red-hot poker would heat your face if somebody decided to let you have it there. I stared from the Sergeant to the Inspector and back again with my whole inside fluttering in consternation.

It seems that our mutual friend Finnucane is in the environs, Joe said.

'Certainly I did,' said the Sergeant.

Very strange. How could he if he has been out with us after the bicycle for the last four hours?

'And what steps have you taken and how many steps?' barked the Inspector.

'Long steps and steps in the right direction,' replied the Sergeant evenly. 'I know who the murderer is.'

'Then why is he not arrested into custody?'

'He is,' said the Sergeant pleasantly.

'Where?'

'Here.'

This was the second thunderbolt. After I had glanced fearfully to my rear without seeing a murderer it became clear to me that I myself was the subject of the private conversation of the two Policemen. I made no protest because my voice was gone and my mouth was bone-dry.

Inspector O'Corky was too angry to be pleased at anything so surprising as what the Sergeant said.

'Then why is he not confined under a two-way key and padlock in the cell?' he roared.

For the first time the Sergeant looked a bit crestfallen and shame-faced. His face got a little redder than it was and he put his eyes on the stone floor.

'To tell you the truth,' he said at last, 'I keep my bicycle there.'

'I see,' said the Inspector.

He stooped quickly and rammed black clips on the extremities of his trousers and stamped on the floor. For the first time I saw that he had been leaning by one elbow on the counter.

'See that you regularise your irregularity instantaneously,' he called as his good-bye, 'and set right your irrectitude and put the murderer in the cage before he rips the bag out of the whole countryside.'

After that he was gone. Sounds came to us of coarse scraping on the gravel, a sign that the Inspector favoured the old-fashioned method of mounting from the back-step.

'Well, now,' the Sergeant said.

He took off his cap and went over to a chair and sat on it, easing himself on his broad pneumatic seat. He took a red cloth from his fob and decanted the globes of perspiration from his expansive countenance and opened the buttons of his tunic as if to let out on wing the trouble that was imprisoned there. He then took to carrying out a scientifically precise examination of the soles and the toes of his constabulary boots, a sign that he was wrestling with some great problem.

'What is your worry?' I inquired, very anxious by now that what had happened should be discussed.

'The bicycle,' he said.

'The bicycle?'

'How can I put it out of the cell?' he asked.

'I have always kept it in solitary confinement when I am not riding it to make sure it is not leading a personal life inimical to my own inimitability. I cannot be too careful. I have to ride long rides on my constabulary ridings.'

'Do you mean that I should be locked in the cell and kept there and hidden from the world?'

'You surely heard the instructions of the Inspector?' *Ask is it all a joke?* Joe said.

'Is this all a joke for entertainment purposes?'

'If you take it that way I will be indefinitely beholden to you,' said the Sergeant earnestly, 'and I will remember you with real emotion. It would be a noble gesture and an unutterable piece of supreme excellence on the part of the deceased.'

'What!' I cried.

'You must recollect that to turn everything to your own advantage is one of the regulations of true wisdom as I informed you privately. It is the following of this rule on my part that makes you a murderer this today evening.

'The Inspector required a captured prisoner as the least tiniest minimum for his inferior *bonhomie* and *mal d'esprit*. It was your personal misfortune to be present adjacently at the time but it was likewise my personal good fortune and good luck. There is no option but to stretch you for the serious offence.'

'Stretch me?'

'Hang you by the windpipe before high breakfast time.'

'That is most unfair,' I stuttered, 'it is unjust . . . rotten . . . fiendish.' My voice rose to a thin tremolo of fear.

'It is the way we work in this part of the country,' explained the Sergeant.

'I will resist,' I shouted, 'and will resist to the death and fight for my existence even if I lose my life in the attempt.'

The Sergeant made a soothing gesture in deprecation.

He took out an enormous pipe and when he stuck it in his face it looked like a great hatchet.

'About the bicycle,' he said when he had it in commission.

'What bicycle?'

'My own one. Would it inconvenience you if I neglected to bar you into the inside of the cell? I do not desire to be selfish but I have to think carefully about my bicycle. The wall of this day-room is no place for it.'

'I do not mind,' I said quietly.

'You can remain in the environs on parole and ticket of leave till we have time to build the high scaffold in the backyard.'

'How do you know I will not make excellent my escape?' I asked, thinking that it would be better to discover all the thoughts and intentions of the Sergeant so that my escape would in fact be certain.

He smiled at me as much as the weight of the pipe would let him.

'You will not do that,' he said. 'It would not be honourable but even if it was we would easily follow the track of your rear tyre and besides the rest of everything Policeman Fox would be sure to apprehend you single-handed on the outskirts. There would be no necessity for a warrant.'

Both of us sat silent for a while occupied with our thoughts, he thinking about his bicycle and I about my death.

By the bye, Joe remarked, *I seem to remember our friend saying that the law could not lay a finger on us on account of your congenital anonymity.*

'Quite right,' I said. 'I forgot that.'

As things are I fancy it would not be much more than a debating point.

'It is worth mentioning,' I said.

O Lord, yes.

'By the way,' I said to the Sergeant, 'did you recover my American watch for me?'

'The matter is under consideration and is receiving attention,' he said officially.

'Do you recall that you told me that I was not here at

all because I had no name and that my personality was invisible to the law?'

'I said that.'

'Then how can I be hanged for a murder, even if I did commit it and there is no trial or preliminary proceedings, no caution administered and no hearing before a Commissioner of the Public Peace?'

Watching the Sergeant, I saw him take the hatchet from his jaws in surprise and knot his brows into considerable corrugations. I could see that he was severely troubled with my inquiry. He looked darkly at me and then doubled his look, giving me a compressed stare along the line of his first vision.

'Well great cripes!' he said.

For three minutes he sat giving my representations his undivided attention. He was frowning so heavily with wrinkles which were so deep that the blood was driven from his face leaving it black and forbidding.

Then he spoke.

'Are you completely doubtless that you are nameless?' he asked.

'Positively certain.'

'Would it be Mick Barry?'

'No.'

'Charlemange O'Keeffe?'

'No.'

'Sir Justin Spens?'

'Not that.'

'Kimberley?'

'No.'

'Bernard Fann?'

'No.'

'Joseph Poe or Nolan?'

'No.'

'One of the Garvins or the Moynihans?'

'Not them.'

'Rosencranz O'Dowd?'

'No.'

'Would it be O'Benson?'

'Not O'Benson.'

' The Quigleys, The Mulrooneys or the Hounimen?'
' No.'
' The Hardimen or the Merrimen?'
' Not them.'
' Peter Dundy?'
' No.'
' Scrutch?'
' No.'
' Lord Brad?'
' Not him.'
' The O'Growneys, the O'Roartys or the Finnehys?'
' No.'
' That is an amazing piece of denial and denunciation,' he said.

He passed the red cloth over his face again to reduce the moisture.

' An astonishing parade of nullity,' he added.

' My name is not Jenkins either,' I vouchsafed.

' Roger MacHugh?'
' Not Roger.'
' Sitric Hogan?'
' No.'
' Not Conroy?'
' No.'
' Not O'Conroy?'
' Not O'Conroy.'

' There are very few more names that you could have, then,' he said. ' Because only a black man could have a name different to the ones I have recited. Or a red man. Not Byrne?'

' No.'

' Then it is a nice pancake,' he said gloomily. He bent double to give full scope to the extra brains he had at the rear of his head.

' Holy suffering senators,' he muttered.

I think we have won the day.

We are not home and dried yet, I answered.

Nevertheless I think we can relax. Evidently he has never heard of Signor Bari, the golden-throated budgerigar of Milano.

I don't think this is the time for pleasantries.

Or J. Courtney Wain, private investigator and member of the inner bar. Eighteen thousand guineas marked on the brief. The singular case of the red-headed men.

'By Scot!' said the Sergeant suddenly. He got up to pace the flooring.

'I think the case can be satisfactorily met,' he said pleasantly, 'and ratified unconditionally.'

I did not like his smile and asked him for his explanation.

'It is true,' he said, 'that you cannot commit a crime and that the right arm of the law cannot lay its finger on you irrespective of the degree of your criminality. Anything you do is a lie and nothing that happens to you is true.'

I nodded my agreement comfortably.

'For that reason alone,' said the Sergeant, 'we can take you and hang the life out of you and you are not hanged at all and there is no entry to be made in the death papers. The particular death you die is not even a death (which is an inferior phenomenon at the best) only an insanitary abstraction in the backyard, a piece of negative nullity neutralised and rendered void by asphyxiation and the fracture of the spinal string. If it is not a lie to say that you have been given the final hammer behind the barrack, equally it is true to say that nothing has happened to you.'

'You mean that because I have no name I cannot die and that you cannot be held answerable for death even if you kill me?'

'That is about the size of it,' said the Sergeant.

I felt so sad and so entirely disappointed that tears came into my eyes and a lump of incommunicable poignancy swelled tragically in my throat. I began to feel intensely every fragment of my equal humanity. The life that was bubbling at the end of my fingers was real and nearly painful in intensity and so was the beauty of my warm face and the loose humanity of my limbs and the racy health of my red rich blood. To leave it all without good reason and to smash the little empire into small fragments was a thing too pitiful even to refuse to think about.

The next important thing that happened in the day-room

was the entry of Policeman MacCruiskeen. He marched in to a chair and took out his black notebook and began perusing his own autographed memoranda, at the same time twisting his lips into an article like a purse.

'Did you take the readings?' the Sergeant asked.

'I did,' MacCruiskeen said.

'Read them till I hear them,' the Sergeant said, 'and until I make mental comparisons inside the interior of my inner head.'

MacCruiskeen eyed his book keenly.[7]

'Ten point five,' he said.

'Ten point five,' said the Sergeant. 'And what was the reading on the beam?'

'Five point three.'

'And how much on the lever?'

'Two point three.'

'Two point three is high,' said the Sergeant. He put the back of his fist between the saws of his yellow teeth and commenced working at his mental comparisons. After five minutes his face got clearer and he looked again to Mac-Cruiskeen.

'Was there a fall?' he asked.

'A light fall at five-thirty.'

'Five-thirty is rather late if the fall was a light one,' he said. 'Did you put charcoal adroitly in the vent?'

'I did,' said MacCruiskeen.

---

[7] From a chance and momentary perusal of the Policeman's note-book it is possible for me to give here the relative figures for a week's readings. For obvious reasons the figures themselves are fictitious:

PILOT READING	READING ON BEAM	READING ON LEVER	NATURE OF FALL (if any) with time
10.2	4.9	1.25	Light 4.15
10.2	4.6	1.25	Light 18.16
9.5	6.2	1.7	Light 7.15 (with lumps)
10.5	4.25	1.9	Nil
12.6	7.0	3.73	Heavy 21.6
12.5	6.5	2.5	Black 9.0
9.25	5.0	6.0	Black 14.45 (with lumps)

'How much?'

'Seven pounds.'

'I would say eight,' said the Sergeant.

'Seven was satisfactory enough,' MacCruiskeen said, 'if you recollect that the reading on the beam has been falling for the past four days. I tried the shuttle but there was no trace of play or looseness in it.'

'I would still say eight for safety-first,' said the Sergeant, 'but if the shuttle is tight, there can be no need for timorous anxiety.'

'None at all,' said MacCruiskeen.

The Sergeant cleared his face of all the lines of thought he had on it and stood up and clapped his flat hands on his breast pockets. 'Well now,' he said.

He stooped to put the clips on his ankles.

'I must go now to where I am going,' he said, 'and let you,' he said to MacCruiskeen, 'come with me to the exterior for two moments till I inform you about recent events officially.'

The two of them went out together, leaving me in my sad and cheerless loneliness. MacCruiskeen was not gone for long but I was lonely during that diminutive meantime. When he came in again he gave me a cigarette which was warm and wrinkled from his pocket.

'I believe they are going to stretch you,' he said pleasantly.

I replied with nods.

'It is a bad time of the year, it will cost a fortune,' he said. 'You would not believe the price of timber.'

'Would a tree not suffice?' I inquired, giving tongue to a hollow whim of humour.

'I do not think it would be proper,' he said, 'but I will mention it privately to the Sergeant.'

'Thank you.'

'The last hanging we had in this parish,' he said, 'was thirty years ago. It was a very famous man called MacDadd. He held the record for the hundred miles on a solid tyre. I need to tell you what the solid tyre did for him. We had to hang the bicycle.'

'Hang the bicycle?'

'MacDadd had a first-class grudge against another man called Figgerson but he did not go near Figgerson. He knew how things stood and gave Figgerson's bicycle a terrible thrashing with a crowbar. After that MacDadd and Figgerson had a fight and Figgerson—a dark man with glasses—did not live to know who the winner was. There was a great wake and he was buried with his bicycle. Did you ever see a bicycle-shaped coffin?'

'No.'

'It is a very intricate piece of wood-working, you would want to be a first-class carpenter to make a good job of the handlebars to say nothing of the pedals and the back-step. But the murder was a bad piece of criminality and we could not find MacDadd for a long time or make sure where the most of him was. We had to arrest his bicycle as well as himself and we watched the two of them under secret observation for a week to see where the majority of MacDadd was and whether the bicycle was mostly in MacDadd's trousers *pari passu* if you understand my meaning.'

'What happened?'

'The Sergeant gave his ruling at the end of the week. His position was painful in the extremity because he was a very close friend of MacDadd after office hours. He condemned the bicycle and it was the bicycle that was hanged. We entered a *nolle prosequi* in the day-book in respect of the other defendant. I did not see the stretching myself because I am a delicate man and my stomach is extremely reactionary.'

He got up and went to the dresser and took out his patent music-box which made sounds too esoterically rarefied to be audible to anybody but himself. He then sat back again in his chair, put his hands through the handstraps and began to entertain himself with the music. What he was playing could be roughly inferred from his face. It had a happy broad coarse satisfaction on it, a sign that he was occupied with loud obstreperous barn-songs and gusty shanties of the sea and burly roaring marching-songs. The silence in the room was so unusually quiet that the beginning of it seemed rather loud when the utter stillness of the end of it had been encountered.

How long this eeriness lasted or how long we were listening intently to nothing is unknown. My own eyes got tired with inactivity and closed down like a public house at ten o'clock. When they opened again I saw that MacCruiskeen had desisted from the music and was making preparations for mangling his washing and his Sunday shirts. He had pulled a great rusty mangle from the shadow of the wall and had taken a blanket from the top of it and was screwing down the pressure-spring and spinning the hand wheel and furbishing the machine with expert hands.

He went over then to the dresser and took small articles like dry batteries out of a drawer and also an instrument like a prongs and glass barrels with wires inside them and other cruder articles resembling the hurricane lamps utilised by the County Council. He put these things into different parts of the mangle and when he had them all satisfactorily adjusted, the mangle looked more like a rough scientific instrument than a machine for wringing out a day's washing.

The time of the day was now a dark time, the sun being about to vanish completely in the red west and withdraw all the light. MacCruiskeen kept on adding small well-made articles to his mangle and mounting indescribably delicate glass instruments about the metal legs and on the superstructure. When he had nearly finished this work the room was almost black, and sharp blue sparks would fly sometimes from the upside-down of his hand when it was at work.

Underneath the mangle in the middle of the cast-iron handiwork I noticed a black box with coloured wires coming out of it and there was a small ticking sound to be heard as if there was a clock in it. All in all it was the most complicated mangle I ever saw and to the inside of a steam thrashing-mill it was not inferior in complexity.

Passing near my chair to get an additional accessory, MacCruiskeen saw that I was awake and watching him.

'Do not worry if you think it is dark,' he said to me, 'because I am going to light the light and then mangle it for diversion and also for scientific truth.'

'Did you say you were going to mangle the light?'

'Wait till you see now.'

What he did next or which knobs he turned I did not ascertain on account of the gloom but it happened that a queer light appeared somewhere on the mangle. It was a local light that did not extend very much outside its own brightness but it was not a spot of light and still less a bar-shaped light. It was not steady completely but it did not dance like candlelight. It was light of a kind rarely seen in this country and was possibly manufactured with raw materials from abroad. It was a gloomy light and looked exactly as if there was a small area somewhere on the mangle and was merely devoid of darkness.

What happened next is astonishing. I could see the dim contours of MacCruiskeen in attendance at the mangle. He made adjustments with his cunning fingers, stooping for a minute to work at the lower-down inventions on the iron work. He rose then to full life-size and started to turn the wheel of the mangle, slowly, sending out a clamping creakiness around the barrack. The moment he turned the wheel, the unusual light began to change its appearance and situation in an extremely difficult fashion. With every turn it got brighter and harder and shook with such a fine delicate shaking that it achieved a steadiness unprecedented in the world by defining with its outer shakes the two lateral boundaries of the place where it was incontrovertibly situated. It grew steelier and so intense in its livid pallor that it stained the inner screen of my eyes so that it still confronted me in all quarters when I took my stare far away from the mangle in an effort to preserve my sight. MacCruiskeen kept turning slowly at the handle till suddenly to my sick utter horror, the light seemed to burst and disappear and simultaneously there was a loud shout in the room, a shout which could not have come from a human throat.

I sat on the chair's edge and gave frightened looks at the shadow of MacCruiskeen, who was stooping down again at the diminutive scientific accessories of the mangle, making minor adjustments and carrying out running repairs in the dark.

'What was that shouting?' I stuttered over at him.

'I will tell you that in a tick,' he called, 'if you will inform me what you think the words of the shout were. What would you say was said in the shout now?'

This was a question I was already working with in my own head. The unearthly voice had roared out something very quickly with three or four words compressed into one ragged shout. I could not be sure what it was but several phrases sprang into my head together and each of them could have been the contents of the shout. They bore an eerie resemblance to commonplace shouts I had often heard such as *Change for Tinahely and Shillelagh! Two to one the field! Mind the step! Finish him off!* I knew, however, that the shout could not be so foolish and trivial because it disturbed me in a way that could only be done by something momentous and diabolical.

MacCruiskeen was looking at me with a question in his eye.

'I could not make it out,' I said, vaguely and feebly, 'but I think it was railway-station talk.'

'I have been listening to shouts and screams for years,' he said, 'but I can never surely catch the words. Would you say that he said "Don't press so hard"?'

'No.'

'Second favourites always win?'

'Not that.'

'It is a difficult pancake,' MacCruiskeen said, 'a very compound crux. Wait till we try again.'

This time he screwed down the rollers of the mangle till they were whining and till it was nearly out of the question to spin the wheel. The light that appeared was the thinnest and sharpest light that I ever imagined, like the inside of the edge of a sharp razor, and the intensification which came upon it with the turning of the wheel was too delicate a process to be watched even sideways.

What happened eventually was not a shout but a shrill scream, a sound not unlike the call of rats yet far shriller than any sound which could be made by man or animal. Again I thought that words had been used but the exact meaning of them or the language they belonged to was quite uncertain.

'"Two bananas a penny"?'

'Not bananas,' I said.

MacCruiskeen frowned vacantly.

'It is one of the most compressed and intricate pancakes I have ever known,' he said.

He put the blanket back over the mangle and pushed it to one side and then lit a lamp on the wall by pressing some knob in the darkness. The light was bright but wavery and uncertain and would be far from satisfactory for reading with. He sat back in his chair as if waiting to be questioned and complimented on the strange things he had been doing.

'What is your private opinion of all that?' he asked.

'What were you doing?' I inquired.

'Stretching the light.'

'I do not understand your meaning.'

'I will tell you the size of it,' he said, 'and indicate roughly the shape of it. It is no harm if you know unusual things because you will be a dead man in two days and you will be held incognito and incommunicate in the meantime. Did you ever hear tell of omnium?'

'Omnium?'

'Omnium is the right name for it although you will not find it in the books.'

'Are you sure that is the right name?' I had never heard this word before except in Latin.

'Certain.'

'How certain?'

'The Sergeant says so.'

'And what is omnium the right name for?'

MacCruiskeen smiled at me indulgently.

'You are omnium and I am omnium and so is the mangle and my boots here and so is the wind in the chimney.'

'That is enlightening,' I said.

'It comes in waves,' he explained.

'What colour?'

'Every colour.'

'High or low?'

'Both.'

The blade of my inquisitive curiosity was sharpened but I saw that questions were putting the matter further into doubt instead of clearing it. I kept my silence till Mac-

Cruiskeen spoke again.

'Some people,' he said, 'call it energy but the right name is omnium because there is far more than energy in the inside of it, whatever it is. Omnium is the essential inherent interior essence which is hidden inside the root of the kernel of everything and it is always the same.'

I nodded wisely.

'It never changes. But it shows itself in a million ways and it always comes in waves. Now take the case of the light on the mangle.'

'Take it,' I said.

'Light is the same omnium on a short wave but if it comes on a longer wave it is in the form of noise, or sound. With my own patents I can stretch a ray out until it becomes sound.'

'I see.'

'And when I have a shout shut in that box with the wires, I can squeeze it till I get heat and you would not believe the convenience of it all in the winter. Do you see that lamp on the wall there?'

'I do.'

'That is operated by a patent compressor and a secret instrument connected with that box with the wires. The box is full of noise. Myself and the Sergeant spend our spare time in the summer collecting noises so that we can have light and heat for our official life in the dark winter. That is why the light is going up and down. Some of the noises are noiser than the others and the pair of us will be blinded if we come to the time when the quarry was working last September. It is in the box somewhere and it is bound to come out of it in the due course inevitably.'

'Blasting operations?'

'Dynamiteering and extravagant combustions of the most far-reaching kind. But omnium is the business-end of everything. If you could find the right wave that results in a tree, you could make a small fortune out of timber for export.'

'And policemen and cows, are they all in waves?'

'Everything is on a wave and omnium is at the back of the whole shooting-match unless I am a Dutchman from the distant Netherlands. Some people call it God and there are other names for something that is identically resembling it and that thing is omnium also into the same bargain.'

'Cheese?'

'Yes. Omnium.'

'Even braces?'

'Even braces.'

'Did you ever see a piece of it or what colour it is?'

MacCruiskeen smiled wryly and spread his hands into red fans.

'That is the supreme pancake,' he said. 'If you could say what the shouts mean it might be the makings of the answer.'

'And storm-wind and water and brown bread and the feel of hailstones on the bare head, are those all omnium on a different wave?'

'All omnium.'

'Could you not get a piece and carry it in your waistcoat so that you could change the world to suit you when it suited you?'

'It is the ultimate and the inexorable pancake. If you had a sack of it or even the half-full of a small matchbox of it, you could do anything and even do what could not be described by that name.'

'I understand you.'

MacCruiskeen sighed and went again to the dresser, taking something from the drawer. When he sat down at the table again, he started to move his hands together, performing intricate loops and convolutions with his fingers as if they were knitting something but there were no needles in them at all, nothing to be seen except his naked hands.

'Are you working again at the little chest?' I asked.

'I am,' he said.

I sat watching him idly, thinking my own thoughts. For the first time I recalled the wherefore of my unhappy visit to the queer situation I was in. Not my watch but the black box. Where was it? If MacCruiskeen knew the answer, would he tell me if I asked him? If by chance I did not escape safely from the hangman's morning, would I ever see it or know what was inside it, know the value of the money I could never spend, know how handsome could have been my volume on de Selby? Would I ever see John Divney again? Where was he now? Where was my watch?

You have no watch.

That was true. I felt my brain cluttered and stuffed with questions and blind perplexity and I also felt the sadness of my position coming back into my throat. I felt completely alone, but with a small hope that I would escape safely at the tail end of everything.

I had made up my mind to ask him if he knew anything about the cashbox when my attention was distracted by another surprising thing.

The door was flung open and in came Gilhaney, his red face puffed from the rough road. He did not quite stop or sit down but kept moving restlessly about the day-room, paying no attention to me at all. MacCruiskeen had reached a meticulous point in his work and had his head nearly on the table to make sure that his fingers were working correctly and making no serious mistakes. When he had passed the difficulty he looked up somewhat at Gilhaney.

' Is it about a bicycle?' he asked casually.

' Only about timber,' said Gilhaney.

' And what is your timber news?'

' The prices have been put up by a Dutch ring, the cost of a good scaffold would cost a fortune.'

' Trust the Dutchmen,' MacCruiskeen said in a tone that meant that he knew the timber trade inside out.

' A three-man scaffold with a good trap and satisfactory steps would set you back ten pounds without rope or labour,' Gilhaney said.

' Ten pounds is a lot of money for a hanger,' said MacCruiskeen.

' But a two-man scaffold with a push-off instead of the mechanical trap and a ladder for the steps would cost the best majority of six pound, rope extra.'

' And dear at the same price,' said MacCruiskeen.

' But the ten-pound scaffold is a better job, there is more class about it,' said Gilhaney. ' There is a charm about a scaffold if it is well-made and satisfactory.'

What occurred next I did not see properly because I was

listening to this pitiless talk even with my eyes. But something astonishing happened again. Gilhaney had gone near MacCruiskeen to talk down at him seriously and I think he made the mistake of stopping dead completely instead of keeping on the move to preserve his perpendicular balance. The outcome was that he crashed down, half on bent MacCruiskeen and half on the table, bringing the two of them with him into a heap of shouts and legs and confusion on the floor. The policeman's face when I saw it was a frightening sight. It was the colour of a dark plum with passion, but his eyes burned like bonfires in the forehead and there were frothy discharges at his mouth. He said no words for a while, only sounds of jungle anger, wild grunts and clicks of demoniacal hostility. Gilhaney had cowered to the wall and raised himself with the help of it and then retreated to the door. When MacCruiskeen found his tongue again he used the most unclean language ever spoken and invented dirtier words than the dirtiest ever spoken anywhere. He put names on Gilhaney too impossible and revolting to be written with known letters. He was temporarily insane with anger because he rushed ultimately to the dresser where he kept all his properties and pulled out a patent pistol and swept it round the room to threaten the two of us and every breakable article in the house.

'Get down on your four knees, the two of you, on the floor,' he roared, 'and don't stop searching for that chest you have knocked down till you find it!'

Gilhaney slipped down to his knees at once and I did the same thing without troubling to look at the Policeman's face because I could remember distinctly what it looked like the last time I had eyed it. We crawled feebly about the floor, peering and feeling for something that could not be felt or seen and that was really too small to be lost at all.

This is amusing. You are going to be hung for murdering a man you did not murder and now you will be shot for not finding a tiny thing that probably does not exist at all and which in any event you did not lose.

I deserve it all, I answered, for not being here at all, to quote the words of the Sergeant.

How long we remained at our peculiar task, Gilhaney and

I, it is not easy to remember. Ten minutes or ten years, perhaps, with MacCruiskeen seated near us, fingering the iron and glaring savagely at our bent forms. Then I caught Gilhaney showing his face to me sideways and giving me a broad private wink. Soon he closed his fingers, got up erect with the assistance of the door-handle and advanced to where MacCruiskeen was, smiling his gappy smile.

'Here you are and here it is,' he said with his closed hand outstretched.

'Put it on the table,' MacCruiskeen said evenly.

Gilhaney put his hand on the table and opened it.

'You can now go away and take your departure,' MacCruiskeen told him, 'and leave the premises for the purpose of attending to the timber.'

When Gilhaney was gone I saw that most of the passion had ebbed from the Policeman's face. He sat silent for a time, then gave his customary sigh and got up.

'I have more to do tonight,' he said to me civilly, 'so I will show you where you are to sleep for the dark night-time.'

He lit a queer light that had wires to it and a diminutive box full of minor noises, and led me into a room where there were two white beds and nothing else.

'Gilhaney thinks he is a clever one and a master mind,' he said.

'He might be or maybe not,' I muttered.

'He does not take much account of coincidental chances.'

'He does not look like a man that would care much.'

'When he said he had the chest he thought he was making me into a prize pup and blinding me by putting his thumb in my eye.'

'That is what it looked like.'

'But by a rare chance he *did* accidentally close his hand on the chest and it was the chest and nothing else that he replaced in due course on the table.'

There was some silence here.

'Which bed?' I asked.

'This one,' said MacCruiskeen.

VIII

AFTER MACCRUISKEEN had tiptoed delicately
from the room like a trained nurse and shut the door without
a sound, I found myself standing by the bed and wondering
stupidly what I was going to do with it. I was weary in body
and my brain was numb. I had a curious feeling about my
left leg. I thought that it was, so to speak, spreading—that
its woodenness was slowly extending throughout my whole
body, a dry timber poison killing me inch by inch. Soon my
brain would be changed to wood completely and I would
then be dead. Even the bed was made of wood, not metal.
If I were to lie in it—

*Will you sit down for Pity's sake and stop standing there
like a gawm,* Joe said suddenly.

I am not sure what I do next if I stop standing, I
answered. But I sat down on the bed for Pity's sake.

*There is nothing difficult about a bed, even a child can
learn to use a bed. Take off your clothes and get into bed and
lie on it and keep lying on it even if it makes you feel foolish.*

I saw the wisdom of this and started to undress. I felt
almost too tired to go through that simple task. When all
my clothes were laid on the floor they were much more numerous than I had expected and my body was surprisingly
white and thin.

I opened the bed fastidiously, lay into the middle of it,
closed it up again carefully and let out a sigh of happiness
and rest. I felt as if all my weariness and perplexities of the
day had descended on me pleasurably like a great heavy
quilt which would keep me warm and sleepy. My knees
opened up like rosebuds in rich sunlight, pushing my shins
two inches further to the bottom of the bed. Every joint became loose and foolish and devoid of true utility. Every inch
of my person gained weight with every second until the total
burden on the bed was approximately five hundred thousand
tons. This was evenly distributed on the four wooden legs of
the bed, which had by now become an integral part of the

universe. My eyelids, each weighing no less than four tons, slewed ponderously across my eyeballs. My narrow shins, itchier and more remote in their agony of relaxation, moved further away from me till my happy toes pressed closely on the bars. My position was completely horizontal, ponderous, absolute and incontrovertible. United with the bed I became momentous and planetary. Far away from the bed I could see the outside night framed neatly in the window as if it were a picture on the wall. There was a bright star in one corner with other smaller stars elsewhere littered about in sublime profusion. Lying quietly and dead-eyed, I reflected on how new the night[1] was, how distinctive and unaccustomed its individuality. Robbing me of the reassurance of my eyesight, it was disintegrating my bodily personality into a flux of colour, smell, recollection, desire—all the strange uncounted essences of terrestrial and spiritual existence. I was deprived of definition, position and magnitude and my significance was considerably diminished. Lying there, I felt the weariness ebbing from me slowly, like a tide retiring over limitless sands. The feeling was so pleasurable and profound that I sighed again a long sound of happi-

[1] Not excepting even the credulous Kraus (see his *De Selbys Leben*), all the commentators have treated de Selby's disquisitions on night and sleep with considerable reserve. This is hardly to be wondered at since he held (a) that darkness was simply an accretion of 'black air', i.e., a staining of the atmosphere due to volcanic eruptions too fine to be seen with the naked eye and also to certain 'regrettable' industrial activities involving coal-tar by-products and vegetable dyes; and (b) that sleep was simply a succession of fainting-fits brought on by semi-asphyxiation due to (a). Hatchjaw brings forward his rather facile and ever-ready theory of forgery, pointing to certain unfamiliar syntactical constructions in the first part of the third so-called 'prosecanto' in *Golden Hours*. He does not, however, suggest that there is anything spurious in de Selby's equally damaging rhodomontade in the *Layman's Atlas* where he inveighs savagely against 'the insanitary conditons prevailing everywhere after six o'clock' and makes the famous *gaffe* that death is merely 'the collapse of the heart from the strain of a lifetime of fits and fainting'. Bassett (in *Lux Mundi*) has gone to considerable pains to establish the date of these passages and shows that de Selby was *hors de combat* from his long-standing gall-bladder disorders at least immediately before the passages were composed. One cannot lightly set aside Bassett's formidable table of dates and his corroborative extracts from contemporary newspapers which treat of an unnamed 'elderly man' being assisted into private houses after having fits in the street. For those who wish to hold the balance for

ness. Almost at once I heard another sigh and heard Joe murmuring some contented incoherency. His voice was near me, yet did not seem to come from the accustomed place within. I thought that he must be lying beside me in the bed and I kept my hands carefully at my sides in case I should accidentally touch him. I felt, for no reason, that his diminutive body would be horrible to the human touch—scaly or slimy like an eel or with a repelling roughness like a cat's tongue.

That's not very logical—or complimentary either, he said suddenly.

What isn't?

That about my body. Why scaly?

That's only my joke, I chuckled drowsily. I know you have no body. Except my own, perhaps.

But why scaly?

I don't know. How can I know why I think my thoughts?

By God I won't be called scaly.

His voice to my surprise had become shrill with petulance. Then he seemed to fill the world with his resentment, not by speaking but by remaining silent after he had spoken.

---

themselves, Henderson's *Hatchjaw and Bassett* is not unuseful. Kraus, usually unscientific and unreliable, is worth reading on this point. (*Leben,* pp. 17-37.)

As in many other of de Selby's concepts, it is difficult to get to grips with his process of reasoning or to refute his curious conclusions. The 'volcanic eruptions', which we may for convenience compare to the infra-visual activity of such substances as radium, take place usually in the 'evening' are stimulated by the smoke and industrial combustions of the 'day' and are intensified in certain places which may, for the want of a better term, be called 'dark places'. One difficulty is precisely this question of terms. A 'dark place' is dark merely because it is a place where darkness 'germinates' and 'evening' is a time of twilight merely because the 'day' deteriorates owing to the stimulating effect of smuts on the volcanic processes. De Selby makes no attempt to explain why a 'dark place' such as a cellar need be dark and does not define the atmospheric, physical or mineral conditions which must prevail uniformly in all such places if the theory is to stand. The 'only straw offered', to use Bassett's wry phrase, is the statement that 'black air' is highly combustible, enormous masses of it being instantly consumed by the smallest flame, even an electrical luminance isolated in a vacuum. 'This,' Bassett observes, 'seems to be an attempt to protect the theory from the shock it can be dealt by simply striking

Now, now, Joe, I murmured soothingly.

Because if you are looking for trouble you can have your bellyful, he snapped.

You have no body, Joe.

Then why do you say I have? And why scaly?

Here I had a strange idea not unworthy of de Selby. Why was Joe so disturbed at the suggestion that he had a body? What if he *had* a body? A body with another body inside it in turn, thousands of such bodies within each other like the skins of an onion, receding to some unimaginable ultimum? Was I in turn merely a link in a vast sequence of imponderable beings, the world I knew merely the interior of the being whose inner voice I myself was? Who or what was the core and what monster in what world was the final uncontained colossus? God? Nothing? Was I receiving these wild thoughts from Lower Down or were they brewing newly in me to be transmitted Higher Up?

From Lower Down, Joe barked.

Thank you.

I'm leaving.

What?

---

matches and may be taken as the final proof that the great brain was out of gear.'

A significant feature of the matter is the absence of any authoritative record of those experiments with which de Selby always sought to support his ideas. It is true that Kraus (see below) gives a forty-page account of certain experiments, mostly concerned with attempts to bottle quantities of 'night' and endless sessions in locked and shuttered bedrooms from which bursts of loud hammering could be heard. He explains that the bottling operations were carried out with bottles which were, 'for obvious reasons', made of black glass. Opaque porcelain jars are also stated to have been used 'with some success'. To use the frigid words of Bassett, 'such information, it is to be feared, makes little contribution to serious deselbiana (*sic*).'

Very little is known of Kraus or his life. A brief biographical note appears in the obsolete *Bibliographie de de Selby*. He is stated to have been born in Ahrensburg, near Hamburg, and to have worked as a young man in the office of his father, who had extensive jam interests in North Germany. He is said to have disappeared completely from human ken after Hatchjaw had been arrested in a Sheephaven hotel following the unmasking of the de Selby letter scandal by *The Times,* which made scathing references to Kraus's 'discreditable' machinations in Hamburg and clearly suggested his complicity. If it is remem-

Clearing out. We will see who is scaly in two minutes.

These few words sickened me instantly with fear although their meaning was too momentous to be grasped without close reasoning.

The scaly idea—where did I get that from? I cried.

Higher Up, he shouted.

Puzzled and frightened I tried to understand the complexities not only of my intermediate dependence and my catenal unintegrity but also my dangerous adjunctiveness and my embarrassing unisolation. If one assumes—

Listen. Before I go I will tell you this. I am your soul and all your souls. When I am gone you are dead. Past humanity is not only implicit in each new man born but is contained in him. Humanity is an ever-widening spiral and life is the beam that plays briefly on each succeeding ring. All humanity from its beginning to its end is already present but the beam has not yet played beyond you. Your earthly successors await dumbly and trust to your guidance and mine and all my people inside me to preserve them and lead the light further. You are not now the top of your people's line any more than your mother was when she had you inside her. When I leave you I take with me all that has made you what

---

bered that these events occurred in the fateful June when the *Country Album* was beginning to appear in fortnightly parts, the significance of the whole affair becomes apparent. The subsequent exoneration of Hatchjaw served only to throw further suspicion on the shadowy Kraus.

Recent research has not thrown much light on Kraus's identity or his ultimate fate. Bassett's posthumous *Recollections* contains the interesting suggestion that Kraus did not exist at all, the name being one of the pseudonyms adopted by the egregious du Garbandier to further his 'campaign of calumny'. The *Leben*, however, seems too friendly in tone to encourage such a speculation.

Du Garbandier himself, possibly pretending to confuse the characteristics of the English and French languages, persistently uses 'black hair' for 'black air', and makes extremely elaborate fun of the raven-headed lady of the skies who deluged the world with her tresses every night when retiring.

The wisest course on this question is probably that taken by the little-known Swiss writer, Le Clerque. 'This matter,' he says, 'is outside the true province of the conscientious commentator inasmuch as being unable to say aught that is charitable or useful, he must preserve silence.'

you are—I take all your significance and importance and all the accumulations of human instinct and appetite and wisdom and dignity. You will be left with nothing behind you and nothing to give the waiting ones. Woe to you when they find you out! Good-bye!

Although I thought this speech was rather far-fetched and ridiculous, he was gone and I was dead.

Preparations for the funeral were put in hand at once. Lying in my dark blanket-padded coffin I could hear the sharp blows of a hammer nailing down the lid.

It soon turned out that the hammering was the work of Sergeant Pluck. He was standing smiling at me from the doorway and he looked large and lifelike and surprisingly full of breakfast. Over the tight collar of his tunic he wore a red ring of fat that looked fresh and decorative as if it had come directly from the laundry. His moustache was damp from drinking milk.

Thank goodness to be back to sanity, Joe said.

His voice was friendly and reassuring, like pockets in an old suit.

' Good morning to you in the morning-time,' the Sergeant said pleasantly.

I answered him in a civil way and gave particulars of my dream. He leaned listening on the jamb, taking in the difficult parts with a skilled ear. When I had finished he smiled at me in pity and good humour.

' You have been dreaming, man,' he said.

Wondering at him, I looked away to the window. Night was gone from it without a trace, leaving in substitution a distant hill that lay gently against the sky. Clouds of white and grey pillowed it and on its soft shoulder trees and boulders were put pleasingly to make it true. I could hear a morning wind making its way indomitably throughout the world and all the low unsilence of the daytime was in my ear, bright and restless like a caged bird. I sighed and looked back at the Sergeant, who was still leaning and quietly picking his teeth, absent-faced and still.

' I remember well,' he said, ' a dream that I had six years ago on the twenty-third of November next. A nightmare would be a truer word. I dreamt if you please that I had a slow puncture.'

'That is a surprising thing,' I said idly, ' but not astonishing. Was it the work of a tintack?'

'Not a tintack,' said the Sergeant. ' but too much starch.'

'I did not know,' I said sarcastically, ' that they starched the roads.'

'It was not the road, and for a wonder it was not the fault of the County Council. I dreamt that I was cycling on official business for three days. Suddenly I felt the saddle getting hard and lumpy underneath me. I got down and felt the tyres but they were unexceptionable and fully pumped. Then I thought my head was giving me a nervous outbreak from too much overwork. I went into a private house where there was a qualified doctor and he examined me completely and told me what the trouble was. I had a slow puncture.'

He gave a coarse laugh and half-turned to me his enormous backside.

'Here, look,' he laughed.

'I see,' I murmured.

Chuckling loudly he went away for a minute and came back again.

'I have put the stirabout on the table,' he said, ' and the milk is still hot from being inside the cow's milk-bag.'

I put on my clothes and went to my breakfast in the day-room where the Sergeant and MacCruiskeen were talking about their figures.

'Six point nine six three circulating,' MacCruiskeen was saying.

'High,' said the Sergeant. 'Very high. There must be a ground heat. Tell me about the fall.'

'A medium fall at midnight and no lumps.'

The Sergeant laughed and shook his head.

'No lumps indeed,' he chuckled, ' there will be hell to pay tomorrow on the lever if it is true there is a ground heat.'

MacCruiskeen got up suddenly from his chair.

'I will give her half a hundredweight of charcoal,' he announced. He marched straight out of the house muttering calculations, not .looking where he was going but staring straight into the middle of his black notebook.

I had almost finished my crock of porridge and lay back

to look fully at the Sergeant.

'When are you going to hang me?' I asked, looking fearlessly into his large face. I felt refreshed and strong again and confident that I would escape without difficulty.

'Tomorrow morning if we have the scaffold up in time and unless it is raining. You would not believe how slippery the rain can make a new scaffold. You could slip and break your neck into fancy fractures and you would never know what happened to your life or how you lost it.'

'Very well,' I said firmly. 'If I am to be a dead man in twenty-four hours will you explain to me what these figures in MacCruiskeen's black book are?'

The Sergeant smiled indulgently.

'The readings?'

'Yes.'

'If you are going to be dead completely there is no insoluble impedimentum to that proposal,' he said, 'but it is easier to show you than to tell you verbally. Follow behind me like a good man.'

He led the way to a door in the back passage and threw it open with an air of momentous revelation, standing aside politely to give me a complete and unobstructed view.

'What do you think of that?' he asked.

I looked into the room and did not think much of it. It was a small bedroom, gloomy and not too clean. It was in great disorder and filled with a heavy smell.

'It is MacCruiskeen's room,' he explained.

'I do not see much,' I said.

The Sergeant smiled patiently.

'You are not looking in the right quarter,' he said.

'I have looked everywhere that can be looked,' I said.

The Sergeant led the way in to the middle of the floor and took possession of a walking-stick that was convenient.

'If I ever want to hide,' he remarked, 'I will always go upstairs in a tree. People have no gift for looking up, they seldom examine the lofty altitudes.'

I looked at the ceiling.

'There is little to be seen there,' I said, 'except a blue-bottle that looks dead.'

The Sergeant looked up and pointed with his stick.

'That is not a bluebottle,' he said, 'that is Gogarty's out-house.'

I looked squarely at him in a mixed way but he was paying me no attention but pointing to other tiny marks upon the ceiling.

'That,' he said, 'is Martin Bundle's house and that is Tiernahins and that one there is where the married sister lives. And here we have the lane from Tiernahins to the main telegraph trunk road.' He drew his stick along a waver-ing faint crack that ran down to join a deeper crack.

'A map!' I cried excitedly.

'And here we have the barrack,' he added. 'It is all as plain as a pikestick.'

When I looked carefully at the ceiling I saw that Mr Mathers' house and every road and house I knew were marked there, and nets of lanes and neighbourhoods that I did not know also. It was a map of the parish, complete, reliable and astonishing.

The Sergeant looked at me and smiled again.

'You will agree,' he said, 'that it is a fascinating pan-cake and a conundrum of great incontinence, a phenomenon of the first rarity.'

'Did you make it yourself?'

'I did not and nobody else manufactured it either. It was always there and MacCruiskeen is certain that it was there even before that. The cracks are natural and so are small cracks.'

With my cocked eye I traced the road we came when Gil-haney had found his bicycle at the bush.

'The funny thing is,' the Sergeant said, 'that MacCruis-keen lay for two years staring at that ceiling before he saw it was a map of superb ingenuity.'

'Now that was stupid,' I said thickly.

'And he lay looking at the map for five years more before he saw that it showed the way to eternity.'

'To eternity?'

'Certainly.'

'Will it be possible for us to come back from there?' I whispered.

'Of course. There is a lift. But wait till I show you the

secret of the map.'

He took up the stick again and pointed to the mark that meant the barracks.

'Here we are in the barracks on the main telegraph trunk road,' he said. 'Now use your internal imagination and tell me what left-hand road you meet if you go forth from the barrack on the main road.'

I thought this out without difficulty.

'You meet the road that meets the main road at Jarvis's outhouse,' I said, 'where we came from the finding of the bicycle.'

'Then that road is the first turn on the left-hand latitude?'

'Yes.'

'And here it is—here.'

He pointed out the left-hand road with his stick and tapped Mr Jarvis's outhouse at the corner.

'And now,' he said solemnly, 'kindly inform me what this is.'

He drew the stick along a faint crack that joined the crack of the main road about half-way between the barrack and the road at Mr Jarvis's.

'What would you call that?' he repeated.

'There is no road there,' I cried excitedly, 'the left-hand road at Jarvis's is the first road on the left. I am not a fool. There is no road there.'

By God if you're not you will be. You're a goner if you listen to much more of this gentleman's talk.

'But there *is* a road there,' the Sergeant said triumphantly, 'if you know how to look knowledgeably for it. And a very old road. Come with me till we see the size of it.'

'Is this the road to eternity?'

'It is indeed but there is no signpost.'

Although he made no move to release his bicycle from solitary confinement in the cell, he snapped the clips adroitly on his trousers and led the way heavily into the middle of the morning. We marched together down the road. Neither of us spoke and neither listened for what the other might have to say.

When the keen wind struck me in the face it snatched

away the murk of doubt and fear and wonder that was anchored on my brain like a raincloud on a hill. All my senses, relieved from the agony of dealing with the existence of the Sergeant, became supernaturally alert at the work of interpreting the genial day for my benefit. The world rang in my ear like a great workshop. Sublime feats of mechanics and chemistry were evident on every side. The earth was agog with invisible industry. Trees were active where they stood and gave uncompromising evidence of their strength. Incomparable grasses were forever at hand, lending their distinction to the universe. Patterns very difficult to imagine were made together by everything the eye could see, merging into a supernal harmony their unexceptionable varieties. Men who were notable for the whiteness of their shirts worked diminutively in the distant bog, toiling in the brown turf and heather. Patient horses stood near with their useful carts and littered among the boulders on a hill beyond were tiny sheep at pasture. Birds were audible in the secrecy of the bigger trees, changing branches and conversing not tumultuously. In a field by the road a donkey stood quietly as if he were examining the morning, bit by bit unhurryingly. He did not move, his head was high and his mouth chewed nothing. He looked as if he understood completely these unexplainable enjoyments of the world.

My eye ranged round unsatisfied. I could not see enough in sufficient fulness before I took the left turn for eternity in company with the Sergeant and my thoughts remained entangled in what my eyes were looking at.

You don't mean to say that you believe in this eternity business?

What choice have I? It would be foolish to doubt anything after yesterday.

That is all very well but I think I can claim to be an authority on the subject of eternity. There must be a limit to this gentleman's monkey-tricks.

I am certain there isn't.

Nonsense. You are becoming demoralised.

I will be hung tomorrow.

That is doubtful but if it has to be faced we will make a brave show.

We?

Certainly. I will be there to the end. In the meantime let us make up our minds that eternity is not up a lane that is found by looking at cracks in the ceiling of a country policeman's bedroom.

Then what *is* up the lane?

I cannot say. If he said that eternity was up the lane and left it at that, I would not kick so hard. But when we are told that we are coming back from there in a lift—well, I begin to think that he is confusing night-clubs with heaven. A lift!

Surely, I argued, if we concede that eternity is up the lane, the question of the lift is a minor matter. That is a case for swallowing a horse and cart and straining at a flea.

No. I bar the lift. I know enough about the next world to be sure that you don't get there and come back out of it in a lift. Besides, we must be near the place now and I don't see any elevator-shaft running up into the clouds.

Gilhaney had no handlebars on him, I pointed out.

Unless the word ' lift ' has a special meaning. Like ' drop ' when you are talking about a scaffold. I suppose a smash under the chin with a heavy spade could be called a ' lift '. If that is the case you can be certain about eternity and have the whole of it yourself and welcome.

I still think there is an electric lift.

My attention was drawn away from this conversation to the Sergeant, who had now slackened his pace and was making curious inquiries with his stick. The road had reached a place where there was rising ground on each side, rank grass and brambles near our feet, with a tangle of bigger things behind that, and tall brown thickets beset with green creeper plants beyond.

' It is here somewhere,' the Sergeant said, ' or beside a place somewhere near the next place adjacent.'

He dragged his stick along the green margin, probing at the hidden ground.

' MacCruiskeen rides his bicycle along the grass here,' he said, ' it is an easier pancake, the wheels are surer and the seat is a more sensitive instrument than the horny hand.'

After another walk and more probing he found what he

was searching for and suddenly dragged me into the undergrowth, parting the green curtains of the branches with a practised hand.

'This is the hidden road,' he called backwards from ahead.

It is not easy to say whether road is the correct name for a place that must be fought through inch by inch at the cost of minor wounds and the sting of strained branches slapping back against the person. Nevertheless the ground was even against the foot and some dim distance to each side I could see the ground banking up sharply with rocks and gloominess and damp vegetation. There was a sultry smell and many flies of the gnat class were at home here.

A yard in front of me the Sergeant was plunging on wildly with his head down, thrashing the younger shoots severely with his stick and calling muffled warnings to me of the strong distended boughs he was about to release in my direction.

I do not know how long we travelled or what the distance was but the air and the light got scarcer and scarcer until I was sure that we were lost in the bowels of a great forest. The ground was still even enough to walk on but covered with the damp and rotting fall of many autumns. I had followed the noisy Sergeant with blind faith till my strength was nearly gone, so that I reeled forward instead of walking and was defenceless against the brutality of the boughs. I felt very ill and exhausted. I was about to shout to him that I was dying when I noticed the growth was thinning and that the Sergeant was calling to me, from where he was hidden and ahead of me, that we were there. When I reached him he was standing before a small stone building and bending to take the clips from his trousers.

'This is it,' he said, nodding his stooped head at the little house.

'This is what?' I muttered.

'The entrance to it,' he replied.

The structure looked exactly like the porch of a small country church. The darkness and the confusion of the branches made it hard for me to see whether there was a larger building at the rear. The little porch was old, with green stains on the stonework and warts of moss in its many crannies. The door was an old brown door with ecclesiastical hinges and ornamental ironwork; it was set far back and made to measure in its peaked doorway. This was the entrance to eternity. I knocked the streaming sweat from my forehead with my hand.

The Sergeant was feeling himself sensually for his keys.

' It is very close,' he said politely.

' Is this the entrance to the next world?' I murmured. My voice was lower than I thought it would be owing to my exertions and trepidation.

' But it is seasonable weather and we can't complain,' he added loudly, paying no attention to my question. My voice, perhaps, had not been strong enough to travel to his ear.

He found a key which he rasped in the keyhole and threw the door open. He entered the dark inside but sent his hand out again to twitch me in after him by the coat sleeve.

Strike a match there!

Almost at the same time the Sergeant had found a box with knobs and wires in it in the wall and did whatever was necessary to make it give out a startling leaping light from where it was. But during the second I was standing in the dark I had ample time to get the surprise of my life. It was the floor. My feet were astonished when they trod on it. It was made of platefuls of tiny studs like the floor of a steam-engine or like the railed galleries that run around a great printing press. It rang with a ghostly hollow noise beneath the hobnails of the Sergeant, who had now clattered to the other end of the little room to fuss with his chain of keys and to throw open another door that was hidden in the wall.

' Of course a nice shower of rain would clear the air,' he called.

I went carefully over to see what he was doing in the little closet he had entered. Here he had operated successfully another unsteady light-box. He stood with is back to me examining panels in the wall. There were two of them, tiny things like matchboxes, and the figure sixteen could be seen in one panel and ten in the other. He sighed and came out of the closet and looked at me sadly.

'They say that walking takes it down,' he said, 'but it is my own experience that walking puts it up, walking makes it solid and leaves plenty of room for more.'

I thought at this stage that a simple and dignified appeal might have some prospect of succeeding.

'Will you please tell me,' I said, 'since I will be a dead man tomorrow—where are we and what are we doing?'

'Weighing ourselves,' he replied.

'Weighing ourselves?'

'Step into the box there,' he said, 'till we see what your registration is by plain record.'

I stepped warily on to more iron plates in the closet and saw the figures change to nine and six.

'Nine stone six pounds,' said the Sergeant, 'and a most invidious weight. I would give ten years of my life to get the beef down.'

He had his back to me again opening still another closet in another wall and passing trained fingers over another light-box. The unsteady light came and I saw him standing in the closet, looking at his large watch and winding it absently. The light was leaping beside his jaw and throwing unearthly leaps of shadow on his gross countenance.

'Will you step over here,' he called to me at last, 'and come in with me unless you desire to be left behind in your own company.'

When I had walked over and stood silently beside him in the steel closet, he shut the door on us with a precise click and leaned against the wall thoughtfully. I was about to ask for several explanations when a cry of horror came bounding from my throat. With no noise or warning at all, the floor was giving way beneath us.

'It is no wonder that you are yawning,' the Sergeant said conversationally, 'it is very close, the ventilation is far from satisfactory.'

'I was only screaming,' I blurted. 'What is happening to this box we are in? Where—'

My voice trailed away to a dry cluck of fright. The floor was falling so fast beneath us that it seemed once or twice to fall faster than I could fall myself so that it was sure that my feet had left it and that I had taken up a position for brief intervals half-way between the floor and the ceiling. In panic I raised my right foot and smote it down with all my weight and my strength. It struck the floor but only with a puny tinkling noise. I swore and groaned and closed my eyes and wished for a happy death. I felt my stomach bounding sickeningly about inside me as if it were a wet football filled with water.

Lord save us!

' It does a man no harm,' the Sergeant remarked pleasantly, ' to move around a bit and see things. It is a great thing for widening out the mind. A wide mind is a grand thing, it nearly always leads to farseeing inventions. Look at Sir Walter Raleigh that invented the pedal bicycle and Sir George Stephenson with his steam-engine and Napoleon Bonaparte and George Sand and Walter Scott—great men all.'

' Are—are we in eternity yet?' I chattered.

' We are not there yet but nevertheless we are nearly there,' he answered. ' Listen with all your ears for a little click.'

What can I say to tell of my personal position? I was locked in an iron box with a sixteen-stone policeman, falling appallingly for ever, listening to talk about Walter Scott and listening for a click also.

Click!

It came at last, sharp and terrible. Almost at once the falling changed, either stopping altogether or becoming a much slower falling.

' Yes,' said the Sergeant brightly, ' we are there now.'

I noticed nothing whatever except that the thing we were in gave a jolt and the floor seemed to resist my feet suddenly in a way that might well have been eternal. The Sergeant fingered the arrangement of knob-like instruments on the door, which he opened after a time and stepped out.

' That was the lift,' he remarked.

It is peculiar that when one expects some horrible incalculable and devastating thing which does not materialise, one is more disappointed than relieved. I had expected for one thing a blaze of eye-destroying light. No other expectation was clear enough in my brain to be mentioned. Instead of this radiance, I saw a long passage lit fitfully at intervals by the crude home-made noise-machines, with more darkness to be seen than light. The walls of the passage seemed to be made with bolted sheets of pig-iron in which were set rows of small doors which looked to me like ovens or furnace-doors or safe-deposits such as banks have. The ceiling, where I could see it, was a mass of wires and what appeared to be particularly thick wires or possibly pipes. All the time there was an entirely new noise to be heard, not unmusical, sometimes like water gurgling underground and sometimes like subdued conversation in a foreign tongue.

The Sergeant was already looming ahead on his way up the passage, treading heavily on the plates. He swung his keys jauntily and hummed a song. I followed near him, trying to count the little doors. There were four rows of six in every lineal two yards of wall, or a total of many thousands. Here and there I saw a dial or an intricate nest of clocks and knobs resembling a control board with masses of coarse wires converging from all quarters of it. I did not understand the significance of anything but I thought the scene was so real that much of my fear was groundless. I trod firmly beside the Sergeant, who was still real enough for anybody.

We came to a crossroads in the passage where the light was brighter. A cleaner brighter passage with shiny steel walls ran away to each side, disappearing from view only where the distance brought its walls, floor and roof to the one gloomy point. I thought I could hear a sound like hissing steam and another noise like great cogwheels grinding one way, stopping and grinding back again. The Sergeant paused to take a reading from a clock in the wall, then turned sharply to the left and called for me to follow.

I shall not recount the passages we walked or talk of the one with the round doors like portholes or the other place where the Sergeant got a box of matches for himself by putting his hand somewhere into the wall. It is enough to say that we arrived, after walking at least a mile of plate, into a well-lit airy hall which was completely circular and filled with indescribable articles very like machinery but not quite as intricate as the more difficult machines. Large expensive-looking cabinets of these articles were placed tastefully about the floor while the circular wall was one mass of these inventions with little dials and meters placed plentifully here and there. Hundreds of miles of coarse wire were visible running everywhere except about the floor and there were thousands of doors like the strong-hinged doors of ovens and arrangements of knobs and keys that reminded me of American cash registers.

The Sergeant was reading out figures from one of the many clocks and turning a small wheel with great care. Suddenly the silence was split by the sound of loud frenzied hammering from the far end of the hall where the apparatus seemed thickest and most complex. The blood ran away at once from my startled face. I looked at the Sergeant but he still attended patiently to his clock and wheel, reciting numbers under his breath and taking no notice. The hammering stopped.

I sat down to think and gather my scattered wits on a smooth article like an iron bar. It was pleasantly warm and comforting. Before any thought had time to come to me there was another burst of hammering, then silence, then a low but violent noise like passionately-muttered oaths, then silence again and finally the sound of heavy footsteps approaching from behind the tall cabinets of machinery.

Feeling a weakness in my spine, I went over quickly and stood beside the Sergeant. He had taken a long white instrument like a large thermometer or band conductor's baton out of a hole in the wall and was examining the calibrations on it with a frown of great preoccupation. He paid no attention to me or to the hidden presence that was approaching invisibly. When I heard the clanging steps rounding the last cabinet, against my will I looked up wildly. It was Policeman MacCruiskeen. He was frowning heavily and bearing another large baton or thermometer which was orange-coloured. He made straight for the Sergeant and showed him this instrument, putting a red finger on a marking that was on it. They stood there silently examining each other's instruments. The Sergeant looked somewhat relieved, I thought, when he had the matter thought out and marched away to the hidden place that MacCruiskeen had just come from. Soon we heard the sound of hammering, this time gentle and rhythmical.

MacCruiskeen put his baton away into the wall in the hole where the Sergeant's had been and turned to me, giving me generously the wrinkled cigarette which I had come to regard as the herald of unthinkable conversation.

'Do you like it?' he inquired.

'It is neat,' I replied.

'You would not believe the convenience of it,' he remarked cryptically.

The Sergeant came back to us drying his red hands on a towel and looking very satisfied with himself. I looked at the two of them sharply. They received my glance and exchanged it privately between them before discarding it.

'Is this eternity?' I asked. 'Why do you call it eternity?'

'Feel my chin,' MacCruiskeen said, smiling enigmatically.

'We call it that,' the Sergeant explained, 'because you don't grow old here. When you leave here you will be the same age as you were coming in and the same stature and latitude. There is an eight-day clock here with a patent balanced action but it never goes.'

'How can you be sure you don't grow old here?'

'Feel my chin,' MacCruiskeen said again.

'It is simple,' the Sergeant said. 'The beard does not grow and if you are fed you do not get hungry and if you are hungry you don't get hungrier. Your pipe will smoke all day and will still be full and a glass of whiskey will still be there no matter how much of it you drink and it does not matter in any case because it will not make you drunker than your own sobriety.'

'Indeed,' I muttered.

'I have been here for a long time this today morning,' MacCruiskeen said, 'and my jaw is still as smooth as a woman's back and the convenience of it takes my breath away, it is a great thing to downface the old razor.'

'How big is all this place?'

'It has no size at all,' the Sergeant explained, 'because there is no difference anywhere in it and we have no conception of the extent of its unchanging coequality.'

MacCruiskeen lit a match for our cigarettes and then

threw it carelessly on the plate floor where it lay looking very much important and alone.

'Could you not bring your bicycle and ride through all of it and see it all and draw a chart?' I asked.

The Sergeant smiled at me as if I were a baby.

'The bicycle is easy,' he said.

To my astonishment he went over to one of the bigger ovens, manipulated some knobs, pulled open the massive metal door and lifted out a brand-new bicycle. It had a three-speed gear and an oil-bath and I could see the vaseline still glistening on the bright parts. He put the front wheel down and spun the back wheel expertly in the air.

'The bicycle is an easy pancake,' he said, 'but it is no use and does not matter. Come and I will demonstrate the *res ipsa*.'

Leaving the bicycle, he led the way through the intricate cabinets and round behind other cabinets and in through a doorway. What I saw made my brain shrink painfully in my head and put a paralysing chill across my heart. It was not so much that this other hall was in every respect an exact replica of the one we had just left. It was more that my burdened eye saw that one of the cabinet doors in the wall was standing open and a brand-new bicycle was leaning against the wall, identically like the other one and leaning even at the same angle.

'If you want to take another walk ahead to reach the same place here without coming back you can walk on till you reach the next doorway and you are welcome. But it will do you no good and even if we stay here behind you it is probable that you will find us there to meet you.'

Here I gave a cry as my eye caught a spent match lying clearly on the floor.

'What do you think of the no-shaving?' MacCruiskeen asked boastfully. 'Surely that is an uninterruptible experiment?'

'It is inescapable and highly intractable,' the Sergeant said.

MacCruiskeen was examining some knobs in a central cabinet. He turned his head and called to me.

'Come over here,' he called, 'till I show you something

to tell your friends about.'

Afterwards I saw that this was one of his rare jokes because what he showed me was something that I could tell nobody about, there are no suitable words in the world to tell my meaning. This cabinet had an opening resembling a chute and another large opening resembling a black hole about a yard below the chute. He pressed two red articles like typewriter keys and turned a large knob away from him. At once there was a rumbling noise as if thousands of full biscuit-boxes were falling down a stairs. I felt that these falling things would come out of the chute at any moment. And so they did, appearing for a few seconds in the air and then disappearing down the black hole below. But what can I say about them? In colour they were not white or black and certainly bore no intermediate colour; they were far from dark and anything but bright. But strange to say it was not their unprecedented hue that took most of my attention. They had another quality that made me watch them wild-eyed, dry-throated and with no breathing. I can make no attempt to describe this quality. It took me hours of thought long afterwards to realise why these articles were astonishing. *They lacked an essential property of all known objects.* I cannot call it shape or configuration since shapelessness is not what I refer to at all. I can only say that these objects, not one of which resembled the other, were of no known dimensions. They were not square or rectangular or circular or simply irregularly shaped nor could it be said that their endless variety was due to dimensional dissimilarities. Simply their appearance, if even that word is not inadmissible, was not understood by the eye and was in any event indescribable. That is enough to say.

When MacCruiskeen had unpressed the buttons the Sergeant asked me politely what else I would like to see.

'What else is there?'

'Anything.'

'Anything I mention will be shown to me?'

'Of course.'

The ease with which the Sergeant had produced a bicycle that would cost at least eight pounds ten to buy had set in motion in my head certain trains of thought. My nervousness had been largely reduced to absurdity and nothingness by what I had seen and I now found myself taking an interest in the commercial possibilities of eternity.

'What I would like,' I said slowly, 'is to see you open a door and lift out a solid block of gold weighing half a ton.'

The Sergeant smiled and shrugged his shoulders.

'But that is impossible, it is a very unreasonable requisition,' he said. 'It is vexatious and unconscionable,' he added legally.

My heart sank down at this.

'But you said *anything*.'

'I know, man. But there is a limit and a boundary to everything within the scope of reason's garden.'

'That is disappointing,' I muttered.

MacCruiskeen stirred diffidently.

'Of course,' he said, 'if there would be no objection to me assisting the Sergeant in lifting out the block . . .'

'What! Is that a difficulty?'

'I am not a cart-horse,' the Sergeant said with simple dignity.

'Yet, anyhow,' he added, reminding all of us of his great-grandfather.

'Then we'll all lift it out,' I cried.

And so we did. The knobs were manipulated, the door opened and the block of gold, which was encased in a well-made timber box, was lifted down with all our strength and placed on the floor.

'Gold is a common article and there is not much to see when you look at it,' the Sergeant observed. 'Ask him for something confidential and superior to ordinary pre-eminence. Now a magnifying glass is a better thing because you can look at it and what you see when you look is a third thing altogether.'

Another door was opened by MacCruiskeen and I was handed a magnifying glass, a very ordinary-looking instrument with a bone handle. I looked at my hand through it and saw nothing that was recognisable. Then I looked at several other things but saw nothing that I could clearly see. MacCruiskeen took it back with a smile at my puzzled eye.

'It magnifies to invisibility,' he explained. 'It makes

everything so big that there is room in the glass for only the smallest particle of it—not enough of it to make it different from any other thing that is dissimilar.'

My eye moved from his explaining face to the block of gold which my attention had never really left.

'What I would like to see now.' I said carefully, ' is fifty cubes of solid gold each weighing one pound.'

MacCruiskeen went away obsequiously like a trained waiter and got these articles out of the wall without a word, arranging them in a neat structure on the floor. The Sergeant had strolled away idly to examine some clocks and take readings. In the meantime my brain was working coldly and quickly. I ordered a bottle of whiskey, precious stones to the value of £200,000, some bananas, a fountain-pen and writing materials, and finally a serge suit of blue with silk linings. When all these things were on the floor, I remembered other things I had overlooked and ordered underwear, shoes and banknotes, and a box of matches. MacCruiskeen, sweating from his labour with the heavy doors, was complaining of the heat and paused to drink some amber ale. The Sergeant was quietly clicking a little wheel with a tiny ratchet.

' I think that is all,' I said at last.

The Sergeant came forward and gazed at the pile of merchandise.

' Lord, save us,' he said.

' I am going to take these things with me,' I announced.

The Sergeant and MacCruiskeen exchanged their private glance. Then they smiled.

' In that case you will need a big strong bag,' the Sergeant said. He went to another door and got me a hogskin bag worth at least fifty guineas in the open market. I carefully packed away my belongings.

I saw MacCruiskeen crushing out his cigarette on the wall and noticed that it was still the same length as it had been when lit half an hour ago. My own was burning quietly also but was completely unconsumed. I crushed it out also and put it in my pocket.

When about to close the bag I had a thought. I unstooped and turned to the policemen.

'I require just one thing more,' I said. 'I want a small weapon suitable for the pocket which will exterminate any man or any million men who try at any time to take my life.'

Without a word the Sergeant brought me a small black article like a torch.

'There is an influence in that,' he said, 'that will change any man or men into grey powder at once if you point it and press the knob and if you don't like grey powder you can have purple powder or yellow powder or any other shade of powder if you tell me now and confide your favourite colour. Would a velvet-coloured colour please you?'

'Grey will do,' I said briefly.

I put this murderous weapon into the bag, closed it and stood up again.

'I think we might go home now.' I said the words casually and took care not to look at the faces of the policemen. To my surprise they agreed readily and we started off with our resounding steps till we found ourselves again in the endless corridors, I carrying the heavy bag and the policemen conversing quietly about the readings they had seen. I felt happy and satisfied with my day. I felt changed and regenerated and full of fresh courage.

'How does this thing work?' I inquired pleasantly, seeking to make friendly conversation. The Sergeant looked at me.

'It has helical gears,' he said informatively.

'Did you not see the wires?' MacCruiskeen asked, turning to me in some surprise.

'You would be astonished at the importance of the charcoal,' the Sergeant said. 'The great thing is to keep the beam reading down as low as possible and you are doing very well if the pilot-mark is steady. But if you let the beam rise, where are you with your lever? If you neglect the charcoal feedings you will send the beam rocketing up and there is bound to be a serious explosion.'

'Low pilot, small fall,' MacCruiskeen said. He spoke neatly and wisely as if his remark was a proverb.

'But the secret of it all-in-all,' continued the Sergeant, 'is the daily readings. Attend to your daily readings and your conscience will be as clear as a clean shirt on Sunday morning. I am a great believer in the daily readings.'

'Did I see everything of importance?'

At this the policemen looked at each other in amazement and laughed outright. Their raucous roars careered away from us up and down the corridor and came back again in pale echoes from the distance.

'I suppose you think a smell is a simple thing?' the Sergeant said smiling.

'A smell?'

'A smell is the most complicated phenomenon in the world,' he said, 'and it cannot be unravelled by the human snout or understood properly although dogs have a better way with smells than we have.'

'But dogs are very poor riders on bicycles,' MacCruiskeen said, presenting the other side of the comparison.

'We have a machine down there,' the Sergeant continued, 'that splits up any smell into its sub- and inter-smells the way you can split up a beam of light with a glass instrument. It is very interesting and edifying, you would not believe the dirty smells that are inside the perfume of a lovely lily-of-the mountain.'

'And there is a machine for tastes,' MacCruiskeen put in, 'the taste of a fried chop, although you might not think it, is forty per cent the taste of ...'

He grimaced and spat and looked delicately reticent.

'And feels,' the Sergeant said. 'Now there is nothing so smooth as a woman's back or so you might imagine. But if that feel is broken up for you, you would not be pleased with women's backs, I'll promise you that on my solemn oath and parsley. Half of the inside of the smoothness is as rough as a bullock's hips.'

'The next time you come here,' MacCruiskeen promised, 'you will see surprising things.'

This in itself, I thought, was a surprising thing for anyone to say after what I had just seen and after what I was carrying in the bag. He groped in his pocket, found his cigarette, re-lit it and proffered me the match. Hampered with the heavy bag, I was some minutes finding mine but the match still burnt evenly and brightly at its end.

We smoked in silence and went on through the dim passage till we reached the lift again. There were clock-faces or dials beside the open lift which I had not seen before and another pair of doors beside it. I was very tired with my bag of gold and clothes and whiskey and made for the lift to stand on it and put the bag down at last. When nearly on the threshold I was arrested in my step by a call from the Sergeant which rose nearly to the pitch of a woman's scream.

'Don't go in there!'

The colour fled from my face at the urgency of his tone. I turned my head round and stood rooted there with one foot before the other like a man photographed unknowingly in the middle of a walk.

'Why?'

'Because the floor will collapse underneath the bottom of your feet and send you down where nobody went before you.'

'And why?'

'The bag, man.'

'The simple thing is,' MacCruiskeen said calmly, 'that you cannot enter the lift unless you weigh the same weight as you weighed when you weighed into it.'

'If you do,' said the Sergeant, 'it will extirpate you unconditionally and kill the life out of you.'

I put the bag, clinking with its bottle and gold cubes, rather roughly on the floor. It was worth several million pounds. Standing there on the plate floor, I leaned on the plate wall and searched my wits for some reason and understanding and consolation-in-adversity. I understood little except that my plans were vanquished and my visit to eternity unavailing and calamitous. I wiped a hand on my damp brow and stared blankly at the two policemen, who were now smiling and looking knowledgeable and complacent. A large emotion came swelling against my throat and filling my mind with great sorrow and a sadness more remote and desolate than a great strand at evening with the sea far away at its distant turn. Looking down with a bent head at my broken shoes, I saw them swim and dissolve in big tears that came bursting on my eyes. I turned to the wall and gave loud choking sobs and broke down completely and cried loudly like a baby. I do not know how long I was crying. I think I heard the two policemen discussing me in sympathetic undertones as if they were trained doctors in a hospital. Without lifting my head I looked across the floor and saw MacCruiskeen's legs walking away with my bag. Then I heard an oven door being opened and the bag fired roughly in. Here I cried loudly again, turning to the wall of the lift and giving complete rein to my great misery.

At last I was taken gently by the shoulders, weighed and guided into the lift. Then I felt the two large policemen crowding in beside me and got the heavy smell of blue official broadcloth impregnated through and through with their humanity. As the floor of the lift began to resist my feet, I felt a piece of crisp paper rustling against my averted face. Looking up in the poor light I saw that MacCruiskeen was stretching his hand in my direction dumbly and meekly across the chest of the Sergeant who was standing tall and still beside me. In the hand was a small white paper bag. I glanced into it and saw round coloured things the size of florins.

' Creams,' MacCruiskeen said kindly.

He shook the bag encouragingly and started to chew and suck loudly as if there was almost supernatural pleasure to be had from these sweetmeats. Beginning for some reason to sob again, I put my hand into the bag but when I took a sweet, three or four others which had merged with it in the heat of the policeman's pocket came out with it in one sticky mass of plaster. Awkwardly and foolishly I tried to disentangle them but failed completely and then rammed the lot into my mouth and stood there sobbing and sucking and snuffling. I heard the Sergeant sighing heavily and could feel his broad flank receding as he sighed.

' Lord, I love sweets,' he murmured.

' Have one,' MacCruiskeen smiled, rattling his bag.

' What are you saying, man,' the Sergeant cried, turning to view MacCruiskeen's face, ' are you out of your mind, man alive? If I took one of these—not one but half of a corner of the quarter of one of them—I declare to the Hokey that my stomach would blow up like a live landmine and I would be galvanised in my bed for a full fortnight roaring out profanity from terrible stoons of indigestion and heart-scalds. Do you want to kill me, man?'

'Sugar barley is a very smooth sweet,' MacCruiskeen said, speaking awkwardly with his bulging mouth. 'They give it to babies and it is a winner for the bowels.'

'If I ate sweets at all,' the Sergeant said, 'I would live on the "Carnival Assorted". Now *there* is a sweet for you. There is great sucking in them, the flavour is very spiritual and one of them is good for half an hour.'

'Did you ever try Liquorice Pennies?' asked MacCruiskeen.

'Not them but the "Fourpenny Coffee-Cream Mixture" have a great charm.'

'Or the Dolly Mixture?'

'No.'

'They say,' MacCruiskeen said, 'that the Dolly Mixture is the best that was ever made and that it will never be surpassed and indeed I could eat them and keep eating till I got sick.'

'That may be,' the Sergeant said, 'but if I had my health I would give you a good run for it with the Carnival Mixture.' As they wrangled on about sweets and passed to chocolate bars and sticks of rock, the floor was pressing strongly from underneath. Then there was a change in the pressing, two clicks were heard and the Sergeant started to undo the doors, explaining to MacCruiskeen his outlook on Ju-jubes and jelly-sweets and Turkish Delights.

With sloped shoulders and a face that was stiff from my dried tears, I stepped wearily out of the lift into the little stone room and waited till they had checked the clocks. Then I followed them into the thick bushes and kept behind them as they met the attacks of the branches and fought back. I did not care much.

It was not until we emerged, breathless and with bleeding hands, on the green margin of the main road that I realised that a strange thing had happened. It was two or three hours since the Sergeant and I had started on our journey yet the country and the trees and all the voices of every thing around still wore an air of early morning. There was incommunicable earliness in everything, a sense of waking and beginning. Nothing had yet grown or matured and nothing begun had yet finished. A bird singing had not yet turned finally the last twist of tunefulness. A rabbit emerging still had a hidden tail.

The Sergeant stood monumentally in the middle of the hard grey road and picked some small green things delicately from his person. MacCruiskeen stood stooped in knee-high grass looking over his person and shaking himself sharply like a hen. I stood myself looking wearily into the bright sky and wondering over the wonders of the high morning.

When the Sergeant was ready he made a polite sign with his thumb and the two of us set off together in the direction of the barrack. MacCruiskeen was behind but he soon appeared silently in front of us, sitting without a move on the top of his quiet bicycle. He said nothing as he passed us and stirred no breath or limb and he rolled away from us down the gentle hill till a bend received him silently.

As I walked with the Sergeant I did not notice where we were or what we passed by on the road, men, beasts or houses. My brain was like an ivy near where swallows fly. Thoughts were darting around me like a sky that was loud and dark with birds but none came into me or near enough. Forever in my ear was the click of heavy shutting doors, the whine of boughs trailing their loose leaves in a swift springing and the clang of hobnails on metal plates.

When I reached the barrack I paid no attention to anything or anybody but went straight to a bed and lay on it and fell into a full and simple sleep. Compared with this sleep, death is a restive thing, peace is a clamour and darkness a burst of light.

IX

I **WAS** awakened the following morning by sounds of loud hammering[1] outside the window and found myself immediately recalling—the recollection was an absurd paradox—that I had been in the next world yesterday. Lying there half awake, it is not unnatural that my thoughts should turn to de Selby. Like all the greater thinkers, he has been looked to for guidance on many of the major perplexities of existence. The commentators, it is to be feared, have not succeeded in extracting from the vast store-house of his writings any consistent, cohesive or comprehensive corpus of spiritual belief and praxis. Nevertheless, his ideas of paradise are not without interest. Apart from the contents of the famous de Selby ' Codex ',[2] the main references are to be found in the *Rural Atlas* and in the so-called ' substantive ' appendices to the *Country Album*. Briefly he indicates that the happy state is ' not unassociated with water ' and that ' water is rarely absent from any wholly satisfactory situation '. He does not give any closer definition of this hydraulic elysium but mentions that he has written more fully on the subject else-

[1] Le Clerque (in his almost forgotten *Extensions and Analyses*) has drawn attention to the importance of percussion in the de Selby dialectic and shown that most of the physicist's experiments were extremely noisy. Unfortunately the hammering was always done behind locked doors and no commentator has hazarded even a guess as to what was being hammered and for what purpose. Even when constructing the famous water-box, probably the most delicate and fragile instrument ever made by human hands, de Selby is known to have smashed three heavy coal-hammers and was involved in undignified legal proceedings with his landlord (the notorious Porter) arising from an allegation of strained floor-joists and damage to a ceiling. It is clear that he attached considerable importance to ' hammerwork '. v. *Golden Hours*, p. 48-9). In *The Layman's Atlas* he publishes a rather obscure account of his inquiries into the nature of hammering and boldly attributes the sharp sound of percussion to the bursting of ' atmosphere balls ' evidently envisaging the air as being composed of minute balloons, a view scarcely confirmed by later scientific research. In his disquisitions elsewhere on the nature of night and darkness, he refers in passing to the straining of ' air-skins ', *al.* ' air-balls ' and ' bladders '. His conclusion was that ' hammering is anything but what

it appears to be '; such a statement, if not open to explicit refutation, seems unnecessary and unenlightening.

Hatchjaw has put forward the suggestion that loud hammering was a device resorted to by the savant to drown other noises which might give some indication of the real trend of the experiments. Bassett has concurred in this view, with, however, two reservations.

² The reader will be familiar with the storms which have raged over this most tantalising of holograph survivals. The 'Codex' (first so-called by Bassett in his monumental *De Selby Compendium*) is a collection of some two thousand sheets of foolscap closely hand-written on both sides. The signal distinction of the manuscript is that not one word of the writing is legible. Attempts made by different commentators to decipher certain passages which look less formidable than others have been characterised by fantastic divergencies, not in the meaning of the passages (of which there is no question) but in the brand of nonsense which is evolved. One passage, described by Bassett as being 'a penetrating treatise on old age' is referred to by Henderson (biographer of Bassett) as 'a not unbeautiful description of lambing operations on an unspecified farm'. Such disagreement, it must be confessed, does little to enhance the reputation of either writer.

Hatchjaw, probably displaying more astuteness than scholastic acumen, again advances his forgery theory and professes amazement that any person of intelligence could be deluded by 'so crude an imposition'. A curious contretemps arose when, challenged by Bassett to substantiate this cavalier pronouncement, Hatchjaw casually mentioned that eleven pages of the 'Codex' were all numbered '88'. Bassett, evidently taken by surprise, performed an independent check and could discover no page at all bearing this number. Subsequent wrangling disclosed the startling fact that both commentators claimed to have in their personal possession the 'only genuine Codex'. Before this dispute could be cleared up, there was a further bombshell, this time from far-off Hamburg. The Norddeutsche Verlag published a book by the shadowy Kraus purporting to be an elaborate exegesis based on an authentic copy of the 'Codex' with a transliteration of what was described as the obscure code in which the document was written. If Kraus can be believed, the portentously-named 'Codex' is simply a collection of extremely puerile maxims on love, life, mathematics and the like, couched in poor ungrammatical English and entirely lacking de Selby's characteristic reconditeness and obscurity. Bassett and many of the other commentators, regarding this extraordinary book as merely another manifestation of the mordant du Garbandier's spleen, pretended never to have heard of it notwithstanding the fact that Bassett is known to have obtained, presumably by questionable means, a proof of the work many months before it appeared. Hatchjaw alone did not ignore the book. Remarking dryly in a newspaper article that Kraus's 'aberration' was due to a foreigner's confusion of the two English words code and codex, declared his intention of publishing 'a brief brochure' which would effectively discredit the German's work and all similar 'trumpery frauds'. The failure of this work to appear is popularly attributed to Kraus's machinations in Hamburg and lengthy sessions on the transcontinental wire. In any event, the wretched Hatchjaw was again arrested, this time at the suit of his own pub-

where.[3] It is not clear, unfortunately, whether the reader is expected to infer that a wet day is more enjoyable than a dry one or that a lengthy course of baths is a reliable method of achieving peace of mind. He praises the equilibrium of water, its circumambiency, equiponderance and equitableness, and declares that water, ' if not abused '[4] can achieve ' absolute superiority.' For the rest, little remains save the record of his obscure and unwitnessed experiments. The story is one of a long succession of prosecutions for water wastage at the suit of the local authority. At one hearing it was shown that he had used 9,000 gallons in one day and on another occasion almost 80,000 gallons in the course of a week. The word ' used ' in this context is the important one. The local officials, having checked the volume of water entering the house daily from the street connection, had sufficient curiosity to watch the outlet sewer and made the astonishing discovery that *none of the vast quantity of water drawn in ever left the house*. The commentators have seized avidly on

---

lishers who accused him of the larceny of some of the firm's desk fittings. The case was adjourned and subsequently struck out owing to the failure to appear of certain unnamed witnesses from abroad. Clear as it is that this fantastic charge was without a vestige of foundation, Hatchjaw failed to obtained any redress from the authorities.

It cannot be pretended that the position regarding this ' Codex ' is at all satisfactory and it is not likely that time or research will throw any fresh light on a document which cannot be read and of which four copies at least, all equally meaningless, exist in the name of being the genuine original.

An amusing diversion in this affair was unwittingly caused by the mild Le Clerque. Hearing of the ' Codex ' some months before Bassett's authoritative ' Compendium ' was published, he pretended to have read the ' Codex ' and in an article in the *Zuercher Tageblatt* made many vague comments on it, referring to its ' shrewdness ', ' compelling if novel arguments ', ' fresh viewpoint ', etc. Subsequently he repudiated the article and asked Hatchjaw in a private letter to denounce it as a forgery. Hatchjaw's reply is not extant but it is thought that he refused with some warmth to be party to any further hanky-panky in connection with the ill-starred ' Codex '. It is perhaps unnecessary to refer to du Garbandier's contribution to this question. He contented himself with an article in *l'Avenir* in which he professed to have decyphered the ' Codex ' and found it to be a repository of obscene conundrums, accounts of amorous adventures and erotic speculation, ' all too lamentable to be repeated even in broad outline '.

[3] Thought to be a reference to the ' Codex '.

this statistic but are, as usual, divided in their interpretations. In Bassett's view the water was treated in the patent water-box and diluted to a degree that made it invisible—in the guise of water, at all events—to the untutored watchers at the sewer. Hatchjaw's theory in this regard is more acceptable. He tends to the view that the water was boiled and converted, probably through the water-box, into tiny jets of steam which were projected through an upper window into the night in an endeavour to wash the black 'volcanic' stains from the 'skins' or 'air-bladders' of the atmosphere and thus dissipate the hated and 'insanitary' night. However far-fetched this theory may appear, unexpected colour is lent to it by a previous court case when the physicist was fined forty shillings. On this occasion, some two years before the construction of the water-box, de Selby was charged with playing a fire hose out of one of the upper windows of his house at night, an operation which resulted in several passers-by being drenched to the skin. On another occasion[5] he had to face the curious charge of hoarding water, the police testifying that every vessel in his house, from the bath

---

[4] Naturally, no explanation is given of what is meant by 'abusing' water but it is noteworthy that the savant spent several months trying to discover a satisfactory method of 'diluting' water, holding that it was 'too strong' for many of the novel uses to which he desired to put it. Bassett suggests that the de Selby Water Box was invented for this purpose although he cannot explain how the delicate machinery is set in motion. So many fantastic duties have assigned to this inscrutable mechanism (witness Kraus's absurd sausage theory) that Bassett's speculation must not be allowed the undue weight which his authoritative standing would tend to lend it.

[5] Almost all of the numerous petty litigations in which de Selby was involved afford a salutary example of the humiliations which great minds may suffer when forced to have contact with the pedestrian intellects of the unperceiving laity. On one of the water-wastage hearings the Bench permitted itself a fatuous inquiry as to why the defendant did not avail himself of the metered industrial rate 'if bathing is to be persisted in so immoderately'. It was on this occasion that de Selby made the famous retort that 'one does not readily accept the view that paradise is limited by the capacity of a municipal waterworks or human happiness by water-meters manufactured by unemancipated labour in Holland.' It is some consolation to recall that the forcible medical examination which followed was characterised by an enlightenment which redounds to this day to the credit of the medical profession. De Selby's discharge was unconditional and absolute.

down to a set of three ornamental egg-cups, was brimming with the liquid. Again a trumped-up charge of attempted suicide was preferred merely because the savant had accidentally half-drowned himself in a quest for some vital statistic of celestial aquatics.

It is clear from contemporary newspapers that his inquiries into water were accompanied by persecutions and legal pin-prickings unparalleled since the days of Galileo. It may be some consolation to the minions responsible to know that their brutish and barbaric machinations succeeded in denying posterity a clear record of the import of these experiments and perhaps a primer of esoteric water science that would banish much of our worldly pain and unhappiness. Virtually all that remains of de Selby's work in this regard is his house where his countless taps[6] are still as he left them, though a newer generation of more delicate mind has had the water turned off at the main.

Water? The word was in my ear as well as in my brain. Rain was beginning to beat on the windows, not a soft or friendly rain but large angry drops which came spluttering with great force upon the glass. The sky was grey and stormy and out of it I heard the harsh shouts of wild geese and ducks labouring across the wind on their coarse pinions. Black quails called sharply from their hidings and a swollen stream was babbling dementedly. Trees, I knew, would be angular and ill-tempered in the rain and boulders would gleam coldly at the eye.

I would have sought sleep again without delay were it not for the loud hammering outside. I arose and went on the cold

---

[6] Hatchjaw (in his invaluable *Conspectus of the de Selby Dialectic*) has described the house as 'the most water-piped edifice in the world.' Even in the living-rooms there were upwards of ten rough farmyard taps, some with zinc troughs and some (as those projecting from the ceiling and from converted gas-brackets near the fireplace) directed at the unprotected floor. Even on the stairs a three-inch main may still be seen nailed along the rail of the balustrade with a tap at intervals of one foot, while under the stairs and in every conceivable hiding-place there were elaborate arrangements of cisterns and storage-tanks. Even the gas pipes were connected up with this water system and would gush strongly at any attempt to provide the light.

Du Garbandier in this connection has permitted himself some coarse and cynical observations bearing upon cattle lairages.

floor to the window. Outside there was a man with sacks on his shoulders hammering at a wooden framework he was erecting in the barrack yard. He was red-faced and strong-armed and limped around his work with enormous stiff strides. His mouth was full of nails which bristled like steel fangs in the shadow of his moustache. He extracted them one by one as I watched and hammered them perfectly into the wet wood. He paused to test a beam with his great strength and accidentally let the hammer fall. He stooped awkwardly and picked it up.

Did you notice anything?

No.

The Hammer, man.

It looks an ordinary hammer. What about it?

You must be blind. It fell on his foot.

Yes?

And he didn't bat an eyelid. It might have been a feather for all the sign he gave.

Here I gave a sharp cry of perception and immediately threw up the sash of the window and leaned out into the inhospitable day, hailing the workman excitedly. He looked at me curiously and came over with a friendly frown of interrogation on his face.

'What is your name?' I asked him.

'O'Feersa, the middle brother,' he answered. 'Will you come out here,' he continued, 'and give me a hand with the wet carpentry?'

'Have you a wooden leg?'

For answer he dealt his left thigh a mighty blow with the hammer. It echoed hollowly in the rain. He cupped his hand clownishly at his ear as if listening intently to the noise he had made. Then he smiled.

'I am building a high scaffold here,' he said, 'and it is lame work where the ground is bumpy. I could find use for the assistance of a competent assistant.'

'Do you know Martin Finnucane?'

He raised his hand in a military salute and nodded.

'He is almost a relation,' he said, 'but not completely. He is closely related to my cousin but they never married, never had the time.'

149

Here I knocked my own leg sharply on the wall.

' Did you hear that?' I asked him.

He gave a start and then shook my hand and looked brotherly and loyal, asking me was it the left or the right?

Scribble a note and send him for asistance. There is no time to lose.

I did so at once, asking Martin Finnucane to come and save me in the nick of time from being strangled to death on the scaffold and telling him he would have to hurry. I did not know whether he could come as he had promised he would but in my present danger anything was worth trying.

I saw Mr O'Feersa going quickly away through the mists and threading his path carefully through the sharp winds which were racing through the fields, his head down, sacks on his shoulders and resolution in his heart.

Then I went back to bed to try to forget my anxiety. I said a prayer that neither of the other brothers was out on the family bicycle because it would be wanted to bring my message quickly to the captain of the one-legged men. Then I felt a hope kindling fitfully within me and I fell asleep again.

X

WHEN I awoke again two thoughts came into my head so closely together that they seemed to be stuck to one another; I could not be sure which came first and it was hard to separate them and examine them singly. One was a happy thought about the weather, the sudden brightness of the day that had been vexed earlier. The other was suggesting to me that it was not the same day at all but a different one and maybe not even the next day after the angry one. I could not decide that question and did not try to. I lay back and took to my habit of gazing out of the window. Whichever day it was, it was a gentle day—mild, magical and innocent with great sailings of white cloud serene and impregnable in the high sky, moving along like kingly swans on quiet water. The sun was in the neighbourhood also, distributing his enchantment unobtrusively, colouring the sides of things that were unalive and livening the hearts of living things. The sky was a light blue without distance, neither near nor far. I could gaze at it, through it and beyond it and see still illimitably clearer and nearer the delicate lie of its nothingness. A bird sang a solo from nearby, a cunning blackbird in a dark hedge giving thanks in his native language. I listened and agreed with him completely.

Then other sounds came to me from the nearby kitchen. The policemen were up and about their incomprehensible tasks. A pair of their great boots would clump across the flags, pause and then clump back. The other pair would clump to another place, stay longer and clump back again with heavier falls as if a great weight were being carried. Then the four boots would clump together solidly far away to the front door and immediately would come the long slash of thrown-water on the road, a great bath of it flung in a lump to fall flat on the dry ground.

I arose and started to put on my clothes. Through the window I could see the scaffold of raw timber rearing itself high into the heavens, not as O'Feersa had left it to make his way methodically through the rain, but perfect and ready for its dark destiny. The sight did not make me cry or even sigh. I thought it was sad, too sad. Through the struts of the structure I could see the good country. There would be a fine view from the top of the scaffold on any day but on this day it would be lengthened out by five miles owing to the clearness of the air. To prevent my tears I began to give special attention to my dressing.

When I was nearly finished the Sergeant knocked very delicately at the door, came in with great courtesy and bade me good morning.

'I notice the other bed has been slept in,' I said for conversation. 'Was it yourself or MacCruiskeen?'

'That would likely be Policeman Fox. MacCruiskeen and I do not do our sleeping here at all, it is too expensive, we would be dead in a week if we played that game.'

'And where do you sleep then?'

'Down below—over there—beyant.'

He gave my eyes the right direction with his brown thumb. It was down the road to where the hidden left turn led to the heaven full of doors and ovens.

'And why?'

'To save our lifetimes, man. Down there you are as young coming out of a sleep as you are going into it and you don't fade when you are inside your sleep, you would not credit the time a suit or a boots will last you and you don't have to take your clothes off either. That's what charms MacCruiskeen—that and the no shaving.' He laughed kindly at the thought of his comrade. 'A comical artist of a man,' he added.

'And Fox? Where does he live?'

'Beyant, I think.' He jerked again to the place that was to the left. 'He is down there beyant somewhere during the daytime but we have never seen him there, he might be in a distinctive portion of it that he found from a separate ceiling in a different house and indeed the unreasonable jumps of the lever-reading would put you in mind that there is unauthorised interference with the works. He is as crazy as bedamned, an incontestable character and a man of ungovernable inexactitudes.'

'Then why does he sleep here?' I was not at all pleased that this ghostly man had been in the same room with me during the night.

'To spend it and spin it out and not have all of it forever unused inside him.'

'All what?'

'His lifetime. He wants to get rid of as much as possible, undertime and overtime, as quickly as he can so that he can die as soon as possible. MacCruiskeen and I are wiser and we are not yet tired of being ourselves, we save it up. I think he has an opinion that there is a turn to the right down the road and likely that is what he is after, he thinks the best way to find it is to die and get all the leftness out of his blood. I do not believe there is a right-hand road and if there is it would surely take a dozen active men to look after the readings alone, night and morning. As you are perfectly aware the right is much more tricky than the left, you would be surprised at all the right pitfalls there are. We are only at the beginning of our knowledge of the right, there is nothing more deceptive to the unwary.'

'I did not know that.'

The Sergeant opened his eyes wide in surprise.

'Did you ever in your life,' he asked, 'mount a bicycle from the right?'

'I did not.'

'And why?'

'I do not know. I never thought about it.'

He laughed at me indulgently.

'It is nearly an insoluble pancake,' he smiled, 'a conundrum of inscrutable potentialities, a snorter.'

He led the way out of the bedroom to the kitchen where he had already arranged my steaming meal of stirabout and milk on the table. He pointed to it pleasantly, made a motion as if lifting a heavily-laden spoon to his mouth and then made succulent spitty sounds with his lips as if they were dealing with the tastiest of all known delicacies. Then he swallowed loudly and put his red hands in ecstasy to his stomach. I sat down and took up the spoon at this encouragement.

'And why is Fox crazy?' I inquired.

'I will tell you that much. In MacCruiskeen's room there is a litle box on the mantelpiece. The story is that when MacCruiskeen was away one day that happened to fall on the 23rd of June inquiring about a bicycle, Fox went in and opened the box and looked into it from the strain of his unbearable curiosity. From that day to this . . .'

The Sergeant shook his head and tapped his forehead three times with his finger. Soft as porridge is I nearly choked at the sound his finger made. It was a booming hollow sound, slightly tinny, as if he had tapped an empty watering-can with his nail.

'And what was in the box?'

'That is easily told. A card made of cardboard about the size of a cigarette-card, no better and no thicker.'

'I see,' I said.

I did not see but I was sure that my easy unconcern would sting the Sergeant into an explanation. It came after a time when he had looked at me silently and strangely as I fed solidly at the table.

'It was the colour,' he said.

'The colour?'

'But then maybe it was not that at all,' he mused perplexedly.

I looked at him with a mild inquiry. He frowned thoughtfully and looked up at a corner of the ceiling as if he expected certain words he was searching for to be hanging there in coloured lights. No sooner had I thought of that than I glanced up myself, half expecting to see them there. But they were not.

'The card was not red,' he said at last doubtfully.

'Green?'

'Not green. No.'

'Then what colour?'

'It was not one of the colours a man carries inside his head like nothing he ever looked at with his eyes. It was . . . different. MacCruiskeen says it is not blue either and I believe him, a blue card would never make a man batty because what is blue is natural.'

'I saw colours often on eggs,' I observed, 'colours which have no names. Some birds lay eggs that are shaded in a way too delicate to be noticeable to any instrument but the eye, the tongue could not be troubled to find a noise for anything so nearly not-there. What I would call a green sort of complete white. Now would that be the colour?'

'I am certain it would not,' the Sergeant replied immediately, 'because if birds could lay eggs that would put men out of their wits, you would have no crops at all, nothing but scarecrows crowded in every field like a public meeting and thousands of them in their top hats standing together in knots on the hillsides. It would be a mad world completely, the people would be putting their bicycles upside down on the roads and pedalling them to make enough mechanical movement to frighten the birds out of the whole parish.' He passed a hand in consternation across his brow. 'It would be a very unnatural pancake,' he added.

I thought it was a poor subject for conversation, this new colour. Apparently its newness was new enough to blast a man's brain to imbecility by the surprise of it. That was enough to know and quite sufficient to be required to believe. I thought it was an unlikely story but not for gold or diamonds would I open that box in the bedroom and look into it.

The Sergeant had wrinkles of pleasant recollection at his eyes and mouth.

'Did you ever in your travels meet with Mr Andy Gara?' he asked me.

'No.'

'He is always laughing to himself, even in bed at night he laughs quietly and if he meets you on the road he will go into roars, it is a most enervating spectacle and very bad for nervous people. It all goes back to a certain day when Mac-Cruiskeen and I were making inquiries about a missing bicycle.'

'Yes?'

'It was a bicycle with a criss-cross frame,' the Sergeant explained, 'and I can tell you that it is not every day in the week that one like that is reported, it is a great rarity and indeed it is a privilege to be looking for a bicycle like that.'

'Andy Gara's bicycle?'

'Not Andy's. Andy was a sensible man at the time but a

very curious man and when he had us gone he thought he would do a clever thing. He broke his way into the barrack here in open defiance of the law. He spent valuable hours boarding up the windows and making MacCruiskeen's room as dark as night time. Then he got busy with the box. He wanted to know what the inside of it felt like, even if it could not be looked at. When he put his hand in he let out a great laugh, you could swear he was very amused at something.'

'And what did it feel like?'

The Sergeant shrugged himself massively.

'MacCruiskeen says it is not smooth and not rough, not gritty and not velvety. It would be a mistake to think it is a cold feel like steel and another mistake to think it blankety. I thought it might be like the damp bread of an old poultice but no, MacCruiskeen says that would be a third mistake. And not like a bowl-full of dry withered peas, either. A contrary pancake surely, a fingerish atrocity but not without a queer charm all its own.'

'Not hens' piniony under-wing feeling?' I questioned keenly. The Sergeant shook his head abstractedly.

'But the criss-cross bicycle,' he said, 'it is no wonder it went astray. It was a very confused bicycle and was shared by a man called Barbery with his wife and if you ever laid your eye on big Mrs Barbery I would not require to explain this thing privately to you at all.'

He broke off his utterance in the middle of the last short word of it and stood peering with a wild eye at the table. I had finished eating and had pushed away my empty bowl. Following quickly along the line of his stare, I saw a small piece of folded paper lying on the table where the bowl had been before I moved it. Giving a cry the Sergeant sprang forward with surpassing lightness and snatched the paper up. He took it to the window, opened it out and held it far away from him to allow for some disorder in his eye. His face was puzzled and pale and stared at the paper for many minutes. Then he looked out of the window fixedly, tossing the paper over at me. I picked it up and read the roughly printed message:

'ONE-LEGGED MEN ON THEIR WAY TO RESCUE PRISONER.

My heart began to pound madly inside me. Looking at
the Sergeant I saw that he was still gazing wild-eyed into the
middle of the day, which was situated at least five miles
away, like a man trying to memorise forever the perfection
of the lightly clouded sky and the brown and green and
boulder-white of the peerless country. Down some lane of
it that ran crookedly through the fields I could see inwardly
my seven true brothers hurrying to save me in their lame
walk, their stout sticks on the move together.

The Sergeant still kept his eye on the end of five miles
away but moved slightly in his monumental standing. Then
he spoke to me.

'I think,' he said, 'we will go out and have a look at it,
it is a great thing to do what is necessary before it becomes
essential and unavoidable.'

The sounds he put on these words were startling and too
strange. Each word seemed to rest on a tiny cushion and
was soft and far away from every other word. When he had
stopped speaking there was a warm enchanted silence as if
the last note of some music too fascinating almost for com-
prehension had receded and disappeared long before its
absence was truly noticed. He then moved out of the house
before me to the yard, I behind him spellbound with no
thought of any kind in my head. Soon the two of us had
mounted a ladder with staid unhurrying steps and found
ourselves high beside the sailing gable of the barrack, the
two of us on the lofty scaffold, I the victim and he my hangman. I looked blankly and carefully everywhere, seeing for a
time no difference between any different things, inspecting
methodically every corner of the same unchanging sameness.
Nearby I could hear his voice murmuring again:

'It is a fine day in any case,' he was saying.

His words, now in the air and out of doors, had another
warm breathless roundness in them as if his tongue was lined
with furry burrs and they came lightly from him like a string
of bubbles or like tiny things borne to me on thistledown in
very gentle air. I went forward to a wooden railing and

rested my weighty hands on it, feeling perfectly the breeze coming chillingly at their fine hairs. An idea came to me that the breezes high above the ground are separate from those which play on the same level as men's faces: here the air was newer and more unnatural, nearer the heavens and less laden with the influences of the earth. Up here I felt that every day would be the same always, serene and chilly, a band of wind isolating the earth of men from the far-from-understandable enormities of the girdling universe. Here on the stormiest autumn Monday there would be no wild leaves to brush on any face, no bees in the gusty wind. I sighed sadly.

'Strange enlightenments are vouchsafed,' I murmured, 'to those who seek the higher places.'

I do not know why I said this strange thing. My own words were also soft and light as if they had no breath to liven them. I heard the Sergeant working behind me with coarse ropes as if he were at the far end of a great hall instead of at my back and then I heard his voice coming back to me softly called across a fathomless valley:

'I heard of a man once,' he said, 'that had himself let up into the sky in a balloon to make observations, a man of great personal charm but a divil for reading books. They played out the rope till he was disappeared completely from all appearances, telescopes or no telescopes, and then they played out another ten miles of rope to make sure of first-class observations. When the time-limit for the observations was over they pulled down the balloon again but lo and behold there was no man in the basket and his dead body was never found afterwards lying dead or alive in any parish ever afterwards.'

Here I heard myself give a hollow laugh, standing there with a high head and my two hands still on the wooden rail.

'But they were clever enough to think of sending up the balloon again a fortnight later and when they brought it down the second time lo and behold the man was sitting in the basket without a feather out of him if any of my information can be believed at all.'

Here I gave some sound again, hearing my own voice as if I was a bystander at a public meeting where I was myself the main speaker. I had heard the Sergeant's words and understood them thoroughly but they were no more significant than the clear sounds that infest the air at all times— the far cry of gulls, the disturbance a breeze will make in its blowing and water falling headlong down a hill. Down into the earth where dead men go I would go soon and maybe come out of it again in some healthy way, free and innocent of all human perplexity. I would perhaps be the chill of an April wind, an essential part of some indomitable river or be personally concerned in the ageless perfection of some rank mountain bearing down upon the mind by occupying forever a position in the blue easy distance. Or perhaps a smaller thing like movement in the grass on an unbearable breathless yellow day, some hidden creature going about its business—I might well be responsible for that or for some important part of it. Or even those unaccountable distinctions that make an evening recognisable from its own morning, the smells and sounds and sights of the perfected and matured essences of the day, these might not be innocent of my meddling and my abiding presence.

' So they asked where he was and what had kept him but he gave them no satisfaction, he only let out a laugh like one that Andy Gara would give and went home and shut himself up in his house and told his mother to say he was not at home and not receiving visitors or doing any entertaining. That made the people very angry and inflamed their passions to a degree that is not recognised by the law. So they held a private meeting that was attended by every member of the general public except the man in question and they decided to get out their shotguns the next day and break into the man's house and give him a severe threatening and tie him up and heat pokers in the fire to make him tell what happened in the sky the time he was up inside it. That is a nice piece of law and order for you, a terrific indictment of democratic self-government, a beautiful commentary on Home Rule.'

Or perhaps I would be an influence that prevails in water, something sea-borne and far away, some certain arrangement of sun, light and water unknown and unbeheld, something far-from-usual. There are in the great world whirls of fluid and vaporous existences obtaining in their own unpassing time, unwatched and uninterpreted, valid only in their essential un-understandable mystery, justified only in their eyeless and mindless immeasurability, unassailable in their actual abstraction; of the inner quality of such a thing I might well in my own time be the true quintessential pith. I might belong to a lonely shore or be the agony of the sea when it bursts upon it in despair.

'But between that and the next morning there was a stormy night in between, a loud windy night that strained the trees in their deep roots and made the roads streaky with broken branches, a night that played a bad game with root-crops. When the boys reached the home of the balloon-man the next morning, lo and behold the bed was empty and no trace of him was ever found afterwards dead or alive, naked or with an overcoat. And when they got back to where the balloon was, they found the wind had torn it up out of the ground with the rope spinning loosely in the windlass and it invisible to the naked eye in the middle of the clouds. They pulled in eight miles of rope before they got it down but lo and behold the basket was empty again. They all said that the man had gone up in it and stayed up but it is an insoluble conundrum, his name was Quigley and he was by all accounts a Fermanagh man.'

Parts of this conversation came to me from different parts of the compass as the Sergeant moved about at his tasks, now right, now left and now aloft on a ladder to fix the hang-rope on the summit of the scaffold. He seemed to dominate the half of the world that was behind my back with his pre-sence—his movements and his noises—filling it up with himself to the last farthest corner. The other half of the world which lay in front of me was beautifully given a shape of sharpness or roundness that was faultlessly suitable to its nature. But the half behind me was black and evil and composed of nothing at all except the menacing policeman who was patiently and politely arranging the mechanics of my death. His work was now nearly finished and my eyes were faltering as they gazed ahead, making little sense of the distance and taking a smaller pleasure in what was near.

There is not much that I can say.

No.

Except to advise a brave front and a spirit of heroic resignation.

That will not be difficult. I feel too weak to stand up without support.

In a way that is fortunate. One hates a scene. It makes things more difficult for all concerned. A man who takes into consideration the feelings of others even when arranging the manner of his own death shows a nobility of character which compels the admiration of all classes. To quote a well-known poet, ' even the ranks of Tuscany could scarce forbear to cheer '. Besides, unconcern in the face of death is in itself the most impressive gesture of defiance.

I told you I haven't got the strength to make a scene.

Very good. We will say no more about it.

A creaking sound came behind me as if the Sergeant was swinging red-faced in mid-air to test the rope he had just fixed. Then came the clatter of his great hobs as they came again upon the boards of the platform. A rope which would stand his enormous weight would never miraculously give way with mine.

You know, of course, that I will be leaving you soon?

That is the usual arrangement.

I would not like to go without placing on record my pleasure in having been associated with you. It is no lie to say that I have always received the greatest courtesy and consideration at your hands. I can only regret that it is not practicable to offer you some small token of my appreciation.

Thank you. I am very sorry also that we must part after having been so long together. If that watch of mine were found you would be welcome to it if you could find some means of taking it.

But you have no watch.

I forgot that.

Thank you all the same. You have no idea where you are going . . . when all this is over?

No, none.

Nor have I. I do not know, or do not remember, what happens to the like of me in these circumstances. Sometimes I think that perhaps I might become part of . . . the world, if you understand me?

I know.

I mean—the wind, you know. Part of that. Or the spirit of the scenery in some beautiful place like the Lakes of Killarney, the inside meaning of it if you understand me.

I do.

Or perhaps something to do with the sea. ' The light that never was on sea or land, the peasant's hope and the poet's dream.' A big wave in mid-ocean, for instance, it is a very lonely and spiritual thing. Part of that.

I understand you.

Or the smell of a flower, even.

Here from my throat bounded a sharp cry rising to a scream. The Sergeant had come behind me with no noise and fastened his big hand into a hard ring on my arm, started to drag me gently but relentlessly away from where I was to the middle of the platform where I knew there was a trapdoor which could be collapsed with machinery.

Steady now!

My two eyes, dancing madly in my head, raced up and down the country like two hares in a last wild experience of the world I was about to leave for ever. But in their hurry and trepidation they did not fail to notice a movement that was drawing attention to itself in the stillness of everything far far down the road.

' The one-legged men! ' I shouted.

I know that the Sergeant behind me had also seen that the far part of the road was occupied for his grip, though still unbroken, had stopped pulling at me and I could almost sense his keen stare running out into the day parallel with my own but gradually nearing it till the two converged a quarter of a mile away. We did not seem to breathe or be alive at all as we watched the movement approaching and becoming clearer.

' MacCruiskeen, by the Powers! ' the Sergeant said softly.

My lifted heart subsided painfully. Every hangman has an assistant. MacCruiskeen's arrival would make the certainty of my destruction only twice surer.

When he came nearer we could see that he was in a great hurry and that he was travelling on his bicycle. He was lying almost prostrate on top of it with his rear slightly higher than his head to cut a passage through the wind and no eye could travel quickly enough to understand the speed of his flying legs as they thrashed the bicycle onwards in a savage fury. Twenty yards away from the barrack he threw up his head, showing his face for the first time, and saw us standing on the top of the scaffold engaged in watching him with all our attention. He leaped from the bicycle in some complicated leap which was concluded only when the bicycle had been spun round adroitly to form a seat for him with its bar while he stood there, wide-legged and diminutive, looking up at us and cupping his hands at his mouth to shout his breathless message upwards:

' The lever—nine point six nine! ' he called.

For the first time I had the courage to turn my head to the Sergeant. His face had gone instantly to the colour of ash as if every drop of blood had left it, leaving it with empty pouches and ugly loosenesses and laxities all about it. His lower jaw hung loosely also as if it were a mechanical jaw on a toy man. I could feel the purpose and the life running out of his gripping hand like air out of a burst bladder. He spoke without looking at me.

' Let you stay here till I come back reciprocally,' he said.

For a man of his weight he left me standing there alone with a speed that was astonishing. With one jump he was at the ladder. Coiling his arms and legs around it, he slid to the ground out of view with a hurry that was not different in any way from an ordinary fall. In the next second he was seated on the bar of MacCruiskeen's bicycle and the two of them were disappearing into the end of a quarter of a mile away.

When they had gone an unearthly weariness came down upon me so suddenly that I almost fell in a heap on the platform. I called together all my strength and made my way inch by inch down the ladder and back into the kitchen of the barrack and collapsed helplessly into a chair that was near the fire. I wondered at the strength of the chair for my body seemed now to be made of lead. My arms and legs were too heavy to move from where they had fallen and my eyelids could not be lifted higher than would admit through them a small glint from the red fire.

For a time I did not sleep, yet I was far from being awake. I did not mark the time that passed or think about any question in my head. I did not feel the ageing of the day or the declining of the fire or even the slow return of my strength. Devils or fairies or even bicycles could have danced before me on the stone floor without perplexing me or altering by one whit my fallen attitude in the chair. I am sure I was nearly dead.

But when I did come to think again I knew that a long time had passed, that the fire was nearly out and that Mac-Cruiskeen had just come into the kitchen with his bicycle and wheeled it hastily into his bedroom, coming out again without it and looking down at me.

' What has happened?' I whispered listlessly.

' We were just in time with the lever,' he replied, ' it took our combined strengths and three pages of calculations and rough-work but we got the reading down in the nick of zero-hour, you would be surprised at the coarseness of the lumps and the weight of the great fall.'

' Where is the Sergeant?'

' He instructed me to ask your kind pardon for his delays. He is lying in ambush with eight deputies that were sworn in as constables on the spot to defend law and order in the public interest. But they cannot do much, they are out-numbered and they are bound to be outflanked into the same bargain.'

' Is it for the one-leggèd men he is waiting?'

' Surely yes. But they took a great rise out of Fox. He is certain to get a severe reprimand from headquarters over the head of it. There is not seven of them but fourteen. They took off their wooden legs before they marched and tied themselves together in pairs so that there were two men for every two legs, it would remind you of Napoleon on the re-treat from Russia, it is a masterpiece of military techno-cratics.'

This news did more to revive me than would a burning drink of finest brandy. I sat up. The light appeared once more in my eyes.

' Then they will win against the Sergeant and his policemen?' I asked eagerly.

MacCruiskeen gave a smile of mystery, took large keys from his pocket and left the kitchen. I could hear him opening the cell where the Sergeant kept his bicycle. He reappeared almost at once carrying a large can with a bung in it such as painters use when they are distempering a house. He had not removed his sly smile in his absence but now wore it more deeply in his face. He took the can into his bedroom and came out again with a large handkerchief in his hand and his smile still in use. Without a word he came behind my chair and bound the handkerchief tightly across my eyes, paying no attention to my movements and my surprise. Out of my darkness I heard his voice:

' I do not think the hoppy men will best the Sergeant,' he said, ' because if they come to where the Sergeant lies in secret ambush with his men before I have time to get back there, the Sergeant will delay them with military manoeuvres and false alarms until I arrive down the road on my bicycle. Even now the Sergeant and his men are all blindfolded like yourself, it is a very queer way for people to be when they are lying in an ambush but it is the only way to be when I am expected at any moment on my bicycle.'

I muttered that I did not understand what he had said.

' I have a private patent in that box in my bedroom,' he explained, ' and I have more of it in that can. I am going to paint my bicycle and ride it down the road in full view of the hoppy lads.'

He had been going away from me in my darkness while saying this and now he was in his bedroom and had shut the door. Soft sounds of work came to me from where he was.

I sat there for half an hour, still weak, bereft of light and feebly wondering for the first time about making my escape. I must have come back sufficiently from death to enter a healthy tiredness again for I did not hear the policeman coming out of the bedroom again and crossing the kitchen with his unbeholdable and brain-destroying bicycle. I must have slept there fitfully in my chair, my own private darkness reigning restfully behind the darkness of the handkerchief.

XI

I T I S an unusual experience to waken restfully and slowly, to let the brain climb lazily out of a deep sleep and shake itself and yet have no encounter with the light to gaurantee that the sleep is really over. When I awoke I first thought of that, then the scare of blindness came upon me and finally my hand joyously found MacCruiskeen's handkerchief. I tore it off and gazed around. I was still splayed stiffly in my chair. The barrack seemed silent and deserted, the fire was out and the evening sky had the tones of five o'clock. Nests of shadow had already gathered in the corners of the kitchen and in under the table.

Feeling stronger and fresher, I stretched forth my legs and braced my arms with exertions of deep chesty strength. I reflected briefly on the immeasurable boon of sleep, more particularly on my own gift of sleeping opportunely. Several times I had gone asleep when my brain could no longer bear the situations it was faced with. This was the opposite of a weakness which haunted no less a man than de Selby. He, for all his greatness, frequently fell asleep for no apparent reason in the middle of everyday life, often even in the middle of a sentence.[1]

[1] Le Fournier, the conservative French commentator (in his *De Selby —Lieu ou Homme?*) has written exhaustively on the non-scientific aspects of de Selby's personality and has noticed several failings and weaknesses difficult to reconcile with his dignity and eminence as a physicist, ballistician, philosopher and psychologist. Though he did not recognise sleep as such, preferring to regard the phenomenon as a series of 'fits' and heart-attacks, his habit of falling asleep in public earned for him the enmity of several scientific brains of the inferior calibre. These sleeps took place when walking in crowded thorough-fares, at meals and on at least one occasion in a public lavatory. (Du Garbandier has given this latter incident malignant publicity in his pseudo-scientific 'redaction' of the police court proceedings to which he added a virulent preface assailing the savant's moral character in terms which, however intemperate, admit of no ambiguity.) It is true that some of these sleeps occurred without warning at meetings of learned societies when the physicist had been asked to state his views

I arose and stretched my legs up and down the floor. From my chair by the fire I had noticed idly that the front wheel of a bicycle was protruding into view in the passage leading to the rear of the barrack. It was not until I sat down again on the chair after exercising for a quarter of an hour that I found myself staring at this wheel in some surprise. I could have sworn it had moved out farther in the interval because three-quarters of it was now visible whereas I could not see the hub the last time. Possibly it was an illusion due to an altered position between my two sittings but this was quite unlikely because the chair was small and would not permit of much variation of seat if there was any question of studying comfort. My surprise began to mount to astonishment.

I was on my feet again at once and had reached the passage in four long steps. A cry of amazement—now almost a habit with me—escaped from my lips as I looked around. MacCruiskeen in his haste had left the door of the cell wide open with the ring of keys hanging idly in the lock. In the back of the small cell was a collection of paint-cans, old

---

on some abstruse problem but there is no inference, *pace* du Garbandier, that they were 'extremely opportune'.

Another of de Selby's weaknesses was his inability to distinguish between men and women. After the famous occasion when the Countess Schnapper had been presented to him (her *Glauben ueber Ueberalls* is still read) he made flattering references to 'that man', 'that cultured old gentleman', 'crafty old boy' and so on. The age, intellectual attainments and style of dress of the Countess would make this a pardonable error for anybody afflicted with poor sight but it is feared that the same cannot be said of other instances when young shop-girls, waitresses and the like were publicly addressed as 'boys'. In the few references which he ever made to his own mysterious family he called his mother 'a very distinguished gentleman' (*Lux Mundi* p. 307), 'a man of stern habits' (ibid, p. 308) and 'a man's man' (Kraus: *Briefe,* xvii). Du Garbandier (in his extraordinary *Histoire de Notre Temps*) has seized on this pathetic shortcoming to outstep, not the prudent limits of scientific commentary but all known horizons of human decency. Taking advantage of the laxity of French law in dealing with doubtful or obscene matter, he produced a pamphlet masquerading as a scientific treatise on sexual idiosyncracy in which de Selby is arraigned by name as the most abandoned of all human monsters.

Henderson and several lesser authorities on the Hatchjaw-Bassett school have taken the appearance of this regrettable document as the

ledgers, punctured bicycle tubes, tyre repair outfits and a mass of peculiar brass and leather articles not unlike ornamental horse harness but clearly intended for some wholly different office. The front of the cell was where my attention was. Leaning half-way across the lintel was the Sergeant's bicycle. Clearly it could not have been put there by MacCruiskeen because he had returned instantly from the cell with his can of paint and his forgotten keys were proof that he had not gone back there before he rode away. During my absence in my sleep it is unlikely that any intruder would have come in merely to move the bicycle half-way out of where it was. On the other hand I could not help recalling what the Sergeant had told me about his fears for his bicycle and his decision to keep it in solitary confinement. If there is good reason for locking a bicycle in a cell like a dangerous criminal, I reflected, it is fair enough to think that it will try to escape if given the opportunity. I did not quite believe this and I thought it was better to stop thinking about the mystery before I was compelled to believe it because if a man is alone in a house with a bicycle which he thinks is

---

proximate cause of Hatchjaw's precipitate departure for Germany. It is now commonly accepted that Hatchjaw was convinced that the name ' du Garbandier ' was merely a pseudonym adopted for his own ends by the shadowy Kraus. It will be recalled that Bassett took the opposite view, holding that Kraus was a name used by the mordant Frenchman for spreading his slanders in Germany. It may be observed that neither of these theories is directly supported by the writings of either commentator: du Garbandier is consistently virulent and defamatory while much of Kraus's work, blemished as it is by his inaccurate attainments in scholarship, is not at all unflattering to de Selby. Hatchjaw seems to take account of this discrepancy in his farewell letter to his friend Harold Barge (the last he is known to have written) when he states his conviction that Kraus was making a considerable fortune by publishing tepid refutations of du Garbandier's broadsides. This suggestion is not without colour because, as he points out, Kraus had extremely elaborate books on the market—some containing expensive plates—within an incredibly short time of the appearance of a poisonous volume under the name of du Garbandier. In such circumstances it is not easy to avoid the conclusion that both books were produced in collaboration if not written by the one hand. Certainly it is significant that the balance of the engagements between Kraus and du Garbandier was unfailingly to the disadvantage of de Selby.

Too much credit cannot be given to Hatchjaw for his immediate

edging its way along a wall he will run away from it in fright; and I was by now so occupied with the thought of my escape that I could not afford to be frightened of anything which could assist me.

The bicycle itself seemed to have some peculiar quality of shape or personality which gave it distinction and importance far beyond that usually possessed by such machines. It was extremely well-kept with a pleasing lustre on its dark-green bars and oil-bath and a clean sparkle on the rustless spokes and rims. Resting before me like a tame domestic pony, it seemed unduly small and low in relation to the Sergeant yet when I measured its height against myself I found it was bigger than any other bicycle that I knew. This was possibly due to the perfect proportion of its parts which combined merely to create a thing of surpassing grace and elegance, transcending all standards of size and reality and existing only in the absolute validity of its own unexceptionable dimensions. Notwithstanding the sturdy cross-bar it seemed ineffably female and fastidious, posing there like a mannequin rather than leaning idly like a loafer against the

---

and heroic decision to go abroad 'to end once and for all a cancerous corruption which has become an intolerable affront to the decent instincts of humanity.' Bassett, in a note delivered at the quay-side at the moment of departure, wished Hatchjaw every success in his undertaking but deplored the fact that he was in the wrong ship, a sly hint that he should direct his steps to Paris rather than to Hamburg. Hatchjaw's friend Harold Barge has left an interesting record of the last interview in the commentator's cabin. 'He seemed nervous and out of sorts, striding up and down the tiny floor of his apartment like a caged animal and consulting his watch at least once every five minutes. His conversation was erratic, fragmentary and unrelated to the subjects I was mentioning myself. His lean sunken face, imbued with unnatural pallor, was livened almost to the point of illumination by eyes which burned in his head with a sickly intensity. The rather old-fashioned clothes he wore were creased and dusty and bore every sign of having been worn and slept in for weeks. Any recent attempts which he had made at shaving or washing were clearly of the most perfunctory character; indeed, I recall looking with mixed feelings at the sealed port-hole. His disreputable appearance, however, did not detract from the nobility of his personality or the peculiar spiritual exaltation conferred on his features by his selfless determination to bring to a successful end the desperate task to which he had set his hand. After we had traversed certain light mathematical topics (not, alas, with any degree of dialectical elegance), a silence fell between us. Both of

wall, and resting on its prim flawless tyres with irreproachable precision, two tiny points of clean contact with the level floor. I passed my hand with unintended tenderness—sensuously, indeed—across the saddle. Inexplicably it reminded me of a human face, not by any simple resemblance of shape or feature but by some association of textures, some incomprehensible familiarity at the fingertips. The leather was dark with maturity, hard with a noble hardness and scored with all the sharp lines and finer wrinkles which the years with their tribulations had carved into my own countenance. It was a gentle saddle yet calm and courageous, unembittered by its confinement and bearing no mark upon it save that of honourable suffering and honest duty. I knew that I liked this bicycle more than I had ever liked any other bicycle, better even than I had liked some people with two legs. I liked her unassuming competence, her docility, the simple dignity of her quiet way. She now seemed to rest beneath my friendly eyes like a tame fowl which will crouch submissively, awaiting with out-hunched wings the caressing hand. Her saddle seemed to spread invitingly into the most

---

us, I am sure, had heard the last boat-train (run, as it happened, in two sections on this occasion) draw alongside and felt that the hour of separation could not be long delayed. I was searching in my mind for some inanity of a non-mathematical kind which I could utter to break the tension when he turned to me with a spontaneous and touching gesture of affection, putting a hand which quivered with emotion upon my shoulder. Speaking in a low unsteady voice, he said : " You realise, no doubt, that I am unlikely to return. In destroying the evil things which prevail abroad, I do not exclude my own person from the ambit of the cataclysm which will come and of which I have the components at this moment in my trunk. If I should leave the world the cleaner for my passing and do even a small service to that man whom I love, then I shall measure my joy by the extent to which no trace of either of us will be found after I have faced my adversary. I look to you to take charge of my papers and books and instruments, seeing that they are preserved for those who may come after us." I stammered some reply, taking his proffered hand warmly in my own. Soon I found myself stumbling on the quay again with eyes not innocent of emotion. Ever since that evening I have felt that there is something sacred and precious in my memory of that lone figure in the small shabby cabin, setting out alone and almost unarmed to pit his slender frame against the snake-like denizen of far-off Hamburg. It is a memory I will always carry with me proudly so long as one breath animates this humble temple.'

enchanting of all seats while her two handlebars, floating finely with the wild grace of alighting wings, beckoned to me to lend my mastery for free and joyful journeyings, the lightest of light running in the company of the swift ground-winds to safe havens far away, the whir of the true front wheel in my ear as it spun perfectly beneath my clear eye and the strong fine back wheel with unadmired industry raising gentle dust on the dry roads. How desirable her seat was, how charming the invitation of her slim encircling handle-arms, how unaccountably competent and reassuring her pump resting warmly against her rear thigh!

With a start I realised that I had been communing with this strange companion and—not only that—conspiring with her. Both of us were afraid of the same Sergeant, both were awaiting the punishments he would bring with him on his return, both were thinking that this was the last chance to escape beyond his reach; and both knew that the hope of each lay in the other, that we would not succeed unless we went together, assisting each other with sympathy and quiet love.

Barge, it is feared, was actuated more by kindly affection for Hatch-jaw than for any concern for historical accuracy when he says that the latter was 'almost unarmed'. Probably no private traveller has ever gone abroad accompanied by a more formidable armoury and nowhere outside a museum has there been assembled a more varied or deadly collection of lethal engines. Apart from explosive chemicals and the unassembled components of several bombs, grenades and land-mines, he had four army-pattern revolvers, two rook-rifles, angler's landing gear (!), a small machine-gun, several minor firing-irons and an unusual instrument resembling at once a pistol and a shotgun, evidently made to order by a skilled gunsmith and designed to take elephant ball. Wherever he hoped to corner the shadowy Kraus, it is clear that he intended that the 'cataclysm' should be widespread.

The reader who would seek a full account of the undignified fate which awaited the courageous crusader must have recourse to the page of history. Newspaper readers of the older generation will recall the sensational reports of his arrest for *impersonating himself*, being arraigned at the suit of a man called Olaf (var. Olafsohn) for obtaining credit in the name of a world-famous literary 'Gelehrter'. As was widely remarked at the time, nobody but either Kraus or du Garbandier could have engineered so malignant a destiny. (It is noteworthy that du Garbandier, in a reply to a suggestion of this kind made by the usually inoffensive Le Clerque, savagely denied all knowledge of Hatchjaw's whereabouts on the continent but made the peculiar state-

The long evening had made its way into the barrack through the windows, creating mysteries everywhere, erasing the seam between one thing and another, lengthening out the floors and either thinning the air or putting some refinement on my ear enabling me to hear for the first time the clicking of a cheap clock from the kitchen.

By now the battle would be over, Martin Finnucane and his one-leggèd men would be stumbling away into the hills with blinded eyes and crazy heads, chattering to each other poor broken words which nobody understood. The Sergeant would now be making his way inexorably through the twilight homewards, arranging in his head the true story of his day for my amusement before he hanged me. Perhaps Mac-Cruiskeen would remain behind for the present, waiting for the blackest of the night's darkness by some old wall, a wrinkled cigarette in his mouth and his bicycle now draped with six or seven greatcoats. The deputies would also be going back to where they came from, still wondering why they had been blindfolded to prevent them seeing something wonderful—a miraculous victory with no fighting, nothing

---

ment that he had thought for many years that 'a similar impersonation' had been imposed on the gullible public at home many years before there was any question of 'a ridiculous adventure' abroad, implying apparently that Hatchjaw was not Hatchjaw at all but either another person of the same name or an impostor who had successfully maintained the pretence, in writing and otherwise, for forty years. Small profit can accrue from pursuing so peculiar a suggestion.) The facts of Hatchjaw's original incarceration are not now questioned by any variety of fates after being released. None of these can be regarded as verified fact and many are too absurd to be other than morbid conjecture. Mainly they are: (1) that he became a convert to the Jewish faith and entered the ministry of that persuasion; (2) that he had resort to petty crime and drug-peddling and spent much of his time in jail; (3) that he was responsible for the notorious 'Munich Letter' incident involving an attempt to use de Selby as the tool of international financial interests; (4) that he returned home in disguise with his reason shattered; and (5) that he was last heard of as a Hamburg brothel-keeper's nark or agent in the lawless dockland fastnesses of that maritime cosmopolis. The definitive work on this strange man's life is, of course, that of Henderson but the following will also repay study: Bassett's *Recollections*, Part vii; *The Man Who Sailed Away: A Memoir* by H. Barge; Le Clerque's Collected Works, Vol. III, pp. 118-287; Peachcroft's *Thoughts in a Library* and the Hamburg chapter in Goddard's *Great Towns*.

but a bicycle bell ringing madly and the screams of demented men mixing madly in their darkness.

In the next moment I was fumbling for the barrack latch with the Sergeant's willing bicycle in my care. We had travelled the passage and crossed the kitchen with the grace of ballet dancers, silent, swift and faultless in our movements, united in the acuteness of our conspiracy. In the country which awaited us outside we stood for a moment undecided, looking into the lowering night and inspecting the dull sameness of the gloom. It was to the left the Sergeant had gone with MacCruiskeen, to that quarter the next world lay and it was leftwards that all my troubles were. I led the bicycle to the middle of the road, turned her wheel resolutely to the right and swung myself into the centre of her saddle as she moved away eagerly under me in her own time.

How can I convey the perfection of my comfort on the bicycle, the completeness of my union with her, the sweet responses she gave me at every particle of her frame? I felt that I had known her for many years and that she had known me and that we understood each other utterly. She moved beneath me with agile sympathy in a swift, airy stride, finding smooth ways among the stony tracks, swaying and bending skilfully to match my changing attitudes, even accommodating her left pedal patiently to the awkward working of my wooden leg. I sighed and settled forward on her handlebars, counting with a happy heart the trees which stood remotely on the dark roadside, each telling me that I was further and further from the Sergeant.

I seemed to cut an unerring course between two sharp shafts of wind which whistled coldly past each ear, fanning my short side hairs. Other winds were moving about in the stillness of the evening, loitering in the trees and moving leaves and grasses to show that the green world was still present in the dark. Water by the roadside, always over-shouted in the roistering day, now performed audibly in its hidings. Flying beetles came against me in their broad loops and circles, whirling blindly against my chest; overhead geese and heavy birds were calling in the middle of a journey. Aloft in the sky I could see the dim tracery of the stars struggling out here and there between the clouds. And all the time she was under me in a flawless racing onwards, touching the road with the lightest touches, surefooted, straight and faultless, each of her metal bars like spear-shafts superbly cast by angels.

A thickening of the right-hand night told me that we were approaching the mass of a large house by the road. When we were abreast of it and nearly past it, I recognised it. It was the house of old Mathers, not more than three miles from where my own house was. My heart bounded joyfully. Soon I would see my old friend Divney. We would stand in the bar drinking yellow whiskey, he smoking and listening and I telling him my strange story. If he found any part of it difficult to believe completely I would show him the Sergeant's bicycle. Then the next day we could both begin again to look for the black cashbox.

Some curiosity (or perhaps it was the sense of safety which comes to a man on his own hillside) made me stop pedalling and pull gently at the queenly brake. I had intended only to look back at the big house but by accident I had slowed the bicycle so much that she shuddered beneath me awkwardly, making a gallant effort to remain in motion. Feeling that I had been inconsiderate I jumped quickly from the saddle to relieve her. Then I took a few paces back along the road, eyeing the outline of the house and the shadows of its trees. The gate was open. It seemed a lonely place with no life or breath in it, a dead man's empty house spreading its desolation far into the surrounding night. Its trees swayed mournfully, gently. I could see the faint glinting of the glass in the big sightless windows and fainter, the sprawl of ivy at the room where the dead man used to sit. I eyed the house up and down, happy that I was near my own people. Suddenly my mind became clouded and confused. I had some memory of seeing the dead man's ghost while in the house searching for the box. It seemed a long time ago now and doubtless was the memory of a bad dream. I had killed Mathers with my spade. He was dead for a long time. My adventures had put a strain upon my mind. I could not now remember clearly what had happened to me during the last few days. I recalled only that

I was fleeing from two monstrous policemen and that I was now near my home. I did not just then try to remember anything else.

I had turned away to go when a feeling came upon me that the house had changed the instant my back was turned. This feeling was so strange and chilling that I stood rooted to the road for several seconds with my hands gripping the bars of the bicycle, wondering painfully whether I should turn my head and look or go resolutely forward on my way. I think I had made up my mind to go and had taken a few faltering steps forward when some influence came upon my eyes and dragged them round till they were again resting upon the house. They opened widely in surprise and once more my startled cry jumped out from me. A bright light was burning in a small window in the upper storey.

I stood watching it for a time, fascinated. There was no reason why the house should not be occupied or why a light should not be showing, no reason why the light should frighten me. It seemed to be the ordinary yellow light of an oil lamp and I had seen many stranger things than that— many stranger lights, also—in recent days. Nevertheless I could not persuade myself that there was anything the least usual in what my eyes were looking at. The light had some quality which was wrong, mysterious, alarming.

I must have stood there for a long time, watching the light and fingering the reassuring bars of the bicycle which would take me away swiftly at any time I chose to go. Gradually I took strength and courage from her and from other things which were lurking in my mind—the nearness of my own house, the nearer nearness of Courahans, Gillespies, Cavanaghs, and the two Murrays, and not further than a shout away the cottage of big Joe Siddery, the giant blacksmith. Perhaps whoever had the light may have found the black box and would yield it willingly to anyone who had suffered so much in search of it as I had. Perhaps it would be wise to knock and see.

I laid the bicycle gently against the gate-pier, took some string from my pocket and tied her loosely to the bars of the ironwork; then I walked nervously along the crunching gravel towards the gloom of the porch. I recalled the great thickness of the walls as my hand searched for the door in the pitch darkness at the rear of it. I found myself well into the hall before I realised that the door was swinging half-open, idly at the mercy of the wind. I felt a chill come upon me in this bleak open house and thought for a moment of returning to the bicycle. But I did not do so. I found the door and grasped the stiff metal knocker, sending three dull rumbling thuds through the house and out around the dark empty garden. No sound or movement answered me as I stood there in the middle of the silence listening to my heart. No feet came hurrying down the stairs, no door above opening with a flood of lamplight. Again I knocked on the hollow door, got no response and again thought of return-ing to the companionship of my friend who was at the gate. But again I did not do so. I moved farther into the hallway, searched for matches and struck one. The hall was empty with all doors leading from it closed; in a corner of it the wind had huddled a blowing of dead leaves and along the walls was the stain of bitter inblown rain. At the far end I could glimpse the white winding stairway. The match spluttered in my fingers and went out, leaving me again standing in the dark in indecision, again alone with my heart.

At last I summoned all my courage and made up my mind to search the upper storey and finish my business and get back to the bicycle as quickly as possible. I struck an-other match, held it high above my head and marched noisily to the stairs, mounting them with slow heavy foot-falls. I remembered the house well from the night I had spent in it after spending hours searching it for the black box. On the top landing I paused to light another match and gave a loud call to give warning of my approach and awaken anybody who was asleep. The call, when it died away with-out reply, left me still more desolate and alone. I moved for-ward quickly and opened the door of the room nearest me, the room where I thought I once slept. The flickering match showed me that it was empty and had been long unoccupied. The bed was stripped of all its clothes, four chairs were locked together, two up-ended, in a corner and a white sheet was draped over a dressing-table. I slammed the door shut and paused to light another match, listening intently for any sign that I was watched. I heard nothing at all. Then I went along the passage throwing open the door of every room to the front of the house. They were all empty, deserted, with no light or sign of light in any of them. Afraid to stand still, I went quickly to all the other rooms, but found them all in the same way and ended by running down the stairs in growing fright and out of the front door. Here I stopped dead in my tracks. The light from the upper window was still streaming out and lying against the dark. The window seemed to be in the centre of the house. Feeling frightened, deluded, cold and bad-tempered I strode back into the hall, up the stairs and looked down the corridor where the doors of all the rooms to the front of the house were. I had left them all wide open on my first visit yet no light now came from any one of them. I walked the passage quickly to make sure that they had not been closed. They were all still open. I stood in the silence for three or four minutes barely breathing and making no sound, thinking that perhaps whatever was at work would make some move and show itself. But nothing happened, nothing at all.

I then walked into the room which seemed most in the centre of the house and made my way over to the window in the dark, guiding myself with my hands outstretched before me. What I saw from the window startled me painfully. The light was streaming from the window of the room next door on my right-hand side, lying thickly on the misty night air and playing on the dark-green leaves of a tree that stood nearby. I remained watching for a time, leaning weakly on the wall; then I moved backwards, keeping my eyes on the faintly-lighted tree-leaves, walking on my toes and making no sound. Soon I had my back to the rear wall, standing within a yard of the open door and the dim light on the tree still plainly visible to me. Then almost in one bound I was out into the passage and into the next room. I could not have spent more than one quarter of a second in that jump and yet I found the next room dusty and deserted with no life or light in it. Sweat was gathering on my brow, my heart was thumping loudly and the bare wooden floors seemed to tingle still with the echoing noises my feet had made. I moved to the window and looked out. The yellow light was still lying on the air and shining on the same tree-leaves but now it was streaming from the window of the room I had just left. I felt I was standing within three yards of something unspeakably inhuman and diabolical which was using its trick of light to lure me on to something still more horrible.

I stopped thinking, closing up my mind with a snap as if it were a box or a book. I had a plan in my head which seemed almost hopelessly difficult, very nearly beyond the extremity of human effort, desperate. It was simply to walk out of the room, down the stairs and out of the house on to the rough solid gravel, down the short drive and back to the company of my bicycle. Tied down there at the gate she seemed infinitely far away as if now in another world.

Certain that I would be assailed by some influence and prevented from reaching the hall door alive, I put my hands down with fists doubled at my sides, cast my eyes straight at my feet so that they should not look upon any terrible thing appearing in the dark, and walked steadily out of the room and down the black passage. I reached the stairs without mishap, reached the hall and then the door and soon found myself on the gravel feeling very much relieved and surprised. I walked down to the gate and out through it. She was resting where I had left her, leaning demurely against the stone pier; my hand told me that the string was unstrained, just as I had tied it. I passed my hands about her hungrily, knowing that she was still my accomplice in the plot of reaching home unharmed. Something made me turn my head again to the house behind me. The light was still burning peacefully in the same window, for all the world as if there was somebody in the room lying contentedly in bed reading a book. If I had given (or had been able to give) unrestricted rein to either fear or reason I should have turned my back forever on this evil house and rode away there and then upon the bicycle to the friendly home which was waiting for me beyond four bends of the passing road. But there was some other thing interfering with my mind. I could not take my eye from the lighted window and perhaps it was that I could resign myself to going home with no news about the black box so long as something was happening in the house where it was supposed to be. I stood there in the gloom, my hands gripping the handlebars of the bicycle and my great perplexity worrying me. I could not decide what was the best thing for me to do.

It was by accident that an idea came to me. I was shifting my feet as I often did to ease my bad left leg when I noticed that there was a large loose stone on the ground at my feet. I stooped and picked it up. It was about the size of a bicycle-lamp, smooth and round and easily fired. My heart had again become almost audible at the thought of hurling it through the lighted window and thus provoking to open action whoever was hiding in the house. If I stood by with the bicycle I could get away quickly. Having had the idea, I knew that I should have no contentment until the stone was fired; no rest would come to me until the unexplainable light had been explained.

I left the bicycle and went back up the drive with the stone swinging ponderously in my right hand. I paused under the window, looking up at the shaft of light. I could see some large insect flitting in and out of it. I felt my limbs weakening under me and my whole body becoming ill and faint with apprehension. I glanced at the nearby porch half expecting to glimpse some dreadful apparition watching me covertly from the shadows. I saw nothing but the im-penetrable patch of deeper gloom. I then swung the stone a few times to and fro at the end of my straight arm and lobbed it strongly high into the air. There was a loud smash of glass, the dull thuds of the stone landing and rolling along the wooden floor and at the same time the tinkle of broken glass falling down upon the gravel at my feet. Without wait-ing at all I turned and fled at top speed down the drive until I had again reached and made contact with the bicycle.

Nothing happened for a time. Probably it was four or five seconds but it seemed an interminable delay of years. The whole upper half of the glass had been carried away, leaving jagged edges protruding about the sash; the light seemed to stream more clearly through the gaping hole. Sud-denly a shadow appeared, blotting out the light on the whole left-hand side. The shadow was so incomplete that I could not recognise any part of it but I felt certain it was the shadow of a large being or presence who was standing quite still at the side of the window and gazing out into the night to see who had thrown the stone. Then it disappeared, making me realise for the first time what had happened and sending a new and deeper horror down upon me. The certain feeling that something else was going to happen made me afraid to make the smallest move lest I should reveal where I was standing with the bicycle.

The developments I expected were not long in coming. I was still gazing at the window when I heard soft sounds behind me. I did not look round. Soon I knew they were the footsteps of a very heavy person who was walking along the grass margin of the road to deaden his approach. Thinking he would pass without seeing me in the dark recess of the gateway, I tried to remain even more still than my original utter immobility. The steps suddenly clattered out on the roadway not six yards away, came up behind me and then stopped. It is no joke to say that my heart nearly stopped also. Every part of me that was behind me—neck, ears, back and head—shrank and quailed painfully before the presence confronting them, each expecting an onslaught of indescribable ferocity. Then I heard words.

' This is a brave night! '

I swung round in amazement. Before me, almost blocking out the night, was an enormous policeman. He looked a policeman from his great size but I could see the dim sign of his buttons suspended straight before my face, tracing out the curvature of his great chest. His face was completely hidden in the dark and nothing was clear to me except his overbearing policemanship, his massive rearing of wide strengthy flesh, his domination and his unimpeachable reality. He dwelt upon my mind so strongly that I felt many times more submissive than afraid. I eyed him weakly, my hands faltering about the bars of the bicycle. I was going to try to make my tongue give some hollow answer to his salutation when he spoke again, his words coming in thick friendly lumps from his hidden face.

' Will you follow after me till I have a conversation with you privately,' he said, ' if it was nothing else you have no light on your bicycle and I could take your name and address for the half of that.'

Before he had finished speaking he had eased off in the dark like a battleship, swinging his bulk ponderously away the same way as he had come. I found my feet obeying him without question, giving their six steps for every two of his, back along the road past the house. When we were about to pass it he turned sharply into a gap in the hedge and led the way into shrubberies and past the boles of dark forbidding trees, leading me to a mysterious fastness by the gable of the house where branches and tall growings filled the darkness and flanked us closely on both sides, reminding me of my journey to the underground heaven of Sergeant Pluck. In the presence of this man I had stopped wondering or even thinking. I watched the swaying outline of his back in the murk ahead of me and hurried after it as best I could. He said nothing and made no sound save that of the air labouring in his nostrils and the brushing strides of his boots on the grass-tangled ground, soft and rhythmical like a well-wielded scythe laying down a meadow in swaths.

He then turned sharply in towards the house and made for a small window which looked to me unusually low and near the ground. He flashed a torch on it, showing me as I peered from behind his black obstuction four panes of dirty glass set in two sashes. As he put his hand out to it I thought he was going to lift the lower sash up but instead of that he swung the whole window outwards on hidden hinges as if it were a door. Then he stooped his head, put out the light and began putting his immense body in through the tiny opening. I do not know how he accomplished what did not look possible at all. But he accomplished it quickly, giving no sound except a louder blowing from his nose and the groaning for a moment of a boot which had become wedged in some angle. Then he sent the torchlight back at me to show the way, revealing nothing of himself except his feet and the knees of his blue official trousers. When I was in, he leaned back an arm and pulled the window shut and then led the way ahead with his torch.

The dimensions of the place in which I found myself were most unusual. The ceiling seemed extraordinarily high while the floor was so narrow that it would not have been possible for me to pass the policeman ahead if I had desired to do so. He opened a tall door and, walking most awkwardly half-sideways, led the way along a passage still narrower. After passing through another tall door we began to mount an unbelievable square stairs. Each step seemed about a foot in depth, a foot in height and a foot wide. The policeman was walking up them fully sideways like a crab with his face turned still ahead towards the guidance of his torch. We went through another door at the top of the stairs and I found myself in a very surprising apartment. It was slightly wider than the other places and down the middle of it was a table about a foot in width, two yards in length and attached permanently to the floor by two metal legs. There was an oil-lamp on it, an assortment of pens and inks, a number of small boxes and file-covers and a tall jar of official gum. There were no chairs to be seen but all around the walls were niches where a man could sit. On the walls themselves were pinned many posters and notices dealing with bulls and dogs and regulations about sheep-dipping and school-going and breaches of the Firearms Act. With the figure of the policeman, who still had his back to me making an entry on some schedule on the far wall, I had no trouble in know-that I was standing in a tiny police station. I looked around again, taking everything in with astonishment. Then I saw that there was a small window set deeply in the left wall and that a cold breeze was blowing in through a gaping hole in the lower pane. I walked over and looked out. The lamplight was shining dimly on the foliage of the same tree and I knew that I was standing, not in Mathers' house, *but inside the walls of it*. I gave again my surprised cry, supported myself at the table and looked weakly at the back of the policeman. He was carefully blotting the figures he had entered on the paper on the wall. Then he turned round and replaced his pen on the table. I staggered quickly to one of the niches and sat down in a state of complete collapse, my eyes glued on his face and my mouth drying up like a raindrop on a hot pavement. I tried to say something several times but at first my tongue would not respond. At last I stammered out the thought that was blazing in my mind:

' I thought you were dead! '

The great fat body in the uniform did not remind me of

anybody that I knew *but the face at the top of it belonged to old Mathers*. It was not as I had recalled seeing it last whether in my sleep or otherwise, deathly and unchanging; it was now red and gross as if gallons of hot thick blood had been pumped into it. The cheeks were bulging out like two ruddy globes marked here and there with straggles of purple discolouration. The eyes had been charged with unnatural life and glistened like beads in the lamplight. When he answered me it was the voice of Mathers.

'That is a nice thing to say,' he said, 'but it is no matter because I thought the same thing about yourself. I do not understand your unexpected corporality after the morning on the scaffold.'

'I escaped,' I stammered.

He gave me long searching glances.

'Are you sure?' he asked.

Was I sure? Suddenly I felt horribly ill as if the spinning of the world in the firmament had come against my stomach for the first time, turning it all to bitter curd. My limbs weakened and hung about me helplessly. Each eye fluttered like a bird's wing in its socket and my head throbbed, swelling out like a bladder at every surge of blood. I heard the policeman speaking at me again from a great distance.

'I am Policeman Fox,' he said, 'and this is my own private police station and I would be glad to have your opinion on it because I have gone to great pains to make it spick and span.'

I felt my brains struggling on bravely, tottering, so to speak, to its knees but unwilling to fall completely. I knew that I would be dead if I lost consciousness for one second. I knew that I could never awaken again or hope to understand afresh the terrible way in which I was if I lost the chain of the bitter day I had had. I knew that he was not Fox but Mathers. I knew Mathers was dead. I knew that I would have to talk to him and pretend that everything was natural and try perhaps to escape for the last time with my life to the bicycle. I would have given everything I had in the world and every cashbox in it to get at that moment one look at the strong face of John Divney.

'It is a nice station,' I muttered, 'but why is it inside the walls of another house?'

'That is a very simple conundrum, I am sure you know the answer of it.'

'I don't.'

'It is a very rudimentary conundrum in any case. It is fixed this way to save the rates because if it was constructed the same as any other barracks it would be rated as a separate hereditament and your astonishment would be flabbergasted if I told you what the rates are in the present year.'

'What?'

'Sixteen and eightpence in the pound with thruppence in the pound for bad yellow water that I would not use and fourpence by your kind leave for technical education. Is it any wonder the country is on its final legs with the farmers crippled and not one in ten with a proper bull-paper? I have eighteen summonses drawn up for nothing else and there will be hell to pay at the next Court. Why had you no light at all, big or small, on your bicycle?'

'My lamp was stolen.'

'Stolen? I thought so. It is the third theft today and four pumps disappeared on Saturday last. Some people would steal the saddle from underneath you if they thought you would not notice it, it is a lucky thing the tyre cannot be taken off without undoing the wheel. Wait till I take a deposition from you. Give me a description of the article and tell me all and do not omit anything because what may seem unimportant to yourself might well give a wonderful clue to the trained investigator.'

I felt sick at heart but the brief conversation had steadied me and I felt sufficiently recovered to take some small interest in the question of getting out of this hideous house. The policeman had opened a thick ledger which looked like the half of a longer book which had been sawn in two to fit the narrow table. He put several questions to me about the lamp and wrote down my replies very laboriously in the book, scratching his pen noisily and breathing heavily through his nose, pausing occasionally in his blowing when some letter of the alphabet gave him special difficulty. I surveyed him carefully as he sat absorbed in his task of writing. It was beyond all doubt the face of old Mathers but now it seemed to have a simple childlike quality as if the wrinkles of a long lifetime, evident enough the first time I looked at him, had been suddenly softened by some benign influence and practically erased. He now looked so innocent and good-natured and so troubled by the writing down of simple words that hope began to flicker once again within me. Surveyed coolly, he did not look a very formidable enemy. Perhaps I was dreaming or in the grip of some horrible hallucination. There was much that I did not understand and possibly could never understand to my dying day—the face of old Mathers whom I thought I had buried in a field on so great and fat a body, the ridiculous police station within the walls of another house, the other two monstrous policemen I had escaped from. But at least I was near my own house and the bicycle was waiting at the gate to take me there. Would this man try to stop me if I said I was going home? Did he know anything about the black box?

He had now carefully blotted his work and passed the book to me for my signature, proffering the pen by the handle with great politeness. He had covered two pages in a large childish hand. I thought it better not to enter into any discussion on the question of my name and hastily made an intricate scrawl at the bottom of the statement, closed the book and handed it back. Then I said as casually as I could:

' I think I will be going now.'

He nodded regretfully.

' I am sorry I cannot offer you anything,' he said, ' because it is a cold night and it would not do you a bit of harm.'

My strength and courage had been flowing back into my body and when I heard these words I felt almost completely strong again. There were many things to be thought about but I would not think of them at all until I was secure in my own house. I would go home as soon as possible and on the way I would not put my eye to right or left. I stood up steadily.

' Before I go,' I said, ' there is one thing I would like to ask you. There was a black cashbox stolen from me and I have been searching for it for several days. Would you by any chance have any information about it?'

The instant I had this said I was sorry I had said it because if it actually was Mathers brought miraculously back to life he might connect me with the robbery and the murder of himself and wreak some terrible vengeance. But the policeman only smiled and put a very knowing expression on his face. He sat down on the edge of the very narrow table and drummed upon it with his nails. Then he looked me in the eye. It was the first time he had done so and I was dazzled as if I had accidentally glanced at the sun.

'Do you like strawberry jam?' he asked.

His stupid question came so unexpectedly that I nodded and gazed at him uncomprehendingly. His smile broadened.

'Well if you had that box here,' he said, 'you could have a bucket of strawberry jam for your tea and if that was not enough you could have a bathful of it to lie in it full-length and if that much did not satisfy you, you could have ten acres of land with strawberry jam spread on it to the height of your two oxters. What do you thing of that?'

'I do not know what to think of it,' I muttered. 'I do not understand it.'

'I will put it another way,' he said good-humouredly. 'You could have a house packed full of strawberry jam, every room so full that you could not open the door.'

I could only shake my head. I was becoming uneasy again.

'I would not require all that jam,' I said stupidly.

The policeman sighed as if despairing to convey to me his line of thought. Then his expression grew slightly more serious.

'Tell me this and tell me no more,' he said solemnly. 'When you went with Pluck and MacCruiskeen that time downstairs in the wood, what was your private opinion of what you saw? Was it your opinion that everything there was more than ordinary?'

I started at the mention of the other policemen and felt that I was once more in serious danger. I would have to be extremely careful. I could not see how he knew what had happened to me when I was in the toils of Pluck and Mac-Cruiskeen but I told him that I did not understand the underground paradise and thought that even the smallest thing that happened there was miraculous. Even now when I recalled what I had seen there I wondered once more whether I had been dreaming. The policeman seemed pleased at the wonder I had expressed. He was smiling quietly, more to himself than to me.

'Like everything that is hard to believe and difficult to comprehend,' he said at last, 'it is very simple and a neighbour's child could work it all without being trained. It is a pity you did not think of the strawberry jam while you were there because you could have got a barrel of it free of charge and the quality would be extra and superfine, only the purest fruit-juice used and little or no preservatives.'

'It did not look simple—what I saw.'

'You thought there was magic in it, not to mention monkey-work of no mean order?'

'I did.'

'But it can all be explained, it was very simple and the way it was all worked will astonish you when I tell you.'

Despite my dangerous situation, his words fired me with a keen curiosity. I reflected that this talk of the strange underground region with the doors and wires confirmed that it did exist, that I actually had been there and that my memory of it was not the memory of a dream—unless I was still in the grip of the same nightmare. His offer to explain hundreds of miracles in one simple explanation was very tempting. Even that knowledge might repay me for the uneasiness I felt in his company. The sooner the talking stopped the sooner I could attempt my escape.

'How was it done, then?' I asked.

The Sergeant smiled broadly in amusement at my puzzled face. He made me feel that I was a child asking about something that was self-evident.

'The box,' he said.

'The box? *My* box?'

'Of course. The little box did the trick, I have to laugh at Pluck and MacCruiskeen, you would think they had more sense.'

'Did you find the box?'

'It was found and I entered into complete possession of it in virtue of section 16 of the Act of '87 as extended and amended. I was waiting for you to call for it because I know by my own private and official inquiries that you were the party that was at the loss of it but my impatience gave in with your long delay and I sent it to your house today by express bicycle and you will find it there before you when you travel homewards. You are a lucky man to have it because there is nothing so valuable in the whole world and it works like a charm, you could swear it was a question of clockwork. I weighed it and there is more than four ounces in it, enough to make you a man of private means and anything else you like to fancy.

'Four ounces of what?'

'Of omnium. Surely you know what was in your own box?'

'Of course,' I stammered, 'but I did not think there was *four* ounces.'

'Four point one two on the Post Office scales. And that is how I worked the fun with Pluck and MacCruiskeen, it would make you smile to think of it, they had to run and work like horses every time I shoved the readings up to danger-point.'

He chuckled softly at the thought of his colleagues having to do hard work and looked across at me to see the effect of this simple revelation. I sank back on the seat flabbergasted but managed to return a ghostly smile to divert suspicion that I had not known what was in the box. If I could believe him he had been sitting in this room presiding at four ounces of this inutterable substance, calmly making ribbons of the natural order, inventing intricate and unheard of machinery to delude the other policemen, interfering drastically with time to make them think they had been leading their magical lives for years, bewildering, horrifying and enchanting the whole countryside. I was stupefied and appalled by the modest claim he had made so cheerfully, I could not quite believe it, yet it was the only way the terrible recollections which filled my brain could be explained. I felt again afraid of the policeman but at the same time a wild excitement gripped me to think that this box and what was in it was at this moment resting on the table of my own kitchen. What would Divney do? Would he be angry at finding no money, take this awful omnium for a piece of dirt and throw it out on the manure heap? Formless speculations crowded in upon me, fantastic fears and hopes, inexpressible fancies, intoxicating foreshadowing of creations, changes, annihilations and god-like interferences. Sitting at home with my box of omnium I could do anything, see anything and know anything with no limit to my powers save that of my own imagination. Perhaps I could use it even to extend my imagination. I could destroy, alter and improve the universe at will. I could get rid of John Divney, not brutally, but by giving him ten million pounds to go away. I could write the most unbelievable commentaries on de Selby ever written and publish them in bindings unheard of for their luxury and durability. Fruits and crops surpassing anything ever known would flower on my farm, in earth made inconceivably fertile by unparalleled artificial manures. A leg of flesh and bone yet stronger than iron would appear magically upon my left thigh. I would improve the weather to a standard day of sunny peace with gentle rain at night washing the world to make it fresher and more enchanting to the eye. I would present every poor labourer in the world with a bicycle made of gold, each machine with a saddle made of something as yet uninvented but softer than the softest softness, and I would arrange that a warm gale would blow behind every man on every journey, even when two were going in opposite directions on the same road. My sow would farrow twice daily and a man would call immediately offering ten million pounds for each of the piglings, only to be outbid by a second man arriving and offering twenty million. The barrels and bottles in my public house would still be full and inexhaustible no matter how much was drawn out of them. I would bring de Selby himself back to life to converse with me at night and advise me in my sublime undertakings. Every Tuesday I would make myself invisible—

'You would not believe the convenience of it,' said the policeman bursting in upon my thoughts, 'it is very handy for taking the muck off your leggings in the winter.'

'Why not use it for preventing the muck getting on your leggings at all?' I asked excitedly. The policeman looked at me in wide-eyed admiration.

'By the Hokey I never thought of that,' he said. 'You are very intellectual and I am certain that I am nothing but a gawm.'

'Why not use it,' I almost shouted, 'to have no muck anywhere at any time?'

He dropped his eyes and looked very disconsolate.

'I am the world's champion gawm,' he murmured.

I could not help smiling at him, not, indeed, without some pity. It was clear that he was not the sort of person to be entrusted with the contents of the black box. His oafish underground invention was the product of a mind which fed upon adventure books of small boys, books in which every extravagance was mechanical and lethal and solely concerned with bringing about somebody's death in the most elaborate way imaginable. I was lucky to have escaped from his preposterous cellars with my life. At the same time I recalled that I had a small account to settle with Policeman MacCruiskeen and Sergeant Pluck. It was not the fault of these gentlemen that I had not been hanged on the scaffold and prevented from ever recovering the black box. My life had been saved by the policeman in front of me, probably by accident, when he decided to rush up an alarming reading on the lever. He deserved some consideration for that. I would probably settle ten million pounds upon him when I had time to consider the matter fully. He looked more a fool than a knave. But MacCruiskeen and Pluck were in a different class. It would probably be possible for me to save time and trouble by adapting the underground machinery to give both of them enough trouble, danger, trepidation, work and inconvenience to make them rue the day they first threatened me. Each of the cabinets could be altered to contain, not bicycles and whiskey and matches, but putrescent offals, insupportable smells, unbeholdable corruptions containing tangles of gleaming slimy vipers each of them deadly and foul of breath, millions of diseased and decayed monsters clawing the inside latches of the ovens to open them and escape, rats with horns walking upside down along the ceiling pipes trailing their leprous tails on the policemen's heads, readings of incalculable perilousness mounting hourly upon the—

'But it is a great convenience for boiling eggs,' the policeman put in again, 'if you like them soft you get them soft and the hard ones are as hard as iron.'

'I think I will go home,' I said steadily, looking at him almost fiercely. I stood up. He only nodded, took out his torch and swung his leg off the table.

'I do not think an egg is nice at all if it is underdone,' he remarked, 'and there is nothing so bad for heartburn and indigestion, yesterday was the first time in my life I got my egg right.'

He led the way to the tall narrow door, opened it and passed out before me down the dark stairs, flashing the torch ahead and swinging it politely back to me to show the steps. We made slow progress and remained silent, he sometimes walking sideways and rubbing the more bulging parts of his uniform on the wall. When we reached the window, he opened it and got out into the shrubberies first, holding it up until I had scrambled out beside him. Then he went ahead of me again with his light in long swishing steps through the long grass and undergrowth, saying nothing until we had reached the gap in the hedge and were again standing on the hard roadside. Then he spoke. His voice was strangely diffident, almost apologetic.

'There was something I would like to tell you,' he said, 'and I am half-ashamed to tell you because it is a question of principle and I do not like taking personal liberties because where would the world be if we all did that?'

I felt him looking at me in the dark with his mild inquiry. I was puzzled and a little disquieted. I felt he was going to make some further devastating revelation.

'What is it?' I asked.

'It is about my little barrack . . .' he mumbled.

'Yes?'

'I was ashamed of my life of the shabbiness of it and I took the liberty of having it papered the same time as I was doing the hard-boiled egg. It is now very neat and I hope you are not vexed or at any loss over the head of it.'

I smiled to myself, feeling relieved, and told him that he was very welcome.

'It was a sore temptation,' he continued eagerly to reinforce his case, 'it was not necessary to go to the trouble of taking down the notices off the wall because the wallpaper put itself up behind them while you would be saying nothing.'

'That is all right,' I said. 'Good night and thank you.'

'Goodbye to you,' he said, saluting me with his hand, ' and you can be certain I will find the stolen lamp because they cost one and sixpence and you would want to be made of money to keep buying them.'

I watched him withdrawing through the hedge and going back into the tangle of trees and bushes. Soon his torch was only an intermittent flicker between the trunks and at last he disappeared completely. I was again alone upon the roadway. There was no sound to be heard save the languorous stirring of the trees in the gentle night air. I gave a sigh of relief and began to walk back towards the gate to get my bicycle.

XII

THE NIGHT seemed to have reached its middle point of intensity and the darkness was now much darker than before. My brain was brimming with half-formed ideas of the most far-reaching character but I repressed them firmly and determined to confine myself wholly to finding the bicycle and going home at once.

I reached the embrasure of the gateway and moved about it gingerly, stretching forth my hands into the blackness in search of the reassuring bars of my accomplice. At every move and reach I either found nothing or my hand came upon the granite roughness of the wall. An unpleasant suspicion was dawning on me that the bicycle was gone. I started searching with more speed and agitation and investigated with my hands what I am sure was the whole semi-circle of the gateway. She was not there. I stood for a moment in dismay, trying to remember whether I had untied her the last time I had raced down from the house to find her. It was inconceivable that she had been stolen because even if anybody had passed at that unearthly hour, it would not be possible to see her in the pitch darkness. Then as I stood, something quite astonishing happened to me again. Something slipped gently into my right hand. It was the grip of a handlebar—*her* handlebar. It seemed to come to me out of the dark like a child stretching out its hand for guidance. I was astonished yet could not be certain afterwards whether the thing actually had entered my hand or whether the hand had been searching about mechanically while I was deep in thought and found the handlebar without the help or interference of anything unusual. At any other time I would have meditated in wonder on this curious incident but I now repressed all thought of it, passed my hands about the rest of the bicycle and found her leaning awkwardly against the wall with the string hanging loosely from her crossbar. She was not leaning against the gate where I had tied her.

My eyes had become adjusted to the gloom and I could now see clearly the lightish road bounded by the formless obscurities of the ditch on either side. I led the bicycle to the centre, started upon her gently, threw my leg across and settled gently into her saddle. She seemed at once to communicate to me some balm, some very soothing and pleasurable relaxation after the excitements of the tiny police station. I felt once more comfortable in mind and body, happy in the growing lightness of my heart. I knew that nothing in the whole world could tempt me from the saddle on this occasion until I reached my home. Already I had left the big house a far way behind me. A breeze had sprung up from nowhere and pushed tirelessly at my back, making me flit effortlessly through the darkness like a thing on wings. The bicycle ran truly and faultlessly beneath me, every part of her functioning with precision, her gentle saddle-springs giving unexceptionable consideration to my weight on the undulations of the road. I tried as firmly as ever to keep myself free of the wild thought of my four ounces of omnium but nothing I could do could restrain the profusion of half-thought extravagances which came spilling forth across my mind like a horde of swallows—extravagances of eating, drinking, inventing, destroying, changing, improving, awarding, punishing and even loving. I knew only that some of these undefined wisps of thought were celestial, some horrible, some pleasant and benign; all of them were momentous. My feet pressed down with ecstasy on the willing female pedals.

Courahan's house, a dull silent murk of gloom, passed away behind me on the right-hand side and my eyes narrowed excitedly to try to penetrate to my own house two hundred yards further on. It formed itself gradually exactly in the point I knew it stood and I nearly roared and cheered and yelled out wild greetings at the first glimpse of these four simple walls. Even at Courahan's—I admitted it to myself now—I could not quite convince myself beyond all doubt that I would ever again see the house where I was born, but now I was dismounting from the bicycle outside it. The perils and wonders of the last few days seemed magnificent and epic now that I had survived them. I felt enormous, important and full of power. I felt happy and fulfilled.

The shop and the whole front of the house was in darkness. I wheeled the bicycle smartly up to it, laid it against the door and walked round to the side. A light was shining from the kitchen window. Smiling to myself at the thought of John Divney, I tiptoed up and looked in.

There was nothing altogether unnatural in what I saw but I encountered another of those chilling shocks which I thought I had left behind me forever. A woman was standing at the table with some article of clothing neglected in her hands. She was facing up the kitchen towards the fireplace where the lamp was and she was talking quickly to somebody at the fire. The fireplace could not be seen from where I stood. The woman was Pegeen Meers whom Divney had once talked of marrying. Her appearance amazed me far more than her presence in my own kitchen. She seemed to have grown old, very fat and very grey. Looking at her sideways I could see that she was with child. She was talking rapidly, even angrily, I thought. I was certain she was talking to John Divney and that he was seated with his back to her at the fire. I did not stop to think on this queer situation but walked past the window, lifted the latch of the door, opened the door quickly and stood there looking in. In the one glance I saw two people at the fire, a young lad I had never seen before and my old friend John Divney. He was sitting with his back half-towards me and I was greatly startled by his appearance. He had grown enormously fat and his brown hair was gone, leaving him quite bald. His strong face had collapsed to jowls of hanging fat. I could discern a happy glimmer from the side of his fire-lit eye; an open bottle of whiskey was standing on the floor beside his chair. He turned lazily towards the open door, half-rose and gave a scream which pierced me and pierced the house and careered up to reverberate appallingly in the vault of the heavens. His eyes were transfixed and motionless as they stared at me, his loose face shrunk and seemed to crumble to a limp pallid rag of flesh. His jaws clicked a few times like a machine and then he fell forward on his face with another horrible shriek which subsided to heartrending moans.

I was very frightened and stood pale and helpless in the doorway. The boy had jumped forward and tried to lift Divney up; Pegeen Meers had given a frightened cry and rushed forward also. They pulled Divney round upon his back. His face was twisted in a revolting grimace of fear. His eyes again looked in my direction upside down and back-wards and he gave another piercing scream and frothed foully at the mouth. I took a few steps forward to assist in getting him up from the floor but he made a demented con-vulsive movement and choked out the four words 'Keep away, keep away,' in such a tone of fright and horror that I halted in my tracks, appalled at his appearance. The woman pushed the pale-faced boy distractedly and said:

'Run and get the doctor for your father, Tommy! Hurry, hurry!'

The boy mumbled something and ran out of the open door without giving me a glance. Divney was still lying there, his face hidden in his hands, moaning and gibbering in broken undertones; the woman was on her knees trying to lift his head and comfort him. She was now crying and muttered that she knew something would happen if he did not stop his drinking. I went a little bit forward and said:

'Could I be of any help?'

She took no notice of me at all, did not even glance at me. But my words had a strange effect on Divney. He gave a whining scream which was muffled by his hands; then it died down to choking sobs and he locked his face in his hands so firmly that I could see the nails biting into the loose white flesh beside his ears. I was becoming more and more alarmed. The scene was eerie and disturbing. I took another step forward.

'If you will allow me,' I said loudly to the woman Meers, 'I will lift him and get him into bed. There is nothing wrong with him except that he has taken too much whiskey.'

Again the woman took no notice whatever but Divney was seized by a convulsion terrible to behold. He half-crawled and rolled himself with grotesque movements of his limbs until he was a crumpled heap on the far side of the fireplace, spilling the bottle of whiskey on his way and sending it clattering noisily across the floor. He moaned and made cries of agony which chilled me to the bone. The woman followed him on her knees, crying pitifully and trying to mumble soothing words to him. He sobbed convulsively where he lay and began to cry and mutter things disjointedly like a man raving at the door of death. It was about me. He told me to keep away. He said I was not there. He said I was dead. He said that what he had put under the boards in the big house was not the black box but a mine, a bomb. It had gone up when I touched it. He had watched the bursting of it from where I had left him. The house was blown to bits. I was dead. He screamed to me to keep away. I was dead for sixteen years.

' He is dying,' the woman cried.

I do not know whether I was surprised at what he said, or even whether I believed him. My mind became quite empty, light, and felt as if it were very white in colour. I stood exactly where I was for a long time without moving or thinking. I thought after a time that the house was strange and I became uncertain about the two figures on the floor. Both were moaning and wailing and crying.

' He is dying, he is dying,' the woman cried again.

A cold biting wind was sweeping in through the open door behind me and staggering the light of the oil-lamp fitfully. I thought it was time to go away. I turned with stiffer steps and walked out through the door and round to the front of the house to get my bicycle. It was gone. I walked out upon the road again, turning leftwards. The night had passed away and the dawn had come with a bitter searing wind. The sky was livid and burdened with ill omen. Black angry clouds were piling in the west, bulging and glutted, ready to vomit down their corruption and drown the dreary world in it. I felt sad, empty, and without a thought. The trees by the road were rank and stunted and moved their stark leafless branches very dismally in the wind. The grasses at hand were coarse and foul. Waterlogged bog and healthless marsh stretched endlessly to left and right. The pallor of the sky was terrible to look upon.

My feet carried my nerveless body unbidden onwards for mile upon mile of rough cheerless road. My mind was completely void. I did not recall who I was, where I was or what my business was upon earth. I was alone and desolate yet not concerned about myself at all. The eyes in my head were open but they saw nothing because my brain was void.

Suddenly I found myself noticing my own existence and taking account of my surroundings. There was a bend in the road and when I came round it an extraordinary spectacle was presented to me. About a hundred yards away was a house which astonished me. It looked as if it were painted like an advertisement on a board on the roadside and, indeed, very poorly painted. It looked completely false and unconvincing. It did not seem to have any depth or breadth and looked as if it would not deceive a child. That was not in itself sufficient to surprise me because I had seen pictures and notices by the roadside before. What bewildered me was the sure knowledge, deeply rooted in my mind, that this was the house I was searching for and that there were people inside it. I had never seen with my eyes ever in my life before anything so unnatural and appalling and my gaze faltered about the thing uncomprehendingly as if at least one of the customary dimensions were missing, leaving no meaning in the remainder. The appearance of the house was the greatest surprise I had encountered ever, and I felt afraid of it.

I kept on walking but walked more slowly. As I approached, the house seemed to change its appearance. At first, it did nothing to reconcile itself with the shape of an ordinary house but it became uncertain in outline like a thing glimpsed under ruffled water. Then it became clear again and I saw that it began to have some back to it, some small space for rooms behind the frontage. I gathered this from the fact that I seemed to see the front and the back simultaneously from my position approaching what should have been the side. As there was no side that I could see I thought that the house must be triangular with its apex pointing towards me but when I was only fifteen yards away I saw a small window facing me and I knew from that that there must be *some* side to it. Then I found myself almost in the shadow of the structure, dry-throated and timorous from wonder and anxiety. It seemed ordinary enough at close quarters except that it was very white and still. It was momentous and frightening; the whole morning and the whole world seemed to have no purpose at all save to frame it and give it some magnitude and position so that I could find it with my simple senses and pretend to myself that I understood it. A constabulary crest above the door told me that it was a police station. I had never seen a police station like it.

I stopped in my tracks. I heard distant footsteps on the road behind me, heavy footsteps hurrying after me. I did not look round but remained standing motionless ten yards from the police station, waiting for the hurrying steps. They grew louder and louder and heavier and heavier. At last he came abreast of me. It was John Divney. We did not look at each other or say a single word. I fell into step beside him and both of us marched into the police station. We saw, standing with his back to us, an enormous policeman. His back appearance was unusual. He was standing behind a little counter in a neat whitewashed day-room; his mouth was open and he was looking into a mirror which hung upon the wall.

' It's my teeth,' we heard him say abstractedly and half-aloud. ' Nearly every sickness is from the teeth.'

His face, when he turned, surprised us. It was enormously fat, red and widespread, sitting squarely on the neck of his tunic with a clumsy weightiness that reminded me of a sack of flour. The lower half of it was hidden by a violent red moustache which shot out from his skin far into the air like the antennae of some unusual animal. His cheeks were red and chubby and his eyes were nearly invisible, hidden from above by the obstruction of his tufted brows and from below by the fat foldings of his skin. He came over ponderously to the inside of the counter and Divney and I advanced meekly from the door until we were face to face.

' Is it about a bicycle?' he asked.

PUBLISHER'S NOTE

O n St. Valentine's Day, 1940, the author wrote to William Saroyan about this novel, as follows:

' I've just finished another book. The only thing good about it is the plot and I've been wondering whether I could make a crazy . . . play out of it. When you get to the end of this book you realise that my hero or main character (he's a heel and a killer) has been dead throughout the book and that all the queer ghastly things which have been happening to him are happening in a sort of hell which he earned for the killing. Towards the end of the book (before you know he's dead) he manages to get back to his own house where he used to live with another man who helped in the original murder. Although he's been away three days, this other fellow is twenty years older and dies of fright when he sees the other lad standing in the door. Then the two of them walk back along the road to the hell place and start thro' all the same terrible adventures again, the first fellow being surprised and frightened at everything just as he was the first time and as if he'd never been through it before. It is made clear that this sort of thing goes on for ever—and there you are. It is supposed to be very funny but I don't know about that either . . . I think the idea of a man being dead all the time is pretty new. When you are writing about the world of the dead—and the damned—where none of the rules and laws (not even the law of gravity) holds good, there is any amount of scope for back-chat and funny cracks.'

14 February, 1940.

B. O'N.

Elsewhere, the author wrote:

' Joe had been explaining things in the meantime. He said it was again the beginning of the unfinished, the re-discovery of the familiar, the re-experience of the already suffered, the fresh-forgetting of the unremembered. Hell goes round and round. In shape it is circular and by nature it is interminable, repetitive and very nearly unbearable.'